ST KILDA FEVER

F.M.T. Macdonald

June 2019

To Tristan

Hope you enjoy
reading this

Fiona (and George!)

This novel is a work of fiction. Neither the village of Valagarry, nor its inhabitants exist.

First published 2019 by

FMT Macdonald
64 Bayhead Street
Stornoway
Isle of Lewis
HS1 2DX

FMTMacdonald@Outlook.com

ISBN 978-1-9993519-0-8

Printed and bound by
CPI Group (UK) Ltd, Croydon, CR0 4YY

2 4 6 8 10 9 7 5 3 1

Acknowledgements

Firstly, thanks to Heather Birrell, writer, who established a writing group in An Lanntair, Stornoway, our local arts centre. Heather's back home in Canada but the group's still going strong.

Special thanks to John Hayward not only for his encouragement but for his advice, patience and tireless work in the process of birthing this book! Also to Linda Burke for her reading and to Karen at Karen MacKay Design Co. Ltd. for the cover.

Finally, apologies to my family for my absence from real life while I descended into my fictitious world.

Prologue

Outer Hebrides
April 1976

My hand shook as I stubbed out my cigarette. I took the silver pen from his outstretched fingers, my bitten nails contrasting with his carefully filed ones. I hesitated, looking at the document headed *Official Secrets Act*. He coughed, and tapped his foot.

His lips pursed, and he stared at me intently. 'It's up to you, Doctor.' His black leather briefcase sat at his feet, and he bent down and pulled out a thin buff coloured file and placed it on his lap.

Perhaps it held the answers to all my questions. I had no choice but to go ahead and sign it. I was aware of my heart beat accelerating. I scribbled my signature on the line and handed the form back to him. He folded it and placed it in his briefcase then handed me the file.

'Thanks,' I said.

He nodded.

I took a deep breath, opened the file and began to read...

Six Months Earlier

The Outer Hebrides, November 1975

Chapter One

'Shut up! For God's sake! George, will you stop that bloody noise! I've told you about this before. Any more of this and you're banned from the bedroom,' I shouted, my fingers wandering crab-like across the bedside table searching for the light.

Typically, he ignored me. My heart was now pounding and things felt kind of fuzzy. Gin and sleeping pills are never a good combo. I didn't need my medical training to know that. My hand hit something, knocking it over.

'Bugger!'

There was a crash, then a whimper as George, broke the bottle's fall. This spooked him even further, and his barking upped a gear just as my hand found the switch and pressed it.

'Blast!'

In addition to the aural assault, spears of light were now piercing my eyes. If this is what hell is like, I thought, thank God I'm an atheist.

'Are you okay?' I asked George, who was now crouched facing the door, ears flapped back, tail erect. He ignored me, in his Jack Russell, small dog syndrome sort of way.

I threw back the scratchy woollen blankets, and eased myself out of bed. My foot caught the empty gin bottle sending it carouselling across the room where it ended its journey skidding under the wardrobe. The rough floorboards caught my thick woollen bed socks as I padded towards the door. Oh, for the bliss of a fitted carpet!

Since I'd arrived in the Outer Hebrides two months ago, I'd resorted, old-lady like, to wearing extra layers of clothing. I was living temporarily in my cousin Mairi and her husband Alasdair's croft house. Situated on the edge of the beach, close to the machair, it was cold and damp.

Something squid-like wrapped itself round my ankles. Was this a nightmare? No! I screamed and fell backwards onto the bed, frantically tearing at the beast with my nails. Looking down, I saw that attached to my leg was my pink nylon bra. Idiot! I stood up quickly. My head swam, and I let out a groan. The large peony roses on the wallpaper swam out of and then back into focus. Losing my balance I grabbed the chair back, and hopping on one leg managed to grab the grubby bra and flung it onto the bed. Shivering, I grabbed Alasdair's large red tartan dressing-gown from the hook behind the door. I slipped it on and pulled the cord tightly round my waist. I caught a glimpse of myself in the wardrobe mirror. I looked like a dented tin of shortbread.

'Okay, killer—let's go sort this out,' I muttered to George, flinging open the bedroom door, which immediately rebounded off my toes.

'Damn!'

My synapses were clearly in good working order, as the jolt of pain journeyed quickly from my toe to my brain. I yelped loudly and George's barking ceased as he lay quivering, eyes closed, paws covering his nose.

I limped down the narrow, creaking staircase, gripping the wooden bannister to steady myself, George's nose touching the back of my leg. A low growling noise was emanating from his throat, hardly audible, like the noise of a distant underground train approaching a station. Something was spooking him big-time, and loud unhappy hen squawking noises were coming from the barn. George gave me one of his *I told you so* looks, as he walked past nose in the air. He sat down and waited beside the back door. If he'd had fingers, he would have been drumming them on the floor.

Right, now I'd two early warning systems going off—hysterical hens and a jumpy Jack Russell. I was a single woman living alone. At this point if I was in Glasgow, I'd phone the cops. But this was the Outer Hebrides, and all this racket probably meant one thing—mink in the henhouse. Okay, so now I was seriously frightened. My cousin Mairi had warned me about the wild mink. Years ago they'd been brought onto the island to be farmed for their coats, but they'd either been let loose or escaped from the now defunct mink farm. I'm terrified of anything wee and rodenty at the best of times, so the thought of facing a hen-killer mink in the middle of the night was a seriously scary business.

Every light in the cottage was now on. But what should I do next? I swallowed hard. I'd need to go outside to check the hens. I'm a city girl at heart—I don't do rodents. Were mink related to ferrets? Did they run up your trouser legs? I shuddered as I jammed my feet into Mairi's wellies, lying beside the back door, and carefully tucked my pyjama trousers inside them—that should keep them out. I hoped. I grabbed Alasdair's black rubber torch, and struggled with the back door key. There was a rush of cold air as the door swung open. I inhaled the salty tang, and shivered involuntarily. I could just hear the sea over the rising chicken crescendo. George, who usually rushed passed me heading for the great outdoors, suddenly developed an unheard dose of chivalry, and tucked himself behind my legs.

'Okay killer! Let's go and get 'em,' I said to my canine coward. I couldn't see anything, and I stumbled on the uneven path. The weak yellow disc of my torchlight barely lit the path to the barn where the hens were housed. As I approached the noise got even louder. The barn door was wide open and the smell of chicken shit assailed my nose. I gagged and the taste of gin filled my mouth. I swallowed hard. I could have sworn that I'd closed and bolted the barn door before going to bed, but sometimes after a

11

few drinks things got a bit hazy. I wasn't too keen to corner a mink, so before going in I gave the barn door a hard whack with the torch, hoping that the noise would scare it off.

The torch bulb smashed and darkness enveloped me. For George, it was the final straw. He yelped, and shot back towards the triangle of light leading into the kitchen. By the weak moonlight, I could just see the barn door. I pulled it shut, found the bolt, and forced the rusty catch closed. I followed George back into the house, slamming the door and letting out a sigh of relief. The thudding in my chest began to lessen. I made sure I locked the back door before trying to remove Mairi's wellies, which had stuck themselves to my feet and were resisting my attempts to pull them off. I gave up and thumped up the stairs, smearing chicken dirt over the treads. When I reached the bedroom, the bump and trembling of the blankets showed that George was now hogging the centre of the bed.

'Move over, fearless,' I instructed. Reluctantly he burrowed deeper under the covers, and I sat down on the bed. With a struggle I pulled off the wellies, and threw them across the room. Picking up the small brown pill bottle from the bedside table, I twisted the top off, shook out a couple of sleeping pills into my hand, and swallowed them. I looked for the gin bottle to wash them down. Realising it was lying under the wardrobe, I swore inwardly, switched off the light and fell back into a dreamless sleep.

Well, not exactly. The excitement had kick-started my adrenal glands. They were now in overdrive, and sending signals to my head which was pounding along in time to my heartbeat. I tried counting sheep. Where better than the Hebrides to do that?

I suspected George was more successful, as canine snoring was now emanating from under the covers. Finally, the tablets kicked in and things began to fade.

Chapter Two

Something was hurting me. Light was beaming directly into my eyes and there was a loud ringing noise from somewhere. I peeled open my dry, crisp-like eyes. I'd forgotten to close the bedroom curtains last night, and now light was tap dancing on my eye balls, keeping perfect time with the ringing phone. I stood up, holding my head, swearing as my swollen toe made contact with the floor. I felt queasy at the sight of the chicken dirt, and I tried to avoid standing on it as I hobbled downstairs. The ringing continued as I shuffled across the kitchen floor. I picked up the receiver from the wall phone. Blissful silence...broken by an authoritative female voice announcing, 'Good morning, Doctor MacAllister. It is quarter past nine and there are patients waiting in the surgery.' I held the phone further from my ear.

'Damn,' I muttered. Sometimes mother's little helpers can be just too efficient at knocking you out. Perhaps I shouldn't have taken the extra ones on top of the gin last night.

'Pardon, Doctor?' she said.

'I can...yes. Sorry, I can be with you shortly, Mrs Murray.'

Mrs Murray was the person in charge of my life—the practice receptionist and dispenser who'd been with my predecessor, Dr Robertson, for nearly thirty years, until he had suffered a heart attack. She'd been his handmaiden rather than receptionist, and hadn't taken kindly to me as his locum replacement. Being neither local, nor male, were two large black marks in Mrs Murray's eyes.

Mrs Murray was now sounding very unhappy, and if Mrs Murray wasn't happy today then I knew that I wasn't going to be happy either.

I limped back upstairs and into the bedroom. Clothes, I needed clothes. Those lying on the chair and scattered across the floor were all crushed and badly needing a wash. Needs must— I picked up my push-up bra and folded in my drooping breasts. Why had I been at the end of the queue when they'd been handing out the perky breasts? I sniffed my knickers—they'd do. But in the interest of hygiene I turned them inside out before pulling on my thankfully unladdered tights. Thank goodness my mother couldn't see this. Finally, I struggled into yesterday's skirt and jumper which were lying on the top of the bundle.

I made my way slowly back downstairs, still swearing under my breath. This time George was leading the way. This was usually the case when food might be involved. But he was in for disappointment; I already knew that the dog food tin was empty. I poured some cornflakes into his bowl. Sniffing the bottle of milk, I recoiled and poured the curdled contents down the sink, then bent down and patted his head.

'Look, I'll get your food today. Promise.'

He looked at me disbelievingly, turned his back and sat facing the wall. I shrugged. Things weren't going to get any easier today.

My make-up bag lay on the mantelpiece, its contents cascading from its unzipped mouth. I quickly dabbed some concealer onto the shadows under my eyes. I took a look in the mirror then applied a second thicker coat, trying to avoid the stare of the pale hollow-eyed woman looking back at me. Applying blusher only succeeded in giving me a mortician like glow. I gathered up the lank hair from my shoulders and pulled it back into a ponytail with an elastic band, grimacing as it pulled at my hair. Did that dry shampoo stuff work? Probably, but I didn't have any of it anyway. A quick squirt of my cousin Mairi's perfume and I was ready to face the world, or more importantly Mrs Murray.

On the way to the car, I unlocked the barn door and threw some seed on the ground. There was a rush of feathers and clucking. I noticed a patch of dried blood on the ground but couldn't see any obvious injury to the birds who were pecking enthusiastically around my feet.

'Bloody mink,' I muttered. The hens ignored me, being myopically focused on their seed. I stuck my hand in my pocket. 'Damn! No car keys.' Then I remembered they were already inside my yellow Beetle. Car theft was unknown on the island and I'd quickly got into the island habit of leaving the keys in the ignition.

I squinted against the light bouncing off the grey sea as I drove along the single track cliff road to work, praying that I wouldn't meet anyone coming in the opposite direction as I wasn't quite sure how quick my reactions would be. Ten minutes later I pulled into the surgery car park. About a dozen vehicles were scattered outside, all in various stages of disintegration. Metal plus sea air equals rust, or oxidation as Mr Crawford, my chemistry teacher, had taught us. He'd been the teacher in Glasgow who'd inspired me to choose science which had led to me becoming a doctor. Though I sometimes wished Mrs Jackson, our Home Economics teacher, could have inspired me more towards cooking and housework. Perhaps then my house wouldn't smell, there would be food in the fridge and I wouldn't have to face an aggressive, menopausal, medical receptionist.

My stomach knotted. I took a deep breath and pushed open the surgery door. There was a smell of disinfectant. The figure of Mrs Murray in her white medical coat lurked behind the reception desk. If Hitchcock's Bates Motel had ever been looking for a receptionist, then this was the woman for the job. One day, shortly after starting at the practice, I'd accidentally brushed against her coat. It felt as starched and unyielding as its wearer.

Underneath she was wearing her customary grey Harris Tweed skirt and black polo neck jumper. The key to the medicine cupboard hung talisman-like around her neck. New patients could easily mistake her for a doctor and there was no doubt in her mind who was in charge of the surgery. Her eyebrows arched questioningly as I struggled inside, my medical bag bouncing off the doorframe and hitting my leg. I swore. She grimaced. Her face wore an expression reminiscent of the one my mother wore the night I was poured home drunk from the sixth year school dance.

'Good morning, Mrs Murray. Sorry I'm a bit late. Bit of a problem with the hens this morning,' I croaked. 'Any chance of a coffee?' I smiled ingratiatingly. Mrs Murray nodded grimly.

'Two sugars and a biscuit if you have one,' I added, edging past Mrs Murray as her lips pursed tighter.

The waiting room had one male patient, sitting in the corner reading a thick book, and five female patients sitting dressed uniformly in black, ranged along the wooden seats like crows on a telegraph wire. Everyone was deep in conversation in Gaelic as I hurried past clutching their patient notes. They broke off their conversation and chorused, 'Good morning, Doctor,' but had resumed it before I'd even closed the surgery door.

The morning surgery flowed smoothly. One patient, with a rumbling appendix needed an urgent appointment with the hospital surgeon. I phoned his secretary and she agreed that Mr MacDonald would see him in the afternoon. I scribbled a quick letter with his details. I had to ask Mrs Murray for an envelope which she produced with ill grace.

At eleven o'clock there was a knock at the door and Mrs Murray brought in a cup of coffee and, joy of joys, a homemade scone and raspberry jam. I would have kissed her, but I wasn't sure that I could cope with the forest of black hairs on her top lip.

I looked at the scone and hesitated, as my skirt waistband silently chastised me for all the weight I'd acquired in the last two months. Most home visits ended with the offer of a cup of tea and some home baking, a custom which I'd happily embraced and for which my straining waistband was now paying the price. But I was starving as I hadn't had any breakfast. *Important to keep your blood sugar levels up*, I assured myself as I sat back and took a mouthful, and my mind began to wander.

Chapter 3

It was only two months since I'd arrived on the island to replace the late Doctor Robertson, but it seemed an age.

It'd been the last week of September. My ferry trip from Ullapool to Stornoway had been smooth and I'd happily consumed bacon rolls and mugs of tea, despite the lingering smell from the sheep trucks on the car deck that I'd been unable to shake from my nostrils. But the next morning it'd been pouring with rain and blowing a gale. This was more like the stormy Hebridean weather that I'd only heard about on the late night shipping forecast. *Hebrides, Bailey southwest 5 to 6: occasional gale 8.* Mrs Murray hadn't made any attempt to hide her disapproval as I'd barrelled through the surgery door, my hair soaked and plastered to my skull and my errant skirt attempting a Marilyn Monroe tribute act.

'Good morning, Doctor MacAllister?' she'd sniffed.

I'd nodded and smiled. She hadn't. I'd seen cheerier faces on bodies lying waiting for dissection on a mortuary table.

'It's nice to meet you,' I ventured.

She nodded. 'You'll be wanting to get the surgery started, Doctor.' She'd shown me into my consulting room. I'd hesitated at the door. Someone with a sense of humour had painted it a shade of what could only be described as diarrhoea yellow. But a quick inspection revealed that the equipment appeared up-to-date. Mrs Murray picked up a small black object from the desk.

'You'll be dictating the patients' letters into this. I'll bring you a cup of tea at ten thirty.' I suppressed the urge to snap my heels together and salute. She put down the dictaphone and as she walked out the door, she stopped and turned. 'I'll send in the first patient in ten minutes?' This was couched as a question but was clearly an instruction. She walked out without looking back.

My shoulders drooped, it was going to be a long six months until the health board found a new doctor. But meanwhile I needed to work to pay off my debts and the money I'd borrowed from my parents to help buy my first flat, so here I was in the Outer Hebrides. It might as well have been the Arctic circle. Did they have penguins here? I knew they had puffins.

I sat down and opened the top drawer. Good, something useful. I pulled out the late Dr Robertson's thistle shaped ash tray. Lighting a cigarette, I sat back and lifted off the first patient file from the top of the pile.

There was a knock at the door. The lone male patient from the waiting room entered. His notes told me his name was Calum Twig Macdonald. He was clutching a medical dictionary, which he put on my desk and opened. My heart sank. I could see at least three pieces of paper bookmarking pages. I knew it was going to be a long appointment.

Now, two months later, I was getting to know the patients and they were getting to know me. Though I'd a sneaking suspicion that, despite me holding their medical records, their information gathering system was probably far more efficient than mine. In my first week I reckoned that at least half a dozen of my male patients were there just to have a good look at the new doctor. Most had made appointments 'just to get my blood pressure checked, Doctor.' My cousin Mairi had warned me that there were some perennial bachelors on the list who were known to be on the lookout for a wife. I'd laughed and pointed out that one sure way to get struck off was to take your work home with you. The General Medical Council took a very dim view of this and I was anxious to avoid their attention after what had happened in Glasgow.

If I was honest I hadn't been surprised when late one Friday afternoon, just as I was packing up to go home for the weekend and glad that I'd avoided the Glasgow rush hour traffic, Dr James, the senior partner, had called me into his office.

'Dr MacAllister, there's been a drugs stocktake and some of the opiates seem to be, how shall I put it, evaporating from the drugs cupboard. Do you know anything about this?'

I'd blushed, and shaken my head, then looked down and examined my bitten nails. He was a kindly soul, and I'm sure he would have tried to help me if I'd confessed the mess I was in. Since being dumped by Tom, my boyfriend, I hadn't been able to sleep or concentrate, and I was in a worse state than many of my depressed patients. I just wanted to find a large black hole and crawl inside. One evening I'd had enough. I was exhausted. It'd been weeks since I'd had a night's sleep. Everyone had gone home and I'd gone into the practice's drugs cabinet and borrowed some tablets—just enough to give me a few nights' rest. They'd worked and I'd started using them to get help me sleep. At that point, I was spending most weekends cocooned in bed. If it wasn't for George and his insistence that he had to go out for walks, I suspect I might have been discovered as a mummified figure and exhibited at the local museum.

But no, I'd kept silent. Standing up and opening the office door, Doctor James suggested that perhaps it was time for a change of scene. He wouldn't report me and I agreed to leave at the end of the month.

For once luck was on my side. Two evenings later my cousin Mairi phoned from the Outer Hebrides to tell me about a locum vacancy on the island. Doctor Robertson's sudden death from a heart attack had been untimely, though I understood he was overweight and heavy on the booze and fags, so perhaps he'd decided against ticking the old age box.

Mairi had been brought up in Glasgow too. We'd watched each other's backs in school, surviving attacks from bullies and the odd psychopathic belt-mad teacher. She'd met her islander husband, Alasdair, while she was working as a nurse in Glasgow. He was studying chemistry at university and desperate to return home to the Hebrides. After graduation he got a post in the local pharmaceutical factory on the island of Lewis. His parents were from Lewis and he'd inherited the old family croft. They'd moved back two years ago with plans to do up the old draughty croft house, but the factory had recently closed, so they'd both gone back to Glasgow where Alasdair was now training to be a teacher.

There was also an element of self-interest in Mairi's wish for me to live in their croft house. I suspected that my most important tasks were keeping the house wind and watertight and looking after her hens. The health of the local populous came a poor second. But it got me out of a jam and well out of the sights of the General Medical Council in London. It was a long drive from deepest London to the Highlands, then a three-and-a-half-hour ferry ride and hopefully the G.M.C. weren't too keen on water.

Chapter 4

It had been a long surgery and a very pregnant Catherine Miller was my last patient of the day. She waddled into the surgery and sat down with a long sigh. The hospital had asked us to keep an eye on her blood pressure and her husband had driven her to the surgery. Given her size, I doubted whether she would fit behind the steering wheel of a car.

'I'll be glad to get this wee soul into the outside world,' she smiled, wanly. 'I haven't had a good night's sleep for the last month, Doctor. Kicking like a lamb this one.'

Her blood pressure was fine and the baby's heartbeat was strong.

'The head's engaged—not long to go now. Next time I see you, you'll be pushing a pram.'

She smiled and I gave her a reassuring pat on the shoulder as she heaved herself from the examination couch.

At four o'clock the noise of my rumbling stomach almost drowned out the dictation of some letters. I still hadn't done any shopping, so I thought that I would nip out before the shop closed.

Avoiding Mrs Murray, who was speaking loudly in Gaelic to someone on the phone, I hurried out of the surgery, nodding as I went past. She didn't look up.

Once in my car, with one hand on the wheel, I searched around with my other hand and eventually pulled out my Eagles tape from the clutter. I fed it into the cassette player, hoping that it wouldn't jam. I wasn't in the mood to stop the car, and start fiddling with a pencil to rewind a spaghetti-aspiring tape. I whistled along as I drove. Now that I'd escaped the surgery, my spirits were starting to lift. The road wound through the bottom of the glen, Scots pines gripping the sides to prevent themselves sliding unmajestically downwards. Although it was a sunny day, the sides were so steep that no sunlight touched the road in the deepening autumnal shadow. The single track roads were quiet, in comparison to the busy Glasgow ones I was used to, and I'd only to pull off occasionally into a passing place to let an oncoming car whizz past, rewarded by a wave of the hand or the beep of a horn. But I was still concentrating on the road though, watching out for kamikaze sheep, whose favourite trick was to simultaneously launch themselves from each side of the road, executing a crossover manoeuvre that even the Red Arrows would be proud of.

My journey to the shop took me through the dark glen or the *glen dubh* as it's known in Gaelic. Having been brought up in Glasgow, I was still getting used to the strangeness of Gaelic, the local language. Before arriving on the island, my only awareness of it had been occasionally hearing late-evening Gaelic singing competitions on television, which I'd always quickly turned off as the music was so mournful. But here in the village, miles from the town, I'd been surprised to find out that most of my patients and staff spoke Gaelic as their first language. It made me feel like a tourist in my own country.

Strangely the language bears no resemblance to English. It doesn't even have all the letters of the alphabet, lacking J, K, Q, W, X, Y and Z. No Gaelic speaking child was ever going to experience the difficulty of spelling that frequently used word xylophone.

Gaelic was causing me problems too. Despite the fact I'd been good at languages at school, I was struggling with some of the Gaelic place names. I knew that I was mispronouncing some of them big-time. Sometimes I saw the ghost of a smile on a patient's face when I stumbled over their address, but the staff in the surgery were too polite to correct me.

Arriving back at the surgery from a house call, late one afternoon, I'd opened the door to hear my voice loudly reverberating round the office, dictating a letter. I'd walked in on Mrs Murray and Angela, the district nurse, laughing at my woeful mangling of a patient's address. Angela had blushed and Mrs Murray quickly turned off the tape. I was annoyed, but let the incident pass. I didn't have any time to learn Gaelic, and anyway as I wasn't planning to stay I didn't see the point.

I passed a signpost. Confusingly, the only signposts there were on the island, were in English, and these were literally few and far between. Was this because all the locals knew where everywhere was and they didn't want to encourage any intrepid tourists who'd made their way onto the islands?

At the end of the valley, the local shop slid into view, a single petrol pump, standing totem pole like outside. I drew off the road and parked next to three other vehicles, two of which looked as if they were glued together by rust.

The rain started again as I crunched across the rough gravel. Since I'd arrived on the island two months ago, it seemed there had been constant rain with intermittent dry spells. They say that Eskimos have thirty words for snow. Well, I presumed there must be at least fifty words in Gaelic for rain.

In the surgery, each appointment began with at least a couple of minutes discussing meteorological matters before we could move onto anything medical. I suspected that when local people totted up their lifetime activities, after sleeping and eating there would be six months of weather discussion, five of which would be allocated to rain.

In front of the shop I skirted round a seagull picking over the remnants of a bacon roll. It fixed me with an aggressive stare as I hurried past. The faded black and red sign above the door read *MacLeod's Store—Goods and Feed*. The words *suppliers of local gossip and character assassination* could have been added, but perhaps they ran out of space. Coming from the inside was the sound of male voices. I took a deep breath and pushed open the smeary glass door. The bell jangled loudly as I walked in, and the conversation stopped.

The heady aroma of paraffin and cheese hung in the air. The owner Mr MacLeod, a man in his fifties, tweed cap on his head, cigarette pinched between his thumb and forefinger, was in his usual position behind the wooden counter, and two male customers were slouched on the other side.

'Good afternoon, Dr MacAllister,' said Mr Macleod, exhaling smoke.

'Em, afternoon. Just in for a few things,' I muttered, grabbing a wire basket.

This place, or rather its occupants, always made me feel uncomfortable. I felt such an outsider. I just wanted to get in and out as soon as possible. Even as I moved around the shop I was aware of three sets of eyes, tracking my movements.

'... and when they pulled him into the boat they had to use a net, he was so badly mangled. Face smashed in by the rocks. His own mother wouldn't recognise him,' said the taller of the two customers, who I recognised as Lulu; weatherbeaten with an unruly black beard, he wouldn't have looked out of place behind the wheel of a Spanish galleon. There was little resemblance to the diminutive Glaswegian singer of his nickname. Apparently, he'd been called after her as he was always shouting.

I was still getting used to most of the men having nicknames. Often the nicknames were garnered in school where there could be two or three Donald MacDonalds or Calum Morrisons in the same class, and the name stayed with them for life. I'd noticed that Doctor Robertson had sometimes written a patient's nick-name in his notes.

'The fiscal and a doctor from the mainland are on their way over from town to look at the body. They've been told not to move it from the lifeboat till they get here. Couple of cops from the town are on board, keeping an eye on it,' said the smaller one, who was wearing a blue, stained, woolly jumper, fraying at the cuffs.

'Aye, Sandy the cox is not well chuffed. You know how clean he keeps that boat. You could eat your dinner off the deck,' said Mr MacLeod taking a drag on his cigarette and flicking the ash onto the floor.

The conversation lapsed into Gaelic, and I could only make out the odd word as I wandered round the shop grabbing essentials: tonic, crisps, shampoo, dog food. I smiled to myself when I saw they had George's favourite brand. He would be pleased. I wasn't sure if dogs were capable of awarding brownie points, but I reckoned I had just totted up a few. What else did I need? Washing powder; a large box. This would prevent the biohazard that was my dirty clothing spreading further. I spotted firelighters—now I could try putting on the stove. The house was starting to get cold at night, and I felt that George and I could do with an evening sitting together in front of the stove. Shopping completed, I headed towards the till and dumped the heavy wire basket on the counter, but the men were so engrossed in their conversation they didn't notice me and the conversation had lapsed back into English.

'...Calum said it had no fingerprints. They'd been burned off sometime within the last couple of months,' said the jumper wearer, shaking his head.

'Burnt off?' said Mr MacLeod, flicking more ash.

'Difficult to tell as he had been in the water for a few days.

Poor bugger wouldn't have lasted long even with his wet suit.'

'Lucky if he managed twenty minutes,' Lulu added. He was dressed in a blue boiler suit, and had probably popped in to give himself a break from working at the croft. 'Reckon the tide brought him.'

'Where from?' asked the short man.

'Kilda,' said Lulu

'Balls! Sorry, Doctor,' said MacLeod glancing in my direction. 'Forgot you were there. No way had he come all the way in a wetsuit from Kilda and looking as fresh as he does. A boat must have brought him.'

'There's been no word on the radio that the army has lost anyone from the St. Kilda station.'

'Aye, but suppose he isn't one of ours?' said Mr MacLeod, as he turned and started to ring my basket of shopping through the till. The other customers subjected my shopping to a level of scrutiny that Sherlock Holmes would have been proud of.

But now the part, that I had been dreading since I walked into the shop.

'Anything else?' asked MacLeod.

'Em—three bottles of Gordon's gin and a hundred Benson and Hedges please,' I muttered.

A quick look was exchanged between MacLeod and the two customers, which I pretended not to see as I fiddled with my purse.

He selected the bottles and cigarettes from the shelves behind him, rang them through and pushed them across the scratched wooden counter, but not before he had put the gin in a brown paper bag.

'That all, Doctor?'

'Yes, that's all thanks,' I said, opening my purse. I paid, declined the offer of help to the car, and headed for the door.

Mr Macleod restarted the conversation. 'Okay, so if he's nae navy, then who is he?'

'I think...'

The shop door slammed behind me. I was relieved to get out and back to my car. I dumped the shopping in the boot and decided that I would take the scenic route home, along the coast road, my favourite part of my journey back to the cottage. When I reached the top, I stopped the car at the lookout point close to the cliff edge and stared out towards the Atlantic. The wind was scything off the tops of the grey foaming waves as they completed the last few yards of their journey from America. I pulled out my cigarettes and reached for some matches. My fingers touched something cold and metallic. I pulled it out. It was a lighter; Tom's lighter. Then I looked down at the silver, heart shaped ring indenting my finger and began slowly turning it round with my thumb, remembering the last dinner Tom and I'd shared in our flat before he'd left.

It'd been my birthday and he'd given the ring to me. It was small. The only finger it fitted properly was my wedding-ring finger, so I'd slipped it on there. But I'd thought that one day soon I'd be wearing the real thing. How stupid I'd been. A single tear escaped onto my cheek. I flicked the lighter and lit a cigarette, leant forward and turned off the music. The greyness of the waves was reflected in my mood. I took an even deeper drag on the cigarette and fought the impulse to think back to happier times. What was the point?

Chapter 5

My plans to have an evening by the fire with George were thwarted by a recalcitrant stove which sat in the kitchen and gloomily refused to light. Mairi had left me a set of handwritten instructions which I'd managed to mislay, so eventually I'd given up and spent the evening facing a one-bar electric fire instead. I'd found a pile of old magazines and had flipped my way through them as I sipped my gin and tonics. Eventually, I'd given in to the cold and retreated upstairs to bed.

The next day was busy. Lunch was an aspiration rather than a fact and I was running on coffee and a couple of Mrs Murray's scones. But thankfully it was Friday, and I was looking forward to a long lie-in tomorrow. After my last house call, I popped back to the surgery to write up my notes and stock up my bag with drugs, just in case I'd an emergency callout over the weekend. One of the advantages of being a country practice so far away from the local chemist's shop in Stornoway was that we dispensed our own prescriptions. The patients collected them directly from the surgery not the chemist. They were left lying on a table just inside the surgery door. Mrs Murray and I were the only people that held the keys to the drugs' cupboard. So far, I'd not 'borrowed' any of the drugs, relying on gin and cigarettes to get me through the evenings and the stock of sleeping pills that I'd brought with me from Glasgow. I knew that sooner rather than later I'd need some more, but I'd cross that bridge when I came to it.

Mrs Murray had left a note on my desk: 'Remember church is at noon on Sunday'. I scrunched the paper into a ball and threw it in the bin. I had no intention of going to church on a regular basis. I made an exception for patients' funerals, but the only one I'd attended so far had been a bit of a trial.

I'd been the only woman in the church without a hat. The service was in Gaelic. There was no organ, no hymns, only psalms. The singing was led by a man at the front of the church and the congregation followed his lead. The music was haunting and beautiful in equal amounts, and had made the hairs stand up on the back of my neck. I'd asked Angela, the district nurse, why everything was so sparse and she'd explained that it all related back to the land clearances and the oppression of the crofters: a time when the land-owning gentry who were in league with the established church had cleared the land for sheep and the people were forced to worship where they could.

There wasn't even a wreath of flowers and the coffin sat at the back of the church. It completely contrasted with my memories of a central belt Church of Scotland. A place where colouring-in, Easter eggs and Christmas parties fused happy memories. It also perhaps explained why, as a small child, I got Santa Claus and God confused, not to mention elves and disciples. No, I'd be giving church a miss. I was going to spend this weekend tucked up in the cottage with George and a good book if I could find one.

It was late by the time I got home. My plan to sneak out of the surgery at five while Mrs Murray was deep in discussion with one of her cronies at reception was thwarted when I received a very wheezy call from Archie Campbell. Between gasps, I could just make out that he was having problems breathing and his inhaler was empty and that he was in the house on his own. I promised to pop in with a new inhaler and check that he was okay on my way home, although this meant a ten-mile round trip on single track roads in the opposite direction from George and the fireside.

Arriving at Mr Campbell's house half an hour later, I knocked and went in through the unlocked back door. I was still getting used to the fact that on the island no one locked their house doors. Theft and housebreaking were unknown and front doors were rarely used, except by travelling salesmen and those travelling to the cemetery.

From his notes I knew that Mr Campbell was elderly and lived alone. A wise looking collie lifted its head and gave me a stern stare as I entered the living room. Mr Campbell was crouched in his chair wheezing over the peat fire, the smell of which helped mask the permeating odour of kippers, dirty socks and worse. Old Mr Campbell smiled when I walked in, although at first any communication on his part was restricted to wheezes, nods and shakes of his grey-topped head. I suspected part of the problem might be due to the pipe resting on the ashtray on the fireplace.

Gradually, with puffs of the new inhaler, the wheezing reduced but I stayed with him till I was happy we'd got his breathing back under control. Then I made him a cup of tea. His kitchen, unlike mine, at least had some clean mugs and fresh milk in his fridge. Whilst we had this, he told me that his sister would be back from town shortly. We arranged that his sister would drive him over to the surgery next week for a check up, and I left sensing that although I may not have passed the testing gaze of his collie I had gained a patient ally.

The light was fading from the sky by the time I left his house. I'd intended to pop into the shop on my way home—I'd forgotten to buy a torch when I was last there. It was now well after seven and the shop closed at six, but, as I was driving past, I saw the lights were still on. What was greater, my fear of Mr MacLeod, or of marauding mink in a dark henhouse? The mink won hands down. I braked, turned the car round and headed back towards the shop. The car park was empty apart from Mr MacLeod's mud-caked Land Rover. The notice on the door said 'closed'. I peered in and was about to walk away when I saw Mr MacLeod beckoning me in from behind the counter. I took a deep breath and stuck my head round the door. I could see that the shelves were looking a lot barer than yesterday.

'Come in, Doctor. Don't be standing there out in the cold,' he smiled. 'We're expecting a storm and tomorrow's ferry will probably be cancelled. Lot of panic buying whenever the ferry doesn't go.' He nodded at the empty shelves. 'Here, you'll be needing some more bread and milk. I've some in the back shop.' He returned with a loaf, two pints of milk and a large steak pie, and put them on the counter.

'Anything else?' He glanced in the direction of the cigarettes and alcohol. 'I can always deliver things and just leave them for you in your porch. Often did that for Dr Robertson and for the odd minister too, save you coming into the shop. You can just phone me,' he added.

His manner towards me had changed, but why?

'It was good of you to go and see my cousin Archie,' he said. 'That asthma of his is a real worry.'

Mystery solved, I'd forgotten that Mairi had told me how everybody was related to each other.

'Bag of coal and a torch please,' I said. 'Mine got broken when I went to check on the hens. I'm not sure if it was a mink.'

'Aye, these mink will have them all. The idiot that brought them over should be shot,' he said, and he handed me a luminous yellow torch that could have had a lighthouse keeper running for cover it was so bright.

'A lambing torch,' he explained. 'Need them on the hills. But take this smaller one too and keep it in your car, just in case.' He pushed a black rubber torch across the counter. 'I hear they're sending some bigwigs up from London to investigate that body they pulled out of the water. Bit unusual that, it'll put some local

32

noses out of joint. Inspector MacLean in Stornoway willnae be happy at that. Aye, and strange they didnae call you out to certify the death. Dr Robertson used to do that. Always complaining that it used to happen just as he was sitting down to his dinner. Aye, he was fond of a good feed and some female company so he was. But something's going on,' he muttered.

I nodded, not wanting to get involved in a conversation about unidentified bodies, though he was right; usually the local doctor does certify deaths on their patch and sends a report to the local procurator fiscal. I knew from Alasdair that Ewan, his cousin, was the fiscal and that his office was in the town of Stornoway.

I paid, and as I turned round I fell over a large open sack which was leaning against the counter.

'Careful, Doctor! Can't have you breaking anything! That's the supplies for the navy boys on St Kilda. Top secret island, very hush, hush.'

He tapped the side of his nose and winked.

'Scooby takes the stuff out to them on his boat on Thursday, if the weather's not too bad. Bugger—sorry, Doctor—of a place to land with the fetch of the waves. Aye, there was one winter the navy had to bring a helicopter over from the mainland to deliver emergency supplies to them. The boat hadn't been able to make deliveries for nearly two months, and the rumour was that they had been down to a tin of soup and two tea bags,' he said, coming round the counter and picking up the bag of coal which he carried out to my car and stuck in the boot. I followed him, looking out to sea. The clouds were an ominous palette of black, grey and streaks of white.

'Aye, Doctor, we always get a big one at the equinox. Make sure that there's nothing loose lying around outside the croft and that you've plenty of candles and coal as chances are the power will go off. Power cuts can last for days out here. They always get the town's power on first. Now you get home before the wind gets up,' he said, thumping the car roof.

Reaching the house, I started to unpack the car despite George's concerted attempts to trip me up. He'd smelt the steak pie and was running around excitedly. I got my drugs bag and the shopping into the house, then hauled the sack of coal and, straining, tipped it into the coal bunker just outside the back door. I could already feel the wind rising and the barn door was banging. Before the wind got up further, I went back out and walked slowly round the house shining the torch from side to side. The beam caught a couple of empty buckets, and I put them into the barn to stop them disappearing out to sea. Then I checked that the hens were all in, and bolted the barn door. 'No mink tonight, girls. You'll be safe and sound,' I assured my feathered charges who looked up blinking and clucking softly from their straw slumbers.

Back inside, I walked from room to room turning on all the lights. I hated coming home to a dark cold house. Still at least there was George standing at the kitchen door, tail wagging as I filled his bowl with dog-food. Now on a domestic roll, I ran upstairs and harvested the dirty clothes from the bedroom floor, stripped the bed and stuffed it all into the washing machine. In the kitchen, while the washing machine was struggling with its bio-chemical hazard load, I found a pair of yellow rubber gloves under the sink and tackled that week's washing-up. The smell of the steak pie, warming in the oven, began to drift around the kitchen, and George sat guarding the oven door and occasionally wagging his tail in anticipation.

Meanwhile I'd commenced another battle of wills with the stove. But this time I was determined. I'd found Mairi's hand-written instructions which had fallen under the coffee table and carefully read them. Kneeling down in front of it with offerings of firelighters, kindling sticks, rolled up newspapers and coal, I followed her instructions religiously, and after half an hour I finally succeeded. The red glow had expanded, crackling had started and the smell of burning peat was now filling the kitchen.

'Eureka!' I shouted, startling George who shot under the kitchen table. Warm water began pumping round the radiators and warmth slowly began to seep out of their metal bodies. An hour later I was slumped on the settee in the kitchen, in front of the stove, with George resting on my lap. We were full of steak pie, and I lay with a glass of gin and tonic resting on George's back. There was an air of tropical rain forest as the pulley was draped with all my washing and my brightly coloured socks and knickers gently steamed on the radiators. There was no tv as it was impossible to get reception in the cottage and the radio signal came and went depending on the weather, so I'd been spending evenings listening to music. My favourite Blondie tape was now playing on the hifi, but in the background the wind was making a low moaning sound which was getting gradually louder. I turned the hifi up higher to drown out the eerie noise. My tape finished and I spent some time looking for something else to play. Mairi's tapes which lined the shelves were mainly of classical music, but I discovered a pile of ceilidh music albums stacked in the corner. These must belong to Alasdair. Most of the covers were adorned by cheery looking men with accordions and fiddles who all appeared to be enjoying a party; any hand not holding a musical instrument was clutching a glass of whisky. Some of the records were scratched and a bit dusty, but I wiped a couple with my sleeve to get the worst of the dust off, and soon Andy Stewart was singing about a whisky flavoured loch.

The wind was getting stronger and outside there was the odd interesting bang which I chose to ignore. At one point George raised a quizzical eyebrow, stretched and walked to the back door. I stood up to open it but he returned to his former position and soon added to the orchestra of noise with his sonorous solo. Despite the growing storm, I spent a very pleasant evening along with a book and some gin and tonics. The warmth of the fire was making us both drowsy and at ten o'clock I decided to head for bed. So I loaded up the stove with a mix of peat and coal, and knocked back a couple of sleeping tablets with the remnants of a glass of gin. I'd just turned out the light when I remembered that I'd left the torch on the kitchen table. I went back down, retrieved it and stuck it on the bedside table. If the power went off and one of the patients phoned during the night. I didn't want to go head-first down the stairs.

The wind was now rising to a level that I'd never experienced as a city dweller. It was the first time in my life I heard wind howling and it was very eerie. It sounded like the painful cry of a prehistoric animal. I shivered and put out the light. I'd read of people pulling blankets over their heads to block out the noise, so I tried that. It only resulted in my discovering I had undiagnosed claustrophobia. So I decided to stick with the wind noise and began to audit my imaginary sheep.

Chapter 6

Deja vu hit me hard. No it didn't just hit me once; it was more of a sustained beating. According to the luminous green hands on my alarm clock it was two o'clock. The gin and pills had done their trick and I'd been deep in the arms of a drug induced stupor. Literally dead to the world, requiring an exceptionally loud noise to wake me up. This is the approximate level of noise which George, the chorus of hens and the wind managed to generate as they welled like an orchestra to a crescendo. But it was the rhythmic banging of what sounded like a door somewhere outside that made further sleep impossible.

'Please will you shut up,' I muttered at George the snoring soloist. No response, so I threw a slipper in his direction. He leapt up startled and growled at the slipper. But my plea for silence was ignored by the hens and the wind. The rain was hammering onto the bedroom windows, and the last thing I wanted to do was get up and go outside, but I knew that I'd have no peace until the banging door was silenced. My hand found the bedside light and pressed the switch.

Nothing.

Okay, so now we had a power cut. Great. Fighting the gin and pills, I struggled into Alasdair's dressing gown, grabbed the torch from the bedside table and padded slowly downstairs. Ever the coward, George decided to stay and guard the bed.

I opened the back door and recoiled. Last night hadn't been much of a dress rehearsal for tonight's weather. The predicted wind was now howling round the cottage; a sound which made my toes curl on the cold linoleum floor. In the torchlight I could see industrial rain passing horizontally in a gravity defying manner. I slammed the door and considered going back to bed, but I knew I had to shut the errant barn door if I was going to get any sleep. Pulling on the wellies and one of Alasdair's waterproofs with a giant hood, I took a deep breath and waving the torch in front of me to light the path, stepped outside and moved forward away from the shelter of the house.

Immediately the hood was ripped off my head and I nearly lost my footing as the elemental force swept against me. The roar was deafening and I retreated back in to the lee of the house. So this was storm force that the shipping forecast sometimes mentioned along with Hebrides and Bailey, and here I was stuck in the middle of it. I made a mental note to do my next locum job on another island, but next time in the southern hemisphere. The wind was coming in strong blasts with lesser gusts between. I stood shivering with cold and fear, waiting in the shelter of the house for the next lull. I'd never been out in such a wind. The coat was slapping against my legs. I was frightened the wind would lift me up Dorothy-style. The wind dropped momentarily and I ran over to the open barn door, holding my hood tightly. How could it be open after I'd locked it? The catch must be faulty. It took all my strength to try to close the door, then something glistened red in the torchlight, catching my eye. Blood. I let the door go and it swung back with a bang. I stepped hesitantly inside, praying that the mink was gone.

The interior of the barn was inky black apart from my torchlight beam which I swept round looking for a dead bird. All the hens were perched facing in one direction, like a weather vane convention, and looking at a large black sack lying just in front of the tarpaulin which was tightly wrapped round Alasdair's pride and joy—his motorbike. He'd been reluctant to take it with him to Glasgow in case it was stolen. Perhaps an injured hen was lying behind it. Cautiously I approached following the path of my torchlight. Suddenly the sack moved. I screamed and almost dropped the torch. The hens began squawking and flapping. Focussing the light of my torch, I saw that it wasn't a sack, it was a body in a black wetsuit. The milk-white face was coated in mud and straw and glistening with sweat. The only way I knew it was male was by the stubble encasing the chin. The eyes were closed. I knelt down to feel his forehead which I already knew would be hot—too hot. As I swept the torchlight along the length of his body I saw a bright smear of red and yellow oozing from the gash on his leg.

The sensible course of action at this point would probably be to withdraw, lock the door and phone the police and an ambulance, but I'm afraid the gin and drugs jammed my common sense dial. My adrenalin started pumping which kick-started my trauma training.

I quickly checked him over. His breathing was laboured, he was fevered and he had a septic wound. He was lying in a freezing cold barn, its floor carpeted in mud, dung and straw, and he was surrounded by attentive, but neurotic, chickens. He couldn't stay here. The door behind me banged again. I jumped. He didn't. He was totally unresponsive. Not good, I told myself, do something. Right, get him into the house. Standing the torch at the door of the barn, and gripping him under the arms I started to pull him across the straw floor towards its light. He was heavier than I expected and I struggled with his dead weight but he couldn't be left here. He groaned but I kept going. At the barn door I paused for breath. Panting heavily, I slowly pulled him across the wet grass. The wind tore open my coat, and rain like gravel hit my face. I was soaking by the time I reached the house. I ran back for the torch and locked the barn door.

When I got back into the house George was standing over the body sniffing the man's hair, then he started licking his face. But despite his dousing by the rain, and George's enthusiastic licking there was still no movement. I wasn't sure who was sweating more—the patient or me. I dumped Alasdair's coat at the back door and dragged him into the kitchen and close to the stove, but I didn't have any strength left to lift him up and onto the sofa. There were still embers glowing in the stove and the kitchen was warm, the faint red glow lighting the room. Thank goodness I'd brought my bag from the car, yesterday evening. I couldn't face going back outside again; the wind seemed to be strengthening. I heard a slate crash from the roof onto the path.

Before I could do anything I needed more light. I lit the lamp and candles and put them along the fireplace and on the kitchen table. Finally, I could take a look at the patient. On the plus side he was breathing. I wasn't sure about the rest; difficult to tell as he was encased in a wetsuit covered in grass, and muck. My next thought was thank goodness house-proud Mairi can't see this; she would go nuts at the mess in her kitchen.

Before I could assess his condition I had to cut off his wetsuit. The surgical scissors in my bag would have been as much use as the proverbial chocolate fireguard. Scrabbling around in the cutlery drawer I found Mairi's large kitchen scissors. It wasn't an easy task, the scissors were designed for cutting fish not rubber, but after ten minutes of hacking through the material I freed him from the rubber casing.

He was a mess. He'd obviously been in the suit for a few days, I tried to breathe through my mouth to avoid the smell. But after a quick assessment it appeared that, luckily, he'd no broken bones. I wiped the worst of the mess off him with the towels that I kept just inside the back door for drying George, but I needed to properly clean the wound, which didn't look great. It was hot and angry looking and clearly infected. Damn! The one thing I didn't have was disinfectant. I checked under the kitchen sink, but there wasn't any there. Then I remembered the gin. Needs must. I poured a generous measure over the wound. It must have stung but still there was no sound from him. I cleaned out the worst of the yellow pus and bandaged it up. Then I washed his body with hot soapy water and stuck a pair of Alasdair's blue pants on him Finally, I injected him with penicillin, keeping my fingers crossed he wasn't allergic to it. It didn't need my thermometer to tell me he had a fever, so to reduce his temperature I dribbled soluble paracetamol into his mouth using one of Mairi's little flowery china milk jugs.

I went into the spare room and grabbed a couple of blankets from the bed and placed them over him. It wasn't ideal but it was an improvement from the chicken house. I knelt back on my heels. What should I do next? Phone the police. They could come and collect him. I picked up the receiver of the wall-phone; the line was dead.

Suddenly, I heard a noise outside the kitchen door. I froze. Was there more than one of them? I looked around. What could I do? I reached over and gently lifted the poker which lay by the stove, trying not to make a sound. I stood up slowly, and crept over to behind the door. I'd seen this done in films. How difficult could it be?

The door creaked open and I raised the poker further above my head. Waiting for him to enter—holding my breath. 'Get out my house. I've called the police,' I shouted. Then George's nose appeared and I laughed as he crept hesitantly across the floor and lay down beside the prone figure. I let out a long sigh. I could do with a drink. I checked my watch. It was four am. Perhaps not now—I could wait until the morning. I tried the light switch again. No luck. I'd better head to bed. But not before I cleaned the foul smelling dirt from the kitchen floor. I scrabbled under the sink for cleaning materials, and as I pulled them out a bottle of whisky tumbled forward. It had been hidden behind the Vim and the bleach. I looked at the label, then I shoved it back in. It was a strange place to keep an expensive bottle of malt, but as I'm not famed for my love of domesticity or cleaning, perhaps Alasdair thought it would be safe to hide it there. I quickly cleaned up the mess from the floor and threw the rags in the fire which was starting to go down. I loaded it with more coal and peats then I went back upstairs to get into bed.

Once upstairs, I had second thoughts and carried my blankets and pillow downstairs and put them on the sofa; it was a lot warmer down here and I could keep an eye on the patient. George opened one eye. I expected him to join me but he was obviously comfortable where he was. The room gradually dimmed as I blew out all the candles and turned down the lantern, leaving a small glow. I lay back onto the sofa, snuggled well under the blankets and flicked off the torch. The performance of the elemental wind orchestra outside was unabated, but exhausted I fell asleep to George's rhythmic snores.

Chapter 7

My head hurt. My neck hurt. My back hurt. Everything...hurt. No wonder—I'd just spent the night on the sofa. This was worrying. I always made it upstairs to bed, no matter how much I'd had to drink. Not good. From now on I'd need to cut down on the pills or the gin or both. Light was filtering through a gap in the curtains. Not bright, clean, shiny light, but dull, grey, anaemic light. I felt like going back to bed. The rain was still pebble-dashing the windows. I stretched. Ouch! More things hurt.

I looked at my watch, my stomach dropped. Damn! It was half past nine. I'd overslept. Why hadn't Mrs Murray phoned? She was usually quick off the mark when I was late; by now she must be fuming. I'd better phone her and tell her I was on my way. I eased myself off the sofa, staggered over to the wall and picked up the phone—no dialling tone. The phones were still off. Then I remembered it was Saturday. There was no surgery apart from emergencies. Thank goodness, I could go back to bed. I yawned. There was something nagging at the back of my brain. Something I had to do...

Turning, I caught sight of the man lying on the floor under the blanket. Damn! I vaguely remembered what had happened. I'd need to sort this out as quickly as possible. I checked, he didn't appear to have moved from where I'd placed him. His chest was still moving. Good—he was still breathing; the most important bit. My bag was lying at his feet, so I knelt down, found a syringe and injected another dose of penicillin into his hip, then made up another paracetamol solution and dribbled it into his mouth. He seemed a bit better than the night before, but time would tell.

George, lying at the end of the rug, resting his nose on his paws had assumed the mantle of a sort of indoors version of Greyfriar's Bobby. He reluctantly moved from his post and slunk outside when I opened the back door. Rain was sweeping horizontally up the valley. Not a living soul could be seen. Even the sheep were hiding behind walls and the seagulls had taken shelter. Back inside I turned on the transistor radio to see if there was any news. Only static. There was a scratching at the back door. A soaking wet George walked into the kitchen and shook himself.

'Sorry, forgot about you,' I tried as he walked past me, clearly unimpressed. My attempt at reconciliation by way of a dog biscuit was rebuffed, and he returned to his post stretched out on the floor beside the man. I shivered. There wasn't much of a glow in the stove. I'd need to get more coal from the bunker outside the back door and peats from the barn. With great reluctance I pulled on the cold, clammy wellies and zipped up Alasdair's oilskin. The wind slammed the kitchen door shut behind me and, leaning into the wind, I went over to the barn and let out the chickens.

You have to admire a chicken—it was blowing a gale and chucking it down and they stood around my feet clucking cheerfully. Was it possible that they put antidepressants in their food, I wondered? Perhaps their reluctance to move away from my feet resulted from the fact that most mornings I'd forgotten about them and it was lunchtime or later before I fed them. But this morning they were in luck and they pecked happily at their seed in the rain. Chicken feeding completed, I dragged an old animal feed bag filled with peats into the kitchen and then ventured out again to fill up the coal bucket.

Thankful to get back into the house, I shook off the oilskin and hung it on the hook behind the door where the drips began to puddle. With the stove catching and the flames licking the glass,

44

I put the kettle onto boil and went upstairs to change. Cursing the scones, I squeezed into my jeans, the zip straining, and threw on a thick Aran jumper of Alasdair's which I'd found in the back of the wardrobe. The clothes were cold and smelt of damp. I pulled on a pair of scratchy hand-knitted bobbin socks which had been given to me by a patient, and I was ready to face my world of one unconscious stranger and a huffy Jack Russell.

Fighting off the urge for a drink, I lit a cigarette and sat on the sofa drinking a mug of strong coffee with two spoons of sugar. Gradually, my brain cells emerged from the chemical fog as the effects of last night's gin and sleeping tablets dissipated.

There was a grunt and the stranger suddenly threw back the covers and struggled to sit upright, then fell backwards onto the rug. I dropped the mug. George barked and shot back upstairs.

I went over and knelt down on the rug making reassuring noises. I could see that the man's eyes were glazed. His forehead still felt too hot on the back of my hand. He was mumbling incoherently. As I pressed his shoulder gently back towards the floor I could only make out one word: Natalia. He repeated it again. I covered him with the blankets. He was still mumbling but the rest was unintelligible for two reasons. Firstly, he was fevered, and secondly the language he was speaking wasn't English or even Gaelic.

It was Russian.

My first boyfriend at university had been studying Russian and I sometimes went with him to the Russian films, though being a frequenter of the back row, the action on the screen sometimes passed me by.

So my patient was Russian. Was he something to do with the body pulled up by the fishing boat? Was he dangerous? Well, in his present condition he wasn't a threat to me, never mind national security. Perhaps I should phone the police. I lifted the phone handset again. Still dead. What should I do? Summoning an ambulance to take him to hospital on rough single-track roads forty miles away wasn't an option in his present condition. He wasn't fit to travel until he regained consciousness and his temperature dropped. Then I could sort things out and get him transferred to hospital in Stornoway. Meanwhile, he'd be better off on the rug with George.

I checked his pulse again, then lay back down on the sofa and pulled the blankets up and picked up a couple of Mairi's paperbacks from the pile on the table. Thomas Hardy or Mills and Boon. Well-written heartbreak or happy piffle. There was no contest. Let's find out what happens when Jennifer's object-ionable, but handsome, new neighbour opens a furniture business next door to her flower shop. I flexed open the paperback and started to read.

It's always a mystery to me, and probably to most of my insomniac patients, why it is almost impossible to fall asleep at night, but sit down for five minutes on a comfy sofa during the day, and stick a book on your lap, there's a guarantee that you'll have a one-way ticket to the land of nod.

When I woke again it was almost noon. I yawned and stretched. My mouth was dry and I was in need of some liquids. My eyes immediately strayed to a half empty gin bottle lying on the floor where I had left it last night. No, I needed a clear head as I'd have to drive to the surgery to get some more antibiotics, and although I'd heard the police never stopped anyone in the medical trade this definitely wasn't the time to take a risk. The power was still off, so I found a tin of tomato soup, poured it into a pan and put it on the stove. At the sound of a tin being opened George woke up and was rewarded with a couple of biscuits.

I was surprised George went near the man. He was usually nervous of men, probably with good reason. The first few weeks of his life hadn't been happy ones, but I remembered vividly the night we first met.

I hadn't been long qualified when I'd been phoned by the cops late one Tuesday evening, and asked to accompany them to an emergency social work call. There was a child care issue involved and it couldn't wait until the morning. The senior partner usually did these calls, but he was off on holiday, and the police sergeant said things would be pretty straight forward. It was dark when I arrived, but I could see that the garden was never going to win any gardening awards. I counted three broken bikes and a pram with no wheels. There were no curtains at any of the windows and dull yellow light eeked out onto the streets.

Neighbours had contacted the police. Both parents were alcoholics, but the granny, who'd lived in the house had held things together. The children were fed and attended school, but things had gone downhill after she'd died three months ago, so we were here to make what is called in social work terms 'an intervention'.

I hate making 'an intervention'. People are never pleased to see you. There is usually a horrible smell. And cats always seem to be involved. Also from my experience any intervention which involves taking an elderly person into care is shorthand for signing their death warrant. The authorities would remove an old person for their protection from a bogging house full of rubbish, piles of newspaper and the obligatory cats. They'd stick them into a bath, then process them into a pristine old folks' home. Odds-on they would be dead within six months. I wondered if perhaps over the years elderly people developed an allergy to cleaning fluids. Perhaps it would be a lot kinder to leave them at home, even if it annoyed the neighbours and social workers.

This Tuesday evening after the parents had been removed by the police, I went in to check on the kids. Sitting on a row on the sofa, like three eggs, they looked malnourished and sat scratching their heads. Their faces had a flat, white, shell-shocked look about them, as they watched with detached interest the parade of police and social workers through their home. After a whispered conversation between the police sergeant and the crumpled looking social worker, it was decided to remove them to a place of safety. I was kneeling examining them when the smallest child who was four and had a face decorated with green tramlines of snot and yellow crusty eyelids, looked at me and asked, 'Whit aboot George?'

'Is that your brother?' I asked.

'Nae,' he said, looking at me as if I was stupid. 'He's in the cupboard cos dad disnae like him an' sometimes hurts him.'

This was getting worse by the minute, another child imprisoned in a cupboard. I relayed the information to the sergeant who went off to fetch poor George. Two minutes later he returned smiling, holding a squirming ball of fur at arm's length.

'What do you want done with this, Doctor? Will I contact the RSPCA?' he asked.

'George?' I asked the children. They all nodded solemnly. While there had been no protest from them when the police had arrested and taken their parents, when the policeman turned to remove the puppy they became agitated and upset. To keep the peace, I volunteered to take George home, and said that he could stay with me, intending to take him to the dog and cat home next morning. This seemed to calm them down. I wrapped the puppy, which was as malnourished and as filthy as the children, in a towel, and stuck him in my car boot for the short journey home. I was scratching my arms by the time I reached home, and hurridly filled the kitchen sink with warm soapy water, and dunked in the bedraggled looking creature. He stood shivering dejectedly as I shampooed him. I looked at the bottle; at least he wouldn't have a dandruff problem. Then I plonked him into a plastic laundry basket lined with newspapers while I went off for a long bath and hoped that I hadn't picked up anything from the puppy or the kids.

Back in the kitchen I heated up some warm milk, and soaked some bread in it, and gave it to the starving puppy. It was either that or baked beans, and I thought the bread would be a safer dietary option. I was unsure of the holding power of puppy bowels.

My boyfriend Tom had been away the previous night for yet another meeting. These overnight meetings had become more frequent in the last few months. When he arrived back the next evening, George looked at him suspiciously.

'What is that?' asked Tom pointing at a quivering George who was backing away from him.

'It's George. I told you how I rescued him.'

'Yes, but I thought he'd be gone by the time I got home. I hate dogs. They smell,' he said, crossing his arms.

George couldn't back away any further and was now in the corner of the room. His tail was firmly between his legs and he was still trying unsuccessfully to growl. He sounded like a child's squeaky toy.

'I think he's frightened of men. He's been badly treated,' I added, picking up the quivering puppy and stroking him. 'Surely we can keep him?' He looked at the puppy again, his face darkened and without another word he'd turned and slammed out of the house. Sometimes living with Tom felt like living with an adolescent who was used to getting his own way, rather than a consultant surgeon who was used to ordering people around.

The puppy had whimpered again, so I took him into the kitchen and placed him in the laundry basket on top of an old towel for the night.

Tom didn't return till well after midnight. He woke me up getting into bed. I lay with my back to him and pretended I was still asleep. And within minutes he was lying on his back snoring like a stranded walrus. A walrus which had spent the evening swimming in beer. But the next day when I'd been loading the washing machine I'd smelt perfume, not mine, on one of his shirts. Like a fool I hadn't tackled him. I loved him and was sure that it was just a passing fling. But, I did decide that George was staying.

A sudden bang, brought me back to the present. I pulled the curtains back and saw my dustbin lid wagon-wheeling down the hill. Then my stomach dropped. There was a police car with blue lights flashing speeding along the valley. Don't be silly, I reassured myself, it's probably off to an accident. Then the car took a sharp left at the bottom of the hill and spun up the road to the croft, skidding to a halt outside. I quickly tugged the curtains shut again. Damn, what should I do? I shook my head and tried to clear my thoughts—drink and pills I could cope with, but lack of sleep was numbing my brain. I had a Russian resting on my rug. I wouldn't open the door, perhaps he'd think I was out. But my car was parked outside. I took a deep breath, I would just have to try and explain what happened. Perhaps they'd believe me. There was a knock at the back door. I froze. I could see the black uniform shadowed in the glass panel. If I could see him, then the policeman could see me.

'Dr MacAllister, it's PC Bain. I need to speak to you urgently,' said the dark shape beyond the glass. Then George started to bark and the knocking became more insistent. I'd have to open the door.

Chapter 8

George's barking was getting louder.

'Dr MacAllister, it's PC Bain. Are you in? Please open the door.' The knocking got louder.

Damn! What should I do? Opening the door to expose the prone figure of a sleeping Russian wasn't perhaps the best option. I froze. He knocked again. He wasn't going to go away.

'Sorry, you'll need to come round to the front door. I can't find the key to this one,' I shouted through the door. I went into the hall, shutting the kitchen door tightly behind me, and went to the wooden front door. There was a large rusty iron key with a piece of blue twine attached in the lock. I struggled to turn the key, and heaved open the swollen door. I wasn't sure how I was going to explain the unconscious Russian spy. I crossed my fingers that he wouldn't make a noise.

I vaguely recognised the tall uniformed cop standing on the doorstep, cap tucked tightly under his arm, being buffeted by the wind. He'd waved to me when driving past on the road. No one was anonymous on the island. I suspected my yellow Beetle had been quickly clocked by him. He looked at me expectantly. It was pouring and I couldn't leave him on the doorstep, and if he'd come to arrest me he would probably barge in anyway.

'Sorry, come in,' I stuttered, stepping back. I realised that he was still talking. This did not bode well. Would he arrest me here or at the police station?

'...so I thought it would be best if I fetched you myself,' he said. My brain still wasn't responding. One half was now deep in panic mode wondering how long you spent in prison for hiding a Russian spy. The other half was trying to understand what the cop was saying in his flat Dingwall accent. He'd stopped talking and was now standing head slightly cocked. He seemed to be waiting for some sort of response. There was no sign of handcuffs being produced. I hedged.

'Sorry, I'm not long up. I'd a bit of a late night last night. Could you just run that by me again?' I chanced a smile. He responded with a smile. Things were starting to look up. There were protesting barks and frantic scratching noises coming from the kitchen. The cop looked towards the door. I decided just to ignore them.

'Sorry for disturbing you, Doctor, but Mrs Stewart up at Bay Cottage has got chest pains. Her husband Donald's in a real panic. I said I would fetch you. All the phones are out. The lines are down and chances are they'll be down for the next couple of days or so till the ferry can bring over the repair boys from Glasgow,' he said, shuffling from foot to foot.

'Right. Em okay, I'll just grab my bag from the kitchen. PC...' I hesitated, remembering that my bag lay two feet away from a possible Russian spy.

'Bain, but Brian will do. Can I give you a hand with your bag?' he said, taking a step towards the kitchen door.

'No.' I moved in front of the door. 'My dog can sometimes be a bit funny with strangers.'

'Do you want to come in my car, or follow in yours and I'll show you where the house is?'

'I'll follow you in my car. Two minutes till I get my bag sorted,' I said, opening the front door and ushering him out. Sticking his hat on, he ran back to his car, one hand holding it on to stop the wind frisbeeing it away. Breathing a sigh of relief, I opened the kitchen door, and an excited George shot into the hall, and stood wagging his tail expectantly.

'Okay, you can come too,' I said. A quick check revealed the

Russian was still dead to the world. I grabbed my bag, and slung on the damp coat hanging behind the kitchen door.

Locking the door was difficult, but I didn't want to come home and discover anyone else in the house. One stranger was enough. I finally managed to get the key to turn and slipped it into my pocket. I ran to the car trying to avoid tripping over George. Struggling against the howling wind to hold open the driver's door, I threw my bag onto the backseat and George hopped onto the front seat in navigator position. The wind snatched the door handle from my hand and slammed the door shut. Just as I started the engine, the police car pulled away, driving along the side of the loch at a speed which I had no chance of attaining in my elderly car. He must have checked his mirror because he slowed down enabling me to catch up.

The roads were greasy and glistening with the rain but at least the usual sheep hazard was absent. They were sheltering behind the dry-stone dykes, walls which jigsawed their way along the side of the road. The beat of my windscreen wipers couldn't keep up with the rain, and it was difficult to see the road. Rivulets were running down the hill and cascading across the road. Strong gusts of wind were tugging at the car and my hands were tightly clenching the steering wheel to stop the car being blown into a ditch. It wasn't quite so bad when we were lower down and sheltered, but as we headed up the hill along the top cliffs one particularly strong blast hit, pushing us towards a ditch and I wrenched the car back from the edge. I was trying not to overcompensate the wheel turns because on the other side of the road was the sea, and a swerve over that would probably been a bit more unforgiving. A loose plastic feed sack flew across the bonnet. George let out a bark and jumped from the seat into the well of the car. I felt like joining him. Ten minutes later, we pulled up outside Bay Cottage. I was sweating, as if I'd run the journey. Leaving George in the car, I followed the cop into the house. In the doorway stood a worried looking man in his sixties, his blue shirt tail escaping his trousers. I followed him up the narrow wooden stairs.

'Thank you for coming out, Doctor,' he said. 'It's Morag. She's in a lot of pain. She's been sick twice and I'm really worried about her.' He pushed open the bedroom door then stood aside to let me in. Morag lying in bed didn't look well; her face, twisted in pain, was the same shade as the magnolia paint on her bedroom walls.

'Thank you for coming out on a Saturday, Doctor,' she smiled wanly. 'Donald, take the doctor's coat,' she instructed. I peeled off the damp waterproof, handed it to Donald who withdrew and closed the bedroom door. Placing my bag on the bed, I sat down.

'How are you feeling?' I said, smiling as I picked up her wrist and checked her pulse. Practice had taught me that patients tended to respond better to a relaxed looking doctor. Even if you didn't feel it, it was always better to pretend.

I opened my bag got out my stethoscope and thermometer and examined her. I suspected a gallstone attack. Extremely painful, but not fatal. We agreed that I'd refer her to the hospital for further action. At the mention of gallstones rather than a heart attack, some of the colour started to creep back into her face, moving her from the magnolia tints in the paint chart to the pale rose ones.

I went downstairs. Donald and PC Bain were sitting on the armchairs either side of the fire, both looking worried. They visibly relaxed at the diagnosis, which was strengthened when Donald admitted that they'd had a large plate of fish and chips last night for tea. Not the ideal dish for a woman with a dicky gall bladder.

Donald stood up and went into the kitchen and returned with a bottle of whisky and three crystal tumblers.

'You'll have a wee dram, Doctor?' I was busy shaking my head when I noticed that Brian was holding a glass and had taken off his hat.

'Nice one this,' he said to Donald.

'Aye, I've been saving it for something special,' he smiled as he handed me a glass and I sat down. A collie slunk out of the kitchen, sniffed my shoes and lay down beside the fire. Time passed, whisky flowed and I relaxed. Donald kept our glasses topped up, and I heard tales, some of which were taller than others. Donald was a natural storyteller, but Brian had one or two interesting police tales of his own that he was happy to share. Outside in the hall a clock chimed two o'clock. I nipped upstairs to check on Morag, who was now fast asleep and breathing more easily.

The two men looked as if they might be exchanging stories for a while longer, so I said my goodbyes. As I was going out the door, Donald pressed a large bag of homegrown potatoes and a gingerbread loaf into my arms.

'Drop in for a cuppa, if you're up this way again,' he shouted, waving as I ran down the path towards the car. George, ignoring the potatoes, sniffed the gingerbread when I placed it beside him on the seat. I decided to call into the surgery on the way home and stock up on drug supplies for my unexpected house guest, in case the wind got back up again and we became housebound.

As I entered the surgery, I automatically flicked the light switch—no power. I went through to the dispensing area to stock up on penicillin. I checked Morag's notes and saw that she'd no allergy to penicillin, so I took some more phials and put them on her records. Suddenly the front door slammed, and the familiar figure of Mrs Murray appeared silhouetted, her black umbrella dripping on the carpet. Bars from *The Flight of the Valkyries* started playing in my head.

'Hello, Mrs Murray,' I said, my stomach clenching. 'Horrible day.'

'Good afternoon, Doctor. I didn't expect to see you here.' She frowned. 'I was passing and I saw the car outside. Is there a problem?' she said, looking at the open door of the drugs cabinet. 'Just popped in to do some paperwork and to stock up on some drugs. The cops called me out.' At my use of the word cops, Mrs Murray had winced. 'Morag Stewart's gallbladder was playing her up, and I've just come back from there. The police arrived at my house with the call.'

'Aye, PC Bain can be pretty handy in a power cut.' She advanced towards the dispensing counter, then stopped and sniffed the air. A look of disapproval crossed her face. Oh God! I'd forgotten about the whisky.

'Tiny sip from Donald. Couldn't get out of the house without one.' I smiled weakly. She didn't respond. 'Well, that's me finished here.' I stood up closing the records and locking the cabinet. 'I'll see you on Monday. Better get home before it's dark.'

She acknowledged the information with a curt nod of her head and I edged round her and got out of the building as quickly as possible. The feeling was reminiscent of that I had as an eight-year old visiting the headmaster's study after breaking a window. The plus side was that I wouldn't have to face an angry set of parents when I reached home—only an unconscious Russian.

56

Chapter 9

Leaving the surgery, something felt different. I couldn't think what it was, then I realised that this was the first time in months that I'd felt remotely happy. I suspected that part of this was probably due to Donald's whisky. The measures he'd poured were extremely generous. But there was more to it. The wind was dropping and sunlight was bouncing off the waves playing hide and seek with the clouds. Easing my grip on the steering wheel, I drove along humming along to the Eagle's tape playing in the car stereo.

I felt as if I was in a bubble. A psychiatrist would probably describe it as a form of dissociative state. Controlling receptionists, sick Russians and dead-beat lovers were momentarily forgotten and a warm glow suffused me. Like the feeling that envelopes you after a couple of drinks or some good sex. Though I wasn't sure if I was still qualified to speak about the latter. It had been so long since I'd had good sex. Yes, I'd had sex in the last year. The 'trying to find a post-coital taxi in the rain sex' or the 'I hope he doesn't want to stay the night as there's nothing in the fridge apart from nail polish and vodka' sex.

But this was different, more like glow you felt when someone special moved into your life. The first time you went into the bathroom and glimpsed two toothbrushes in the tumbler, leaning on each other for mutual support. Or when you came home after a hard day in the surgery, and there was a light in the house, and cooking smells met you as you opened the door.

The glow lasted two minutes then, like the end of the record track, it started to fade. I pulled off the road onto the machair grass, braked and turned off the engine. The Eagles stopped urging me to *Take it Easy* and segued into *Witchy Woman* which for some reason brought an image of Mrs Murray into my brain. I quickly turned off the stereo. George leapt onto the passenger seat, whimpering and scratching at the window. I leaned over, opened the door and he jumped out. I watched him sniffing along the grass, tail in the air, half-heartedly chasing any birds which rose up chattering into the air. I reached for my cigarettes, lit one and inhaled. The buzz of nicotine reached out to me. I took another drag.

'Right, Helen, let's get a grip. What do we do now?' Speaking to yourself is usually frowned upon by my profession. In fact, it sometimes results in sectioning or removal to a mental hospital if the patient persists. But I'd always found a one to one conversation with myself useful when I'd a problem. No confidences were ever breached, there was no waiting list and you didn't have to explain your problem to to a nosey receptionist.

Outside, the waves were now throwing themselves onto the mercy of the beach. Seagulls were flying along the water's edge, coasting effortlessly on the wind as if they were on an elevated conveyor belt. And in the distance I could just make out a large boat balancing on the horizon.

I shook my head. *Concentrate, woman. Go home, phone the police station and tell PC Bain that you've just found an unconscious man in a wetsuit in the barn.* Problem solved. George might be a bit unhappy about his deselection from the role of Greyfriar's Bobby, but in the great scheme of things this would seem to be the best option.

I looked at my watch—it was approaching four. I could have all this done and dusted by tea time and no more worry about the stranger in the living-room. With any luck there would be an old black and white film on television. Scratch that option—I'd forgotten about the power cut. And that I was now living in a house that didn't have a television. Anyway in this part of the world all the programmes were in black and white, as the-powers-that-be hadn't yet decreed that anywhere but the town qualified for a colour transmitter. I laughed remembering Mairi's husband Alasdair regaling us with island tales, one night in the pub in Glasgow. He earnestly explained that the church turned the television transmitter off on a Sunday and only switched it on for 'Songs of Praise'. It was a good leg-puller—I was one of the group that had believed it.

Get it sorted woman, I urged. Right, the sensible option it was. Back home, top the Russian patient up with antibiotics then down to the police station to tell them about my Soviet visitor. I immediately felt better now I'd a plan. I stubbed out the cigarette, wound up the window and turned the key in the ignition. Just in time, I remembered about George. Where was he? There was no sign of him. I wound down my window and whistled, and his head appeared over a dune, and he raced towards the car.

Five minutes later, I pulled up outside the house. Grabbing my bag I headed for the back door, George at my heels. I turned the handle and pushed the door, but couldn't get in. *Idiot!* I'd forgotten that I'd locked it this morning and I'd exited via the front door.

I went round to the front door and turned the handle. Damn! It was still locked too after this morning's episode of hide the patient from the police. Where was the blasted key?

I dumped my bag on the ground and muttered my way back to the car, checking my pockets as I went. Had it fallen out at Donald's house or at the surgery? Eventually, I found the key down the side of the driver's seat. No wonder people on the island left their doors unlocked; it made life a lot easier. Back to the front door and with a bit of a struggle I managed to get it open despite the rusty lock. I kicked it shut. George shot into the kitchen and hid under the sofa.

I went through to check on the Russian. Still out for the count, he was either deeply unconscious or deaf, given the noise I'd made coming in. A quick check over and it was revealed to be the former. Well, before I passed him into the hands of the police I'd better top up his meds as it would take the ambulance a while to get here from town, then they'd need to make the return journey back there to hospital. Another forty miles.

I injected him with more antibiotics, and made up another dose of paracetamol mixture. I drew it into the large plastic syringe which I'd brought from the surgery, and knelt down beside him to administer it. Putting my hand under his head and gently elevating it so that he wouldn't choke, or worse send any liquid into his lungs, I concentrated on gently easing the mixture between his cracked lips. Unexpectedly, there was a change in his breathing pattern. I stopped and his eyelids fluttered. I continued until the syringe was nearly empty, concentrating on maintaining a steady stream and not spilling any. Looking up from his mouth, I was met by a pair of granite grey eyes boring into mine.

Suddenly George growled and, startled, I dropped the syringe. It bounced as it hit the floor then rolled under the sofa. George took off, running out of the kitchen, and I heard his paws scrabbling up the stairs. My first instinct was to join him, but I didn't want to drop the patient's head on the floor, so I continued cradling it and looked around for the milk jug of water that I hoped would help keep him hydrated. Things were going to be moving quicker than I had anticipated. I took a deep breath, not quite sure what to do next.

Chapter 10

As a doctor I've looked into many eyes—some living, some dead. There was something strange about this man's eyes. Cold, flat, they were more reptilian than human. They say that eyes are supposed to be the windows of the soul. Well this soul had bars on the windows, keeping things out—but also in. I shivered.

He moved and muttered something, but I couldn't make it out. I needed to get him hydrated, so I lifted his head and brought the small milk jug of water up to his lips and gently tipped it. Water started dribbling through his white, flaking lips. His eyelids began flickering again. I could see that he was battling to cling to consciousness, but his eyelids began shuttering downwards. Like a sleepy child he slumped back into my arms. I gently deposited his head onto the rug and pulled the blankets back over him. I put my hand on his forehead then took his temperature. It was down a bit, but not enough to stick him in the back of a freezing cold rickety old ambulance for transportation to hospital forty miles away.

Tomorrow was Sunday. Mr Macdonald, the consultant, wouldn't be pleased to receive a patient for admission at this time on a Saturday night. Not long after I'd arrived on the island, I'd sent an emergency admission of a pregnant woman who was unable to keep water down and was becoming dehydrated. My ears were still ringing from the phone call I received from him.

'This could have waited till Monday morning. Can you not manage to insert a drip, lassie? What do they teach you at medical school nowadays?' he said. I mumbled my apology feeling like a first year medical student.

A week later I'd met one of the A and E nurses in J M's, the chemist, in town. I was stocking up on some drugs for the practice. She'd beckoned me to the corner of the shop and told me next time I had an out of hours emergency to ask for a staff nurse not the consultant. I got the feeling that any request or advice would be more sympathetically handled. I'd learnt my lesson. Emergencies were one thing. Sunday emergencies for Mr Macdonald were different and, I suspected, required at minimum some missing limbs. In Mr Macdonald's opinion this patient would definitely not fall into the emergency category as all four limbs were attached.

Nothing moved on the island on Sunday. Mairi had warned me about this before I'd arrived. All the shops were closed. There was hardly any traffic on the roads apart from cars going to and from church. Once for the midday service, then again for the evening service. Even the beaches were deserted. I asked her what she and Alasdair did on a Sunday afternoon.

'We go to bed,' she said, 'to sleep.' Then she'd winked.

When I'd first arrived it'd seemed a good idea to have a day of rest. But now that nights were getting darker I'd have loved to go out and do something on a Sunday. The only buildings open were the churches.

Oh for the luxury of buying loaf of bread or a pint of milk. I couldn't remember the last time I'd read a Sunday paper. They didn't arrive till late Monday afternoon and it wasn't the same as reading it on a Sunday. Once or twice, when I'd had a particularly busy week and some Saturday callouts, the evening had arrived and I'd hardly any food in the house and the shop was closed. This had resulted in George and I having some interesting Sunday lunches. Fishfingers with tinned spaghetti hoops and sweetcorn had been one of our more exotic meals. It had been a miserable Sunday compounded by the fact that I'd run out of gin and was forced to drink vodka and bitter lemon.

On the plus side my patients were pretty good at observing Sunday as a day of rest, and I hadn't yet been called out on a Sunday; only a couple of phone calls for advice. Which reminded me to check to see if the phones were back. I lifted the receiver—still dead. But at least I knew if there was hammering on my door in the middle of the night it was likely to be the police looking for medical assistance of some sort.

My problem was see-sawing. As the man on the rug became less of an emergency he became more of a problem. The prone figure slept on, breathing more steadily. I sat on the settee and watched him, accompanied by George who'd crept back down the stairs to reassume his guard dog position at the patient's side, and was now snoring in an off-tune way.

The furniture in the room seemed to be softening round the edges as the light was fading. I looked out of the window; more storm clouds were gathering. Time to light the candles and to make something to eat for myself and George. First things first—the hens. I went outside, and from the excited greetings realised that I'd forgotten to feed them again this morning. I threw some hen-food on the floor of the barn. They shot inside and I quickly bolted the door. At least tonight I would have no interruptions from them. Back in the kitchen, I had a brain wave, I would write *feed hens* on a piece of paper and pin it to the wall beside the kettle. Problem solved. But I couldn't find any paper, so I used a sheet from my prescription pad. If I had to face the BMA, destruction of a prescription pad would be the least of my worries.

At the back of the cupboard I found a tin of meatballs in tomato sauce. I poured them into a pan and stuck them on top of the stove. Aware of George's nagging nose constantly bumping my leg, I opened a tin of dog-food, sniffed it, then put it on the floor.

'I think you're getting the better deal here, George. This smells a lot better than mine.' He wagged his tail enthusiastically.

While the meatballs were heating up I went round the room lighting the candles, then threw more coal and peats on the fire. Eventually the meatballs started to bubble volcanically, spitting red sauce onto the cooker. I made up some powdered mash from a crushed looking packet. It was a few months out of date, but what harm could powdered potato do? My motto is if it smells good, it's okay; if it don't, it ain't. This had stood me in good stead both in the kitchen and in the surgery.

I poured myself a small gin and tonic, then decanted the meatballs and potato mound onto the plate and took a mouthful. The potato was disgusting, so I washed it down with a large gulp of gin. The meatballs weren't so bad, and I noticed that George had crept over and was now sitting at my feet looking expectantly at my plate. I flicked a meatball with my fork, and he caught it with expertise before it had reached the carpet. The hi-fi wasn't working but I'd found Mairi's battery operated radio cassette. Presumably kept for times when there was a power cut. The candles flickered as I lay on the couch with my plate on my chest listening to Mendelsohn's Hebrides Overture. I presumed this was one of Alasdair's tapes. My musical taste was expanding; I'd never listened to classical music before. I'd always been too busy. But now as I spent most evenings alone I'd started to enjoy classical music. My parents would be very impressed.

When I had first arrived I'd received a flood of duty invitations from the minister, church elders and other well-meaning people in the community. Kindness mixed with curiosity was the catalyst for these invites, which usually resulted in an awkward Sunday lunch. But word must have spread and the invites had dried up. It's difficult to make conversation when work is your only interest and you can't discuss it.

The music swelled, the candles flickered and George snored loudly. Not quite a scene of domestic bliss but the nearest I was likely to get for a while. I wondered what it would be like to to be married and a two point four, not a one point zero. On the kitchen wall was a photograph taken last year at my parents' silver wedding anniversary. Mairi, Alasdair and I were standing our arms linked with huge gin engendered grins. Alasdair, wearing his kilt, sandwiched between Mairi and me. It looked a happy scene, but the smile wasn't reflected in my eyes. It was only two weeks since Tom and I'd split up.

My gorgeous, charming, senior registrar boyfriend of two years had casually announced one weekend that our relationship was over. Things hadn't been going well, and the arrival of George seemed to speed up the disintegration of our relationship. Tom had succumbed to the curse of the nursing handmaiden—something that most female doctors were immune to. I sometimes wondered if there was a section on husband entrapment in the nursing training course. Tom was moving in with the theatre sister.

'Nothing like taking your work home with you,' I'd shouted when he'd told me. 'At last you'll have someone to hand you the correct knife and fork.' He'd left that night. I'd sobbed all weekend. Tom had been my friend and confidante for the last five years. In some ways the loss of his friendship was the most difficult thing to handle. I'd invented a tale of an unattributed allergy to divert attention away from my red eyes. My sleep pattern disappeared hand in hand with my self-esteem and after work I started drinking gin to help me relax. I strayed over the edge one day when a patient brought me in the contents of his deceased mother's medicine cabinet for destruction. I was desperate for a night's sleep, so I'd slipped the Valium and sleeping tablets into my handbag and taken them home. Things had slowly escalated from that. Culminating in my talk with Dr James, the senior partner, who was questioning the evaporation of the practice's sleeping tablets. An escape to the Hebrides had seemed like a good option. I hadn't anticipated that I'd be living under a microscope. Here, it felt like everyone knew who I was and seemed to be aware of my movements, sometimes before I'd even made them. And the loneliness I'd felt in Glasgow was intensifying too. I was missing my friends. I had never been a great one at opening up and pouring out my emotions to all and sundry, but Joyce and Abby who I'd gone through university with were my emotional safety nets. But now they were hundreds of miles away in England, living in flats with no phones and apart from the odd five minute call usually interrupted by the pips. Gradually we'd lost contact over the last couple of years. We were now down to birthday and Christmas cards.

I looked out the window again. The beauty of my surroundings seemed to be bringing to the surface all the emotions that I had tried so hard to suppress and exposed my inner bleakness. Enough, I chided myself as my emotional weeds started to germinate. I doused them with another small gin, but decided to avoid the sleeping tablets just in case I needed to check on the patient during the night.

Kneeling down on the rug beside him, I felt his forehead again. His temperature had dropped and was normal. His breathing was no longer laboured. Well, whoever you are, you're definitely on the mend, I thought. He sighed in his sleep and turned. His arm slipped out from under the blanket and I picked it up to push back into the warmth. The fire flared, and I noticed a dark mark on his left forearm. Septicaemia? Surely not, I thought to myself. But just in case I fetched my torch. Thankfully, it appeared to be an old scar. I'd missed this in the candlelight. Then I took his hands and examined the fingertips. They were scarred as if someone had tried to remove the fingerprints. I remembered the words in the shop. Could this man really be a Soviet spy? I wasn't worried; this man was incapable of peeling a grape in his present condition.

I yawned. Only one more day and I'd deliver the patient to town. Problem resolved. Then, more importantly, I could get on with sorting out my own life.

Chapter 11

I woke up and automatically tensed, waiting for my daily hangover to land. It didn't. Of course! I'd been so busy, last night, that I hadn't drunk much. No sleeping pill induced haze either. It was also my first night of not waking at four in the morning from the nightmare of finding my ex wrapped round a blonde nurse in our bed, and me chasing him with a scalpel. Thankfully, even in my dreams I couldn't run fast enough and I'd never caught him.

I stretched. Light was seeping through the bedroom curtains. I tried the bedside lamp. Still no power. I lay back down again. It was Sunday. I hated Sundays on the island. No ferries sailed. No planes flew. I felt trapped—I couldn't even escape to Inverness or Glasgow for the weekend. It would be nice to be anonymous for a while, to wander round shops without bumping into my patients.

Nothing moved on the island on Sunday, or the Sabbath as Mrs Murray called it. All the shops were closed, and on the sunniest day not a single sock dared dangle from a washing-line. The council locked all its toilets to guard against bodily functions being exercised on a Sunday. Though I'm not sure that this Sabbatarian gesture was appreciated by tourists with small children or older men with large prostates.

In the swing park, the swings didn't swing. They were padlocked together. Much the same as happened in Glasgow when I was child. Maybe one day they would break free and soar skywards accompanied by the sound of childish laughter.

It was quiet, but that was the status quo out here in the country for the other six days of the week as well. I was bored. No, I was probably more lonely than bored. I missed meeting up

68

with friends on a Sunday for a coffee. Life was no was no fun after Tom had left. Tom, Tom, Tom...I had to stop thinking about him. *Get up,* I urged myself.

Things were strangely quiet in the bedroom. No sinal snoring or twitching—George's not mine. His favourite dream seemed to involve chasing something, probably a rabbit. This started with sporadic nose twitching, and culminated in the frantic scrabbling of his paws and undignified yelping. Amusing during the day but not at three o'clock in the morning.

I patted the blankets with my hand. There was no bump. Where was George? I sat up and noticed the bedroom door was open. He must have gone downstairs. During the night he'd been scratching at the bedroom door, but I'd ignored him and gone back to sleep. There were some feral cats living in an abandoned croft house nearby, and they sometimes disturbed him when they came on a visit to check out the henhouse.

My watch said nine o'clock. It was time to take the patient's temperature and do his meds. I slipped on Alasdair's dressing gown and padded downstairs to the kitchen—then stopped. The sofa was empty. My stomach dropped. Where was the patient? Thankfully he wasn't delirious and so he couldn't have wandered off during the night. Perhaps he was stronger than I thought and had left. I smiled—problem solved.

George was lying on top of the pile of blankets, which had fallen off the sofa, rhythmically beating them with his tail. Then I heard the sound of flushing water from the bathroom. The door opened and a gaunt, muscular figure appeared grasping the doorway for support. His only clothing was the faded blue pair of Alasdair's shorts that I'd pulled onto him the night I'd found him. Unaware of me, he slowly staggered from the hall back into the kitchen. Our eyes met briefly as he toppled onto the couch. He lay there breathing heavily and I could see sweat glistening on his upper lip. His mouth moved but I couldn't hear what he was saying. I went over and knelt down beside him.

'Water' he rasped.

'Coming up,' I said, and I filled a glass from the tap. I lifted the glass to his mouth and helped him drink. He gulped it down. Some water ran down from the side of his mouth onto his bare chest. I leant forward to wipe it away. He looked up and I quickly pulled my hand back.

'More,' he grunted.

'Okay, but drink slowly,' I refilled the glass and he quickly drank it. Lying back with a sigh, he closed his eyes for a few moments. I thought he was asleep. Then his eyes slowly opened, and he stared at me intently. His eyes were somehow different today, the coldness of yesterday had gone.

'Do you speak English?' I asked.

He nodded hesitantly as if unsure whether he did or not.

'Good, that'll make things a lot easier,' I smiled. 'My name's Helen. I'm a doctor. I've been looking after you. You're in my house.' I spoke slowly, not sure how much he was taking in. 'You're okay. You've been ill, but you're getting better.' His eyes were following my lips intently. 'Your leg was infected and you've had a fever. Do you understand?' I raised my eyebrows. He nodded. 'I'm going to give you another injection now,' I said, reaching for my bag. 'You're safe here,' I added. I wasn't sure why I said that. Probably my training. I'd been taught to reassure my patients where appropriate. Well, I suppose he was safe—for the moment.

He nodded again. His eyes tracking my every movement as I prepared and gave him the injection. I washed my hands and when I turned back to ask him how he was feeling, his eyelids were closed and he was asleep. I gathered the crumpled blankets from the floor. They were still warm from George's body heat, and I layered them gently over the sleeping man.

There was an insistent nuzzling at the back of my knee, then George started pacing up and down in front of the kitchen cupboard. I stuck the kettle on the stove, and got out the dog food box. The metal lid slid out of my hand and fell to the floor with a clatter. George and I both jumped—but the patient didn't. He was dead to the world.

While the kettle was heating, I went out to feed the chickens. They ran out, wings held horizontally like trainee fighter pilots, clucking cheerfully. I scattered their seed and they began pecking around my feet. The sun was shining. Its light was bouncing off the sea diamond sharp, and I squinted against the glare. The autumn breeze whipped through Alasdair's dressing gown, but it felt good to breathe in some clean air.

Much as I wasn't a fan of cleanliness and housework, I recognised that the fetid odour flowering in the kitchen required some action. There is a saying about cleanliness being next to Godliness. Thank goodness I'd not been required to take an exam on either at university—I would have failed both. Until I resolved the cleanliness issue, I'd take my coffee outside. When the patient next woke up, I could give him a sponge down. I wished I could just get one of the district nurses in, but the patient's presence would require some explanation. Meanwhile I'd have to tackle the task myself.

Doctors are usually pretty hands off when it comes to their patients. Surgeons probably more so. In fact, given a choice, surgeons would probably prefer to have their patients turned inside out for easier access. Skin to surgeons being a packaging that just holds the more interesting contents together.

I carried my coffee and cigarettes outside and found a sheltered spot out of the breeze. Lighting a cigarette I took a drag and absorbed the hit. There was whining from inside the back door, and I let George out to join my nicotine routine. He wandered off then came back and we stood and watched the waves.

I took another drag and slowly exhaled. I'd told my patient he was safe here. Why? He'd looked lost. Fragile. Fragile—I laughed—he was at least six foot tall. He had the look of a man who did a lot of sports. This was not a man who enjoyed sitting behind a desk. He'd been weakened, but he was out of danger. Now was the time to contact the police. Right—I'd get dressed then go to Brian Bain and explain that I'd found a sick Russian in the barn. There would be no need to tell him exactly when I'd found him.

No time like the present. I threw the dregs of the coffee onto the weeds and stubbed out my cigarette on the wall and went back indoors. I quickly pulled on some clothes, and was shrugging my way into my coat when George went over to the patient and nuzzled his hand. Out of the corner of my eye I saw another movement. The patient was stroking George's head. His eyes were open and he was looking at George.

'I have a dog at home,' he said slowly.

He spoke in perfect English. Well, far less accented than my Glaswegian. He wouldn't have been out of place reading the news on Radio 4.

'But he bites strangers,' he said hesitantly.

'George has never bitten anything but bones,' I laughed.

He smiled wanly. 'I thought you were Russian,' I said.

'Why do you think that I am Russian?'

'You were feverish and talking,'

He looked at me sharply. 'Talking?'

'Yes, not much, just a few words in Russian.' He seemed to relax. 'But your English is very good,'

'Years of listening to your World Service on the radio,' he said, trying to pull himself up a little and looking round the room.

'Where am I?'

'You're in Valagarry on the Outer Hebrides. I found you in my barn,' I said.

'A barn. Was I alone?' he asked.

'Yes.' I hesitated, not sure whether to continue, 'But sadly they found a body in the nets of a fishing-boat.'

He looked down, then said. 'Good. That will make things easier.'

'Easier? You knew the dead man?'

He nodded. 'He was the soldier who was guarding me. His orders were to kill me, if I did not do as he instructed.'

'Kill you?'

He nodded again. George continued licking his hand.

There was a sudden click and flash. All the lights turned quickly on and off and the fridge hummed momentarily. All three of us jumped and George hid under the table.

'There's been a power cut. They're trying to fix things,' I said.

'I must go home,' he said, trying to get back off the couch, but failing and falling back.

'To Russia?'

'Yes, before they kill Natalia. They said they would kill her if the mission failed,' he faltered.

'Kill Natalia—your wife?

'No, my daughter. No, my wife's dead. She died in a road accident last year. Natalia is our...my...daughter.' His breathing slowed and he looked into the distance, his eyes seemed to soften and he blinked rapidly. 'She's six and lives with my parents in Minsk.' Once again he tried to push himself off the couch. The plate and mug fell to the floor with a crash and George gave a yelp and hid behind my chair.

'What mission?'

'It is a long story,' he said.

73

'It's Sunday in the Hebrides. You're too ill to move. We're not going anywhere. Are you hungry?' I asked. He nodded. 'I'll make us some tea and toast,' I said.

'Thank you, you English...you English have a thing about your tea,' he smiled.

'Scottish,' I chided. 'You're in Scotland remember.' I stood up and filled the kettle and put it back on the stove. I got out the toaster.

Then a worrying thought hit me...did I have any bread?

Chapter 12

'Tea,' I said, holding out a mug with a picture of a tractor on it. He took it. His hand was shaking.

'The good news is I've found some bread. The bad news is—there's no toast. I forgot there's no electricity, so I've made you some bread and cheese instead. Eat it slowly,' I instructed. He took a tentative bite. George was now sitting, raptly staring at the cheese sandwich, his tail wagging. Cheese was George's favourite food. To prevent any potential dispute, I took his collar and pulled him away from the patient. He lay at my feet, disappointment emanating from every whisker.

The patient took a gulp of tea and spluttered.

'I thought our Russian coffee was strong,' he said grimacing.

'It's how we make tea here in the islands—strong or stronger,' I said. Perhaps it was this excess of tannin that was responsible for Mrs Murray's hairy chin?

I sat down and lit a cigarette. George crept over commando style and assumed his place lying beside the patient. His sandwich finished, the patient hesitated, looked warily at his mug of tea, swallowed a mouthful, then began to speak.

'My name is Andrey. I am...a scientist.' He took another gulp of tea, spilling some onto the blankets. 'I was a lecturer at Moscow University. In our department we were working on developing interception systems.' He coughed and more tea spilt onto the blankets and onto George, who got up, shook himself and moved out of range. 'Your country has been working on developing these systems too,' he said, looking at me. 'But you developed them faster than us.'

'Interception systems. To intercept what?'

'Nuclear missiles,' he said, taking more tea. I dropped ash from the end of my cigarette onto my lap and hurriedly brushed it off.

'It gave your country enough time to shoot down any nuclear missile targeted at it. Your country had installed the device in the tracking station on St. Kilda.'

'Had?' I asked, hesitantly.

'Yes. My job was to uninstall it.' He looked over at me.

'Uninstall it. Did you?' Somehow, I already knew the answer to this question. My stomach was starting to churn.

He looked up and nodded. 'Yes.'

My stomach dropped and more ash fell from my cigarette. 'Nuclear missiles?'

'Yes, it was your country's early warning system,' he said.

'...wa ...was?' I said, stubbing out the cigarette on the ashtray.

How the hell did I get into this mess? This made the possibility of being struck off by the British Medical Council seem like a flea bite. The Russian's weak. I could just run out the door. There's no way he could catch me in his present state. Do they still hang people for espionage? Or was this treason? I remembered as a child seeing a picture of the Tower of London and ravens. They were pecking out someone's eyes and...

He coughed. 'Your country was years ahead of us developing this miniaturised device which was on the base at St Kilda. The plan was to take it back to Russia where we could quickly replicate it and install it. It would take you years to rebuild it as Professor Montgomery, the inventor perished and all his plans were destroyed in a fire.

'I had to do it, I had no choice,' he mumbled.

'No choice?'

'They said they would kill Natalia if I didn't,' he said hoarsely, trying to struggle upright and falling back on the sofa. More tea spilt over the edge of the mug onto the blankets. 'What day is it?

'It's Sunday, why?'

I know that they are planning something big at the end of this month, and we had until then to complete the mission,' he frowned.

The lights flickered again. I jumped. 'These cuts happen all the time at home,' I said.

'Are they on strike? I read that your country is always on strike?'

'No, not this time. There was a storm which knocked out the power.'

'Ah, yes, the storm. I remember, it was...' His head started nodding onto his chest. I put the ashtray down, stood up and lifted the plate and mug from the floor. He looked up, tried to speak some more, but it was unintelligible and gradually his head slumped forward and his breathing became more regular. He was asleep. One hand fell from his chest to the floor, and George crept back and licked any remaining butter from the Russian's fingers then settled down again, nose on paws, beside the couch.

I looked at the Russian. He was sound asleep. I felt his forehead, it was cool. He was no longer in danger. No longer my patient. He could now become someone else's problem. I'd phone Brian Bain. I lifted the phone receiver, holding down the cradle so that the bell wouldn't make a noise. The phone was still dead. I'd need to go to the station. Slipping on Alasdair's grey duffle coat, I whispered George's name. He reluctantly stood up and slowly stretched.

'In your own time,' I whispered angrily. He wagged his tail and followed me to the door. I left the cottage, quietly closing the door behind me and walked slowly over to my car with George trotting at my heels. I turned the key in the ignition. The engine caught. I hesitated, then I turned it off.

I just had to think for a minute to clear my head. I started to drum my fingers on the steering-wheel.

Thinking about it logically, lying asleep on my couch in the kitchen, I had a Russian spy who'd just disabled Britain's nuclear interception capacity. I should contact the police, or at the very least Brian Bain. He could lock him up, and I could get back to work tomorrow as usual. Another week of Mrs Murray loomed. I sighed. The Russian was going to be more difficult to explain than disappearing drugs, but was more pleasant and with more attractive facial hair. What was it about men with stubble? *Get a grip woman*, I chided myself. The country's weapon defence system has just been compromised and you're fixating on his stubble.

But what about his daughter? Surely the Russians wouldn't kill a six-year-old? But the way he'd reacted made me think they might. He had to get back to Russia. But if the police held him here what would happen to Natalia?

I decided to go for a walk along the beach to try to figure out an answer.

I opened the car door, and George, happy to get an unexpected walk, leapt out, tail wagging and ran towards the beach. We walked away from the house over the dunes, sliding down the sandy slope onto the sand. The wind had swung round into the east and was whipping my hair into my eyes. The tide was going out, and the waves were starting their retreat from the shoreline. A lone yellow glove was lying on the sand just beyond the reach of the waves. It had probably fallen from a fishing boat. It looked as if it was trying to claw its way to safety. I wondered if, somewhere out at sea, a fisherman was working with one hand in his pocket.

George had found a ragged strand of seaweed, and was dragging it along the sand and tossing it around his head like bunting. He didn't have a care in the world. I shook my head. How had I suddenly become responsible for the nation's security? My shoulders sagged as I walked slowly to the end of the beach. The cliffs loomed larger as I approached. A small river dribbled its way down the rock face, across the beach and down to the sea. Tufts of grass and lichen clung to the face of the rocks. I chose a large boulder at the bottom, sheltered from the wind and sat down and pulled out my cigarettes. I needed to think... big time.

Chapter 13

My mind was going round in circles like George chasing his tail. 'Why me?' I asked myself. I'd come to the Hebrides to escape trouble, not to dive into the biggest imaginable vat of the stuff. The only sensible thing was to tell the police and then get on with my life. 'Right, I'll drive over and see PC Bain when we get back,' I told George. He looked up, then quickly returned to worrying his rapidly fraying strip of seaweed.

Decision made. I could now get on with my life. I stood up stubbing out my cigarette on the barnacle bearded rock-face. My hands were turning blue with the cold, and I rubbed them together in an effort to warm them. George ran ahead barking and I started to hum *Take it to the Limit*, which is where I'd felt I'd been for the last few days. But now it had to stop. I felt lighter; a weight had lifted. Pulling up my hood and tucking my hands up my sleeves tortoise-like, away from the bitter wind, I started walking back along the edge of the waterline. Splashing through the sea and dodging the larger waves spilling onto the sand, I whistled tunelessly startling some birds which were strutting like little clockwork toys along the water's edge. George ran towards them and they took off skywards with a whir.

Something glinting on the sand caught my eye. Looking down I saw that there were dozens of clear dome-like objects being washed in by the tide. I crouched down for a better look. They were tiny jellyfish, their bodies lucently dissolving onto the sand. Their glistening shapes and insignificant transience caught my attention. Who's to judge the importance of life? I wondered. What's the worth of a six year-old girl against a nation's security?

There was growling at my feet. I looked down. The seaweed

hadn't submitted to George. 'Leave it,' I instructed. He dropped it and we set back off to the house. In the distance I heard a siren. A police car was driving along the side of the loch, at speed, its blue light flashing. Well, if I needed a sign what to do next, I definitely had one now. Shouting George's name, I speeded up my step and started jogging towards the house. They must have found out about the Russian. I reached the house just as the car roared up the track and came to a skidding halt kicking gravel upwards. PC Bain rolled down the window and shouted at me.

'Quick! It's Catherine Miller. The baby's coming. We'll take my car, it'll be quicker.' He looked as anxious as any first time father as he sat revving the engine. 'Hurry, Doctor!'

'I'll get my bag,' I shouted, running indoors. I glanced towards the settee. Andrey was still fast asleep. I left him in George's capable hands, grabbed my bag and locked the door behind me.

'How far apart are the contractions?' I asked as I got into the car. Before I got an answer, I gasped as I was flung back against the seat as the car sped off down the hill. I struggled to pull the door shut.

'About five minutes,' said PC Bain his gaze not leaving the road. 'The ambulance is attending an accident on the other side of the island, so hospital's not an option.' We were driving faster than I thought possible on the narrow roads. I looked at his hands gripping the wheel—his knuckles were white.

'What about Angela? Where's she?' I asked. Angela, our practice nurse, was also a qualified midwife.

'I tried her house on the way here. There was no one in,' he said. My stomach knotted.

'She might be out at church,' he added, 'I spoke to her neighbour and he's going to try to find her.' I mentally crossed my fingers.

The scenery sped past and I was starting to feel queasy. A

couple of times, I closed my eyes and gritted my teeth. Luckily it was after twelve and the church traffic was already in church. This probably saved both their and our lives. Thankfully we arrived before I was ill. I was sure I read somewhere that you could be fined if you were sick in a police car. I was glad I didn't have to put it to the test.

PC Bain ran into the house. I followed at a slightly more leisurely pace as I was hoping my stomach would recede from behind the dam of my tonsils. More importantly, I was desperately trying to remember some of my obs and gynae training from the maternity placement I'd done as part of my medical training. This had been in a small cottage hospital near Glasgow. Fortunately for me it had been a quiet baby month and any emergencies had been quickly shipped off to The Rottenrow. It had given me time to catch up on some badly needed sleep. The maternity nurses treated me as an awkward bystander, and I kept out of their way as much as possible.

Damn—I wished I'd paid a bit more attention. Still this was Catherine's third baby. What could go wrong? By the time I'd reached the door, I'd thought of at least half a dozen serious scenarios and a dozen lesser ones. Oh why, oh why had I ever left Glasgow and the safety net of a large maternity hospital? Mentally throwing up a prayer to any higher being that was listening, I stepped inside.

I didn't have to ask where Catherine was. I could hear deep guttural moans coming from upstairs. I sniffed. I could also smell roast meat. They must have been cooking Sunday lunch when Catherine's labour started. My stomach rumbled.

'I'll be good; just let this be okay,' I bargained, as I went up the stairs. Unlike the cottage they were carpeted which dulled the noise of my footsteps, but not of the occupant upstairs.

'I'll just go and boil the kettle,' muttered Brian Bain in true textbook style as he fled into the kitchen, shutting the door behind him.

I followed the moaning noise which led into a small bedroom with sloping ceilings. Catherine was writhing on the bed, her face was bright red and she was dripping with sweat. Her husband, Calum Mhor, stood in the corner, wringing his hands and looking on anxiously. Birth isn't, in my view, a spectator sport, and rather than having him keel over on top of Catherine I sent him downstairs to keep Brian company. He looked relieved as he hurried from the room. I closed the door behind him and took a deep breath.

'Right, this is your third baby. Third babies are always easier,' I lied. Catherine completed a groan then nodded. I suspected she knew I was lying, but it made us both feel a bit better.

'Breathe,' I kept encouraging, almost as much for my benefit as hers. She panted heavily at intervals. I tried not to.

The next forty-five minutes passed in a blur. It involved some screaming—Catherine's mainly, apart from when she grabbed my hand mid-contraction and crushed my fingers. I realised my error and after that kept my hands well out of her reach. There was some shouting—Catherine's—and a fair amount of swearing which I would have to attribute equally between myself and Catherine. For a church-going woman, she had a repertoire of words that a hardened squaddie would be proud of.

Finally, with a roar from Catherine, that I suspected could be heard on mainland Scotland, the baby slithered into my non-expert hands and immediately started to bawl.

'Thank you,' I said quietly, as I looked at the baby in my arms. 'She's a girl,' I smiled, as I handed her gently to her mother. There was the sound of footsteps running up the stairs, the bedroom door swung open and Angela, our midwife, just stood and smiled.

'Well done, Doctor MacAllister, your first island baby.' She said something in Gaelic to Catherine and they both laughed. 'I'll just nip downstairs and wash my hands before I touch the wee one,' she said. 'Do you want a cup of tea, Catherine?' There was a tired nod from Catherine. 'I'll get Calum to make some tea and toast.'

She left the room. Catherine's hand caught my unguarded bruised hand and held it tightly. I winced.

'Thank you, Doctor. Please don't tell my husband what I said.' She looked at me anxiously.

'Of course not. It's between you and me,' I said, smiling down at the baby which was in her mother's arms. Hopefully her blushes would be spared if the neighbours were still out.

I went downstairs. Two pale faces looked up at me from the armchairs on either side of the fire.

'Everything's fine,' I said. Calum edged past me and up the stairs.

I collapsed on the other chair facing PC Bain.

'You look tired, Doctor,' he said. 'A wee glass of something will help.'

'Thank you, Constable Bain,' I said.

He hesitated. 'Brian's okay, if you're happy with that, Doctor?'

I smiled and nodded and he went into the kitchen. I could hear him talking to Angela followed by the sound of laughter.

I slumped in the chair, totally drained, the responsibility of the last hour sinking in. How precious is a life? I thought of the baby upstairs lying in her mother's arms guarded over by her father. I thought of six year-old Natalia in Russia waiting for the return of her father. I thought of Andrey lying helpless in my kitchen worried about the fate of his daughter. I made a decision. Life is precious, and Natalia's, at this moment, was the only one that I had any hope of helping.

'How are you, Doctor? Any news?' asked Brian Bain. He was standing leaning on the fireplace. I shook my head. I noticed patches of blue paint on the backs of his hands. He followed my glance. 'Was just doing a wee spot of DIY when things kicked off.' He smiled. 'I can often get a wee bit done when everyone's in church.' He put his finger to his lips. 'Don't tell anyone.' He laughed. 'You'll be wanting that wee drink to wet the baby's head,' he said. I nodded. 'Are you okay, Doctor?' he asked picking up the bottle and splashing a generous measure into it and handing it to me.

'I'm okay. Just a bit tired. I'll be okay in a minute.' I leaned back in the threadbare armchair took a gulp of the whisky and closed my eyes.

Chapter 14

It was dark by the time I reached home. After the excitement of the birth, Brian Bain and I had been slowly unwinding with the assistance of Calum's very nice, and I suspected very expensive, bottle of malt whisky. By choice I was a gin drinker, but I'd happily accepted the large glass offered by Brian Bain. It was a Sunday and I was unlikely to be called out again.

I swirled the glass, the whisky gave off a medicinal peaty aroma. I took another sip. In Gaelic I knew it was called *uisge beatha*—the water of life. So what better time to drink it? It loosened both our tongues and I discovered that Brian and I had more in common than I'd initially thought. Soon we were discussing the difficulties of island living. The problems of living amongst the people you not only worked with, but often had intimate knowledge of. We both hated never really being off-duty. Receiving phone calls at any time day or night meant that it was impossible to relax. Though I supposed I did have a certain advantage—people were usually pleased to see me when I appeared on their doorstep, unlike Brian, whose visits were often not well received. But the thing we both missed most, was the anonymity of city life. On the island everyone knew everyone's business.

Brian told me how Lachie the postman had been delivering a parcel to Slipknot's house, one afternoon and had walked into the kitchen to leave it on the table as he thought there was no one in. He knew that Slipknot's wife was on the mainland visiting her sister and Slipknot would be at work. But there sitting at the table was Slipknot having a cup of tea. Sitting opposite him was Janet his next-door-neighbour. Slipknot had blushed and explained she was just trying on her carnival costume. 'Aye, the only problem was that Janet was wearing a dressing-gown and Slipknot had her lipstick all over his face,' Brian told me, grinning. 'And he was wearing a particularly fetching shade of red.' We both laughed.

The talk moved on and, nearing the bottom of his glass, Brian confided that he was having problems with Duncan 'Crusher' Macdonald's behaviour. 'Everyone knows he's drinking too much. Two days ago he drove his car off the road into a ditch. Luckily no one was hurt. He pulled it out the next day with his neighbour's tractor. I went round to have a quiet word about his drinking and driving but he was plastered and wouldn't let me over the door.

'The next time it happens, I've no choice, I'll be summoning assistance from town. He can't go on like this. Someone's going to get hurt,' he said, taking another sip and eying the glass appreciatively. 'From all accounts he's always been a nasty piece of goods. Got some previous when he was in Glasgow. Did a bit of time in Barlinnie for assault—some fracas in a pub. The other guy ended up in hospital for a month. When Duncan got out, he came home and took up fishing. Stayed sober for a few years, but now he's back on the booze. I'll tell you this, Doctor, he's one guy I wouldn't want to arrest on my own,' he said, shaking his head.

We were standing up getting ready to go and draining our glasses when Calum stuck his head round the door.

'You'll both stay for some Sunday lunch. The roast is ready and I can't let good food go to waste,' he insisted. I was about to refuse but saw that Brian was already sitting back down. I was exhausted. Perhaps a good meal was what I needed. The tantalising smell of roast mutton was drifting out of the kitchen and my stomach was growling aggressively.

Angela came bouncing down the stairs and announced that

mum and baby were both fast asleep and quickly got to work setting the table.

Calum said a grace before the meal. This was a habit I was adjusting to. Being token members of a church it was not a habit I'd encountered at home. When I'd first arrived on the island I'd been caught out when attending a patient and forgetting to check to see whether or not a grace would be said even before a cup of tea. So now I just waited for the other person to start. This worked on most occasions only causing a stand-off situation when the other person was particularly polite and was waiting for me to start first. Calum, the proud father, lifted up his glass 'Slainte! Here's to you all and to wee Catherine. May she have a long and happy life.'

We started with lamb broth. A soup so thick with pulses it could be used as a house foundation. That, under normal circumstances would have filled me up, but today I was ravenous. I couldn't remember the last time I'd had a decent meal. The roast lamb melted in my mouth. I wondered at a house that could suddenly feed three unexpected guests for lunch when I would have struggled to produce three cups of tea and biscuits. The afternoon quickly passed as more stories were swapped and I heard more local gossip. At some point Angela made a final check on mother and baby and left.

I was surprised to see it was dark outside. My watch showed nine o'clock. George! I'd forgotten all about George. I'd need to get home. Feeling guilty, I stood up. I was sure George would smell the meat on my breath when I arrived home.

'For the wee dog, Doctor,' said Calum pressing a brown paper bag into my arms. I looked inside; there were scraps of meat wrapped in greaseproof paper. This might buy me some canine goodwill. There was also the small matter of the Russian, but hopefully he was still asleep.

Brian drove me home. The whisky had loosened his tongue and he was busy complaining about the extra work caused by the body recently washed up.

'That bloody captain in charge of the search for the Ruskies. Muscling in, trying to take over. Bloody cheek! They don't even know where they're going half the time. They're in danger of disappearing up their own ars—sorry, Doctor—backsides.'

I daren't look at him and just grunted in agreement at what seemed appropriate gaps.

Thankfully it was dark and he couldn't see my face. The journey home although being done at half the speed, seemed to take four times as long. I was relieved when we drew off the road and headed up the hill to the cottage. Brian dropped me close to the house and I used his headlights' beams to guide me to the door. He waited till I waved the torch, then he drove off. There was no sound as I entered. No George. That was unusual. I whispered his name. Still no George. I went through to the kitchen and shined the torch round the room. The beam caught Andrey who was fast asleep. Lying across his knees was George. They were snoring in unison. The glass of water I'd left beside the settee was empty and the plate of biscuits finished. Good, his appetite was returning. Then I shone the torch on George. One eye opened. He lifted his head and I noticed some biscuit crumbs on his whiskers.

'Did you eat them all?' I asked. There was no reply, just a lowering of his head. I refilled the glass and put out another plate of biscuits, but this time left them out of George's reach. The house was cold. I shivered. Andrey's forehead was cool to the back of my hand. Good, the infection had cleared. I drew the blankets up over his shoulders.

I realised how tired I was when I went to climb the stairs. Giving birth was exhausting, even if you weren't the mother.

Automatically I shook the sleeping pills out on my hand, but tipped them back into the bottle when I remembered that I'd left the bottle of gin in the kitchen. If I was too tired to go back downstairs for the gin, I might get by without any pills. I took off my shoes and flopped onto the bed. It was cold, I couldn't be bothered to take off my clothes. I pulled the blankets up to my nose. The room was quiet. I missed George's canine snores, but soon fell asleep.

Chapter 15

I woke up with a start. I'd been dreaming of Catherine giving birth to a giant baby in a wetsuit who came out of the birth canal clutching a hammer in one hand and a sickle in the other. As if birth wasn't a difficult enough experience. I could hear heavy breathing in the room. My heart rate increased. There was a weight on my chest. I tried to move, but couldn't. I was pinned to the bed. I put my hand out of the bedclothes and felt rough hair. It was George. I let out a sigh and fell back into a dreamless sleep.

My alarm went off at half seven. I tried the light switch—still no power. I slipped Alasdair's dressing-gown on over my clothes and went downstairs. There were still some embers in the stove, and eventually I managed get the stove to catch properly, and stuck the kettle on top. Peering round the door, I could see that Andrey was still fast asleep despite the noise of my raking the stove. George appeared round the door wagging his tail and with a hopeful look on his face. I fed him and then went to let out the hens. The usual rapturous welcome awaited me. I was starting to feel fond of them. Perhaps the quality that most endeared them to me was that they were non-judgmental. It didn't matter that my feeding of them was erratic. Here I was, and they were delighted to see me.

Back inside I ran a bath. The water was still warm from the heat of the stove. I lowered myself into the peaty-coloured water which had brackenish bits floating in it. The vagaries of having your own water supply was something else I was taking a while to get used to. The water came from a loch at the top of the hill. There must be some kind of filter on it...perhaps. I stepped out to dry myself, hoping that I was cleaner than when I went in. Once

I'd dressed and put on some clean clothes, I started to feel a bit more human or at least able to face Mrs Murray. My head was sore, and my guts were complaining about yesterday's meat overdose. The noise of clunking signalled that the stove was heating. I went back downstairs and had some bread and jam with a strong cup of coffee to jump start my day. I made Andrey a cup too and some cheese sandwiches. Before I left the house, I gently shook his shoulder to waken him. I jumped when his hand grasped my arm. I hadn't expected such a strong grip from someone who'd been so ill. His eyes met mine, then he smiled and his grip loosened.

'Coffee, not too strong and some sandwiches,' I said, buttoning my coat. 'I'm off to work but I'll be back later. How do you feel?'

'Better, thank you. Better,' he said, as I handed him the plate.

'Try and eat some of these, before George does,' I smiled, and he nodded.

'I'll lock the doors, but keep the curtains closed in here,' I said, picking up my bag. 'We'll talk later.' I noticed that George was already sitting beside Andrey, his gaze alternating between Andrey's face and the sandwiches. My money's on George, I thought, as I shut the door.

Mrs Murray glanced at the surgery clock as I walked in. It was showing ten to nine.

'Good morning, Mrs Murray. Good weekend? Hopefully we'll get the power back soon,' I said as I picked up the patient notes from the desk.

'Good morning, Doctor MacAllister. Yes, thank you. You're early,' she said still looked slightly bemused. 'Davey from the Hydro called in earlier to say they're hoping to get the power on within the next couple of days. A lot of the poles are down and they're going to have to bring people up from the mainland.'

'What about appointments?'

'The patients know just to turn up, so there shouldn't be too many. Constable Bain will help with emergencies.'

'Yes, I've seen him a couple of times this weekend.' I smiled. She smiled too. This was disconcerting; it was the first time she'd smiled at me since I had arrived.

'Angela told me that you'd delivered my cousin Catherine's baby. Wee Catherine; their first girl. Wee boys are nice but it's lovely that they've got a wee girl. I'm going to see her tonight.' She smiled at me again.

Ah, that explained it. I'd forgotten that everyone was related to each other.

'Some coffee, Doctor?'

'Please...I'll just be sorting through these notes.'

I wasn't sure how to cope with this pleasant Mrs Murray. 'Just let me know when the first patient arrives please.'

Before the first appointment, Mrs Murray appeared with my coffee.

'Here's some of my homemade shortbread, Doctor,' she said putting a large plate of crumbling, sugar-coated biscuits on my desk.

The outside door slammed and she hurried off to check-in the arriving patient. I sat back and looked at the shortbread and wondered how long this pleasant Mrs Murray would last. The words Jekyll and Hyde floated across my consciousness, and I imagined an even more hirsute Mrs Murray, and quickly chided myself for being so unkind. I picked up the piece of shortbread and took a bite, the sugar cascading onto my lap.

Mrs Murray was right. Most of the patients did stay at home. Morning surgery was quicker than usual and I was finished by half eleven. Mrs Murray had dug out her pre-electric typewriter and was typing at speed. It sounded as if a woodpecker with the

DT's had been let loose in reception. I topped up my drugs from the drugs cabinet, signed some letters then left to do a couple of house calls. It was four when I arrived back home.

Opening the door, I stopped and sniffed the air. The malodorous sickly smell had gone. I walked into the kitchen and a very pale Andrey was sitting in the chair beside the stove. He was dressed in Alasdair's Aran jumper and a pair of his pale blue fraying jeans. He was staring intently at a map, and looked up as I entered.

'I found your husband's clothes and put them on after I had a bath. I hope you don't mind?'

'A bath? My husband?' I said puzzled.

'Yes. The bath was full when I got up just after you left this morning. Though the water was a strange colour,' he looked at me questioningly.

'The filter on the water supply isn't great and it tends to be really peaty,' I explained, meanwhile thinking: husband? What husband? Why does he think I'm married? I put my bag on the table. I was still puzzling over the husband remark, then I followed his glance. Ah, the photograph of the three of us with Alasdair in his kilt. Now I understood where my phantom husband had come from. I didn't correct him. Perhaps it would be better if he thought I was married and my husband would appear, at some point.

'What is this peaty?' he asked.

'Peaty. Em, earthy. We burn it in our stoves.' I picked up one of the square dried clods of earth which were heaped in a basket beside the stove. 'This is a peat.'

'Instead of coal?'

'Some people use coal, but crofters have their own peat banks. They cut the peats from them, for free, then they dry them and bring them home and stack them outside their houses. Once

94

they've dried, they burn them over the winter.'

When I'd first arrived, I'd been intrigued by the sight of large carefully constructed peat stacks, sitting outside the houses on the crofts. The Egyptians had their pyramids, the Hebrideans their peat stacks, looking like windowless earthen sheds. The other thing which I'd noticed was the lack of flowers in the garden. I'd thought it was due to the poor climate. Now I knew that it was because many people spent their leisure time in the summer months cutting peat, not gardening. And of course no one did anything on a Sunday. At least not anything that their neighbours could see.

'Are you hungry?' I asked. He nodded.

'Then I'll make us something to eat. But after tea we'll need to talk.' I hesitated. Once more a dark look had flashed across his face. Perhaps in the fading light I had just imagined it. I turned away from him and got out the tin opener, once again wishing I'd taken the cookery option at school.

Chapter 16

Sometimes you pause and reflect how things have brought you to a specific point in time and space. Sometimes it's more important not to reflect, but to decide what to do next. Andrey had his story to tell and before we could move forward I had to hear it.

We were sitting on the pair of battered armchairs on either side of the fire. Every time one of us shifted position the elderly springs rasped mournfully in protest. This noise was almost drowned out by the wind which was beginning to rise again and had started to whistle down the chimney. The draught was causing the candles to flicker, and the rain scatter-gunned the kitchen window. It felt as if we were being enveloped by the elements. We had eaten. Andrey had assured me that he had tasted pasta before, but he'd hesitated when I'd proffered the plate of tinned macaroni cheese. He'd looked at it with the reluctance of a toddler being encouraged to try some new food. And like a toddler hunger had overcome his reticence, and soon the plate was scraped clean.

'That was...interesting,' he said, as I took the plate from him. I presumed that they didn't have such tinned delicacies in Russia.

'Would you like a drink?'

He nodded.

'Some whisky perhaps?'

He nodded more enthusiastically. 'I have heard tales of your Scottish whisky,' he said. 'Yes, I would like to try some.'

'Sorry, I don't have any.' I stopped, remembering Alasdair's bottle which I'd found. 'Hold on, I know where there is some.' I rummaged under the sink.

'You keep your whisky under the sink?' Andrey raised his eyebrows. 'That is another Scottish custom?'

I shook my head, although I knew of some elderly ladies who kept their bottles of port there, 'But only for medicinal matters, Doctor.'

Some doctors are wary of mixing antibiotics and alcohol. My theory was it was a cocktail that could be taken in the correct measures. Some whisky might even perk him up, and I could definitely do with some perking up. I poured some whisky from Alasdair's dusty bottle into two glasses.

'Nothing prepares you for the size of the cliffs,' Andrey said. 'Have you been there?'

I turned round. 'Where?'

'The Island...St Kilda.'

I shook my head. Living in Lewis was remote enough without sailing to an even more remote and desolate island. Although St Kilda was only 40 miles away it could have been in Iceland as far as I was concerned. Uninhabited since the last remaining occupants were evacuated in the 1930s, the only remaining occupants were sheep and, supposedly, soldiers guarding a top secret area. None of the locals visited it. It was off bounds. Even the fishing boats gave it a wide berth. I knew that an army boat took out supplies once a week; I'd seen their green lorry stocking up at Macleod's store. It was a life I definitely didn't envy. There was isolation, and then there was real isolation, and the poor soldiers stuck out there were experiencing the latter. I suspected that it was their equivalent of the Russian front.

I handed him a glass. He took a sip and coughed. 'This whisky, it is strong. Like your tea,' he said.

I laughed.

He continued, 'We'd seen pictures and looked at maps. I knew there would be cliffs, but when you see them up close they are just...' He held out his hands, palm up and shrugged his shoulders. 'So big I cannot describe them. We'd been on the submarine for weeks. It was horrible. So cramped. It smelt of cabbage and unwashed men. I don't know why anyone would choose that job. To live in a box under the sea.' He shook his head and took another swallow.

'The bunks we slept in were so small, they were like shelves, you couldn't even turn over in them. There was not enough space. I was desperate to get out, to breathe air, to get space away from the stink.

'But when we surfaced and they turned off the engine and the hatch opened I was so frightened. I did not want to go on deck. Dimitri pushed me up the ladder and we stepped onto the deck. It was night. It was so slippy I thought that I was going to fall into the water. Although we were both in wetsuits, I knew we wouldn't last long in the cold water. The cliffs towered above us. The submarine could go no closer to the shore. We were lowered into the rubber dinghy. Dimitri was strong and he rowed us towards a landing spot. There was only the light of the moon. We made it to the rocky shore and pulled the boat out of the water. Luckily it was calm and we managed it without any problems. We could see well enough without our torches and Dimitri led the way up the steep cliff. We waited in a hollow until after midnight when the lights had gone out on the building we knew was the base accommodation block.

'It didn't take us long to reach the nearby tracking station. Our map marked its location but we didn't need it. It was a single storey rectangular structure at the edge of the camp with a large mast, which had a flashing red light on the top. The only building on the base with all its lights on. I didn't know what would happen when we got there, but I was as scared of Dimitri as I was of any British soldier. As we neared the building Dimitri pulled out his gun and I followed behind him. When we looked in the window, we saw the soldier who was on guard, on a chair, just inside the entrance. His eyes were shut and his mouth hung wide open. Then Dimitri tried the handle and the door swung open.

'They weren't expecting any visitors,' Dimitri whispered to me.

'We crept inside and Dimitri stood with his gun pointed at the head of the soldier, and gestured with his hand for me to go. I crept slowly through the building, terrified that there would be more soldiers. It was easier than I expected to find the operations room. I followed the loud hum of the machinery. I pushed the door open and edged into the room, but I needn't have worried, there was no one else there. There were banks of electrical equipment but I quickly located the device. I struggled at first as I couldn't loosen it and I was starting to panic. Just as I was about to give up the casing cracked, and I was able to pull it out. I wrapped it carefully in oilskin before placing it in the waterproof bag that Dimitri had given me. Any moment I expected to hear the sound of the gun being fired, but the only sound apart from the humming of the machines was that of the snores which guided me back to the entrance and Dimitri who was still standing with his gun pointing at the sleeping soldier. He was surprised to see me back so quickly. I held out the waterproof bag and he took it and strapped it to his waist. There was no movement from the soldier. We left as we had come and hurried back to the cliffs. I couldn't believe how well things were going. Our schedule was tight for the rendezvous with the submarine, and thankfully we would be there to meet it when it surfaced. We made it back to the cliffs. To save time we attached a rope at the top and began to scramble down.

'But something went wrong. Halfway down, there was a judder and the rope gave way and we both fell. It was so strange. Neither of us made a sound, but as Dimitri fell past me I saw him knock his head on a large rock. Then the weight of his body on the rope snatched me off the cliff too, but I fell into the sea and not onto the rocks like Dimitri. I was so scared. I am not a good swimmer, but I managed to swim back to the shore. I was still attached to Dimitri by the rope. This saved me from being swept out to sea as the rope was wound round some rocks and had anchored me to the shore.

'When I reached Dimitri he was still breathing but unconscious. There was a large cut on his head and it was bleeding.

'I knew that we only had a short time to reach the rendezvous point with the submarine. If we did not appear their orders were to leave. I had injured my leg in the fall and was losing blood. I struggled to get the dinghy back into the water and to hold it close to the shore while I got Dimitri on board. Eventually I managed it but the time was shortening. I pushed us out but it had been Dimitri's job to guide us. I tried my best. Then I saw the waves break and the tower of the submarine as it began to surface. I could see them, but they could not see us and they couldn't use their searchlights in case someone on the base saw them. The noise of the engine and the sea drowned out my shouts and I realised that my torch had been lost when I had fallen into the water. I tried to pull Dimitri's torch from his belt to signal. Finally, it came free and I switched it on but the bulb had smashed when he had hit the rocks. They waited, then I saw the hatch closing and they submerged. They had gone. Our only way home had gone. We were alone.'

He stopped speaking and, blinking, looked down. We sat in silence.

I stood up. 'I'll make us some more coffee,' I said. As I passed his chair I patted him on the shoulder—he flinched at my touch. I returned with the coffee and threw some more peats on the stove.

'What happened next?'

'I didn't know what to do. Dimitri was in charge but he was unconscious. I had to choose whether to go back onto the island and give ourselves up. I could get help for Dimitri. I could see he was badly injured, but I knew if I did this they would kill Natalia, so I decided to keep going. Any chance was better than no chance at all.

'There were oars on the boat and I rowed away from the island. I had to get out of sight before it was light and they discovered that the device had gone. I thought it might take them a while to figure out what had happened, so I had a chance to get us away. I remembered the captain telling us that the weather was calm, but that there was a storm approaching, and I knew that if we didn't land somewhere before the storm arrived then we were dead.'

I couldn't see his face by the shadow of the candles, but his head was starting to droop down towards his chest. I stood up. 'I think you should stop for tonight. You're tired out.'

He nodded.

'There's a bedroom next door. It'll be more comfortable than the sofa.' I helped him up. I could feel the muscles in his arm as I helped him through. This was the room that Alasdair's mother had when she lived with them. The dressing table top was populated with small china animals frozen in time, grazing on glazed grass. One wall was mosaicked with black and white photographs of long dead relatives, posed and taken in photographers' studios. They all had one thing in common. No one was smiling. They all stared at me in a disapproving manner. I pulled back the blankets and Andrey tumbled slowly onto the bed, and I pulled the blankets over him. I doubted if he had the strength to do this by himself.

'Thank you,' he mumbled as he fell asleep.

Then I blew out all the candles and climbed the stairs. I knew that I would be sleeping alone. George had crept into the downstairs bedroom on my heels and had staked himself out on Mairi's fluffy pink rug before I had closed the door.

Chapter 17

Next morning before I left for work I crept into the downstairs bedroom. Andrey was cocooned in blankets and I could only see the top of his head. I left a glass of water and a plate of biscuits on the bedside table, hopefully just out of George's reach. He lay snoring at the foot of the bed. A bowl of dog food lay untouched on the kitchen floor.

Well, some of us have to earn a crust, I thought to myself looking at the two slumbering bodies. I felt strange. I didn't have a hangover and I'd forgotten to take my sleeping pills again last night. My head was clear. Usually it took to midmorning and two strong coffees to get to this stage of clarity. I felt good. Perhaps I should try this more often. I even remembered to feed the hens, but when I went to the back of the barn to get more chicken food I tripped against a small barrel and knocked the top off and spilling white liquid onto my shoes. I picked up the lid and nestling inside were what looked like bits of dead birds and I caught the strong smell of fish. I quickly rammed the lid back on and headed for the car.

Mrs Murray's navy Ford Escort was the only car in the surgery car park. Sitting at reception, she looked up from her typewriter and smiled as I walked in. I was still disconcerted by this behaviour. I suspected the old Mrs Murray, like a volcano, lay dormant just below the surface ready to erupt at any time.

'Ah, Doctor MacAllister. Good morning. Lovely day.'

'Yes, it is,' I agreed, hesitantly. Lovely day? Definitely not to my mainland eyes. There was not a glimmer of sun, which for me is a prerequisite before a day could attain the title of lovely. Still, I suppose it wasn't pouring with rain or blowing a gale.

'Some coffee, Doctor?'

'Please,' I replied, picking up some mail and heading for my surgery. I stopped and turned.

'I don't suppose you'd know why Mairi and Alasdair would have a bucket of birds or fish in their barn? I nearly knocked it over this morning and my shoes are covered in white stuff.'

Mrs Murray looked at my shoes. 'Guga. They keep the guga in brine. That's salt on your shoes.'

'The what?'

'Guga, Doctor. Every year the guga hunters go from Ness to the island of Suilasgeir and spend two weeks harvesting the gannet chicks and salting them, then they bring them home. It's a local delicacy. Alasdair's lucky; he's related to some of the hunters and that's why he gets them.'

Local delicacy, I thought, more like culinary torture. Thank goodness for fish fingers. 'First patient a bit late this morning, Mrs Murray?'

'No, Doctor, you're a bit early,' she said, raising an eyebrow.

I was sorting through some lab results when Mrs Murray came in balancing a mug of coffee and scone on a china plate in one hand. My stomach rumbled a greeting.

She put a piece of paper with a telephone number on my desk. 'The phones came back on this morning—who knows for how long? The fiscal phoned from Stornoway. Could you give him a ring before surgery?' she said.

Ewan Macdonald, the fiscal was Alasdair's first cousin; tall, with sandy hair and a crescent shaped scar above his right eye. He was what my mother would have described as a nice young man. He was the same age as Alasdair, but totally different in personality; quiet to Alasdair's convivial. We'd met two years ago at a wedding in Perth. The day was glorious and I was so happy, hoping that attendance at the wedding would rub off on Tom, and that perhaps he'd finally propose. I'd gazed in envy at the bride and groom, while Tom's eyes had fixed on the well-endowed chest of the chief bridesmaid. Most of the men were in kilts, in their clan tartans. Their sporrans were pretty uniform too although I'd spotted one sporran that looked like roadkill, the poor dead creature dangled from a chain looking rather shocked. The women wore short, stiff, satin outfits, in candy colours, topped with overlarge hats, which they were obliged to hang onto in case they skimmed off in the breeze.

Ewan didn't have a partner and after the meal spent most of his time talking to elderly relatives, an orange juice in his hands. We bumped into each other at the bar, and I'd introduced him to Tom and we stood chatting while we were waiting to be served. Tom had been his usual wise-cracking self. Ewan had smiled politely at his jokes, but had quickly retreated to where Alasdair's grandparents were sitting, and that was the last we'd spoken.

I looked at the paper. I suspected this might be connected with the body found by the fishing boat. In Scotland, the police pass all reports of suspicious or unexplained deaths to the procurator fiscal, a lawyer independent from the police but employed by the Crown Office, to investigate. I dialled his number. It was too early for his secretary, and he answered the phone himself.

'Hello, Ewan, it's Helen MacAllister. I got your message. How are you?' I said, pausing to take a sip of coffee.

'Fine, thanks. It's about the body that the fishing boat found. Now this is completely confidential and off the record, but there appears to be something rather strange about the whole thing.'

A piece of scone caught the back of my throat and I coughed.

He continued, 'The MOD are being very cagey and trying to take over control of the investigation from the police. I'm not sure what's going on, but I'm just letting you know since the body washed up in your area. I know that usually you'd certify the death, and then we'd do a post mortem here in the hospital, but it's been taken out of my hands.'

'Is there anything that I need to do?' I asked hesitantly.

'No, not at this stage. It's really just a courtesy call to let you know that there may be some bigwigs from the military sniffing around. They've arrived from London. Got me out of bed this morning at six o'clock. Something's happened at the base on St. Kilda. I don't know what, but they're keeping it very quiet. It's the area fiscal in Inverness that's dealing with it not me, but I thought I'd keep you in the loop.'

'Okay, thanks for letting me know,' I said.

'That's my other phone. Be in touch.' He hung up.

I sat back. Authorities from London. Things were starting to look even more serious. What was going on? The sooner I got Andrey out of my house and on his way to Russia the better. But first of all I had today's patients to deal with.

Chapter 18

We'd been sitting in silence on either side of the desk for about thirty seconds. After my good morning and expected remark about the weather, I waited to hear what was the reason for the patient's visit.

At forty, Captain Ruaraidh MacDonald, although not in uniform, was still striking. Tall, with cropped dark hair and dark eyes, he'd the look of someone who was used to giving orders. No stubble would dare dally on his smooth chin. When he'd entered the room and sat down, it felt as if he was trying to intimidate me, but I'd held his gaze and eventually he'd dropped his eyes. I looked at him again. His looks ticked my clichéd attractiveness boxes—tall, dark and handsome, but I could see his wedding ring.

Even if he hadn't been married and a patient, despite his attractiveness, I doubt if we would have gelled. He was clearly someone who was aware of his good looks and the effect they had on women. Even Mrs Murray had flushed and fluttered as he'd said 'Thank you, Elizabeth,' when she'd shown him into my surgery. *Elizabeth*—I hadn't even realised that Mrs Murray had a first name, never mind had the temerity to use it.

Captain MacDonald coughed, and crossed and re-crossed his legs. At that point I noticed he was wearing white socks. The final death knell of any potential suitor in my book. At university in our flat, we had a mantra of *never trust a man who wears white socks*. I'm not sure where it evolved from. Probably from Susan whose two-timing boyfriend John not only wore white socks but a dodgy fake leather jacket, which was peeling at the cuffs and smelt of unwashed dog. Unsurprisingly, Tom too had a penchant for white socks. I'd bent my rules on that occasion, and look what had happened.

Captain MacDonald shifted in his seat, but still didn't speak. I tried again. 'What appears to be the problem, Captain Macdonald?' I knew that it was unusual on the island to have a female doctor. It's also sometimes difficult as a younger GP treating older male patients. You can see that they're not comfortable and you have to work a bit harder to ensure they're at their ease.

'How are you feeling today?' I said and waited. No response.

I opened his patient notes and began to read them. Not an easy task as Doctor Robertson's handwriting was appalling even by GPs' standards. GPs are sometimes described as having spidery handwriting. Well this spider looked as if it had consumed a bottle of red wine before tangoing across the page and passing out. His notes told me it had been two years since Captain MacDonald's last visit; a routine one for vaccinations. I knew he was the captain of a deep-sea boat and could be away for months at a time.

He was married to Marion who worked in the council offices in Stornoway. Tall, slim with translucent white skin, she looked as if she'd slipped off the cover of a glossy fashion magazine. She'd been one of the first people I'd met when I'd arrived on the island. I was stocking up on essentials in the local shop, and had been standing looking at the sorry display of fruit and vegetables. Blackened bananas and apples more wizened than any geriatric patients I'd encountered. In Glasgow this fruit would have been in a crate awaiting collection from the bin lorry. Here they were for sale. From the sorry state of the fruit I suspected a number of my patients would be suffering from scurvy. Marion had appeared at my side clutching a wire basket full of lager and bread.

'Hello. You'll be the new doctor,' she said, smiling.

I nodded. 'Yes. How do you know?' I asked.

'Everyone knows,' she laughed. 'Nothing's a secret in the village. You'll soon get used to that. You're Alasdair Dubh's wife's cousin,' she said. 'Hope he gets on okay at the college. It would be even better if he comes back. Our biggest export is our young people. We educate them then whoof they're gone! Nothing for them here.' She stopped for breath. Then started again. 'You're looking at the fruit.'

I nodded.

'It's a disgrace isn't it? Ferry brings it in once a week from Glasgow on a Thursday. There's no point in buying it on a Wednesday. Dead as a dodo,' she laughed. 'Fancy a coffee when you're settled?'

I nodded, unsure if there would be room to squeeze a full sentence into the air space which she had allocated me. There wasn't. She continued. 'We'll bump into each other again.' And off she hurried.

The next time we met was at Thirteen's funeral. Thirteen's real name was Calum Morrison but even as a child he'd been superstitious and had always carried a rabbit's foot, so the boys at school nicknamed him Thirteen.

Because I was late, the only free seat had been near the front of the church. I hurried down the aisle led by Captain MacDonald who guided me to my seat and handed me a psalm book. At that point the door opened and the minister appeared and the service began.

Outside after the service I had squeezed past the groups of women. I was anxious to get back to the surgery. Marion had been on the edge of a group and as I'd gone past she'd turned.

'Coffee soon?' she asked.

'Good idea,' I said. But we hadn't caught up yet.

Another minute passed, and I was aware of the other patients outside waiting for their appointments. I tried again. 'How can I help you, Mr MacDonald?'

'Captain,' he corrected me.

'How can I help you, Captain MacDonald?'

His head came up quickly. 'Anything I tell you is confidential?' he demanded.

'Yes, I have a duty of confidentiality to all my patients,' I replied. 'Nothing you tell me is discussed outside of this room.'

'Will Mrs Murray have access to my notes?' he asked, looking uncomfortable.

'No, I'll ensure that she doesn't,' I replied. 'Now what seems to be the problem?'

'Er, I have a discharge,' he said, blushing.

Good; at last we were getting somewhere. I stood up and pulled a pair of rubber gloves out of the drawer. He looked alarmed. 'If you could just pop behind the screen and drop your trousers, I'll take a swab.'

'A swab!' Perspiration was forming on his brow. 'Just give me some antibiotics. That will do,' he instructed.

'Yes, but before I can prescribe antibiotics, I need to establish that I'm giving you the right ones or they won't cure the infection. Your wife will need to come in too so I can check that she doesn't have the same infection.'

'That won't be necessary. We haven't...since...I've come home. I told her I've got a bladder infection,' he said.

I nodded. 'But you can infect and re-infect each other if you have intercourse.' At the word intercourse, he winced, and I couldn't resist adding 'Captain MacDonald.'

I took the swab. Before he left, I handed him a bottle of antibiotics. 'Results in a week, but you can try these meanwhile. Hopefully they'll do the trick. You can phone Mrs Murray at reception or make an appointment to see me for the results,' I smiled, dropping the rubber gloves into the pedal bin and letting the lid close with a satisfying clang.

'Er... I think it would be better if I came in.' He blushed again.

He left and I placed his file into the bottom drawer of my desk. Mrs Murray wouldn't be pleased. She liked to know everything that happened in the practice. Well she would need to get used to some changes. I turned the key and put it in my pocket. I'd pop the lab request into the postbox on the way home and request a sealed confidential report. I suspected my scone privileges were about to be withdrawn again. Ah well, it was nice while it lasted. I buzzed for the next patient. I could always bring in an emergency packet of chocolate digestives.

Chapter 19

There was a sharp knock on the door but instead of a patient Mrs Murray appeared. Her face was red, lips pursed.

'There are two gentlemen here to see you, Dr MacAllister.'

'Patients?' I asked.

'No. They said it was urgent. Official business. I told them you had a surgery, but they said they had to see you now and couldn't wait.'

My heart sank, these must be the men that Ewan had warned me about. But how could they have found out about Andrey so quickly?

'Send them in,' I said, taking a deep breath and sitting back. Would they put me in handcuffs and take me away in front of the patients, I wondered. There was a loud knock and two men entered and stood in the middle of the room. The taller, blonde one was wearing a long grey wool coat, his RAF cap tucked under his arm. The shorter, balding one was wearing a raincoat and clutching a battered leather briefcase to his chest.

'Doctor MacAllister?' asked the shorter one. 'May we sit down?' His pencil thin moustache reminded me of the whiskers of the pet hamster I'd had as a child.

'Sorry. Yes, of course.' I motioned to the chairs in front of my desk.

They sat down. 'Do you mind if I smoke?' asked the rodenty one, pulling out a pipe and box of matches.

'No, be my guest,' I said, pushing the ashtray across the desk.

'I'm Captain Ellery and this is Mr Simpson,' said the uniformed one. Mr Simpson nodded as he fiddled with his pipe. Captain Ellery smiled exposing a dimple, and once again I wondered why men were more attractive if you stuck them in a uniform. Was it a throwback to my guiding days when I'd fancied Derek Pringle, one of the scouts in the local scout troop?

'We're here about a rather delicate matter and shall require your full cooperation,' Mr Simpson interjected before returning to his pipe. He sniffed the air. I wondered if he could detect guilt.

I paled. 'Of course, where shall I begin?' Perspiration was forming on my upper lip. If I confessed everything perhaps they might not send me to prison.

'I think it would be easier if we explained why we're here,' said Mr Simpson, who had put his unlit pipe on my ashtray. 'You may have heard that there's been a problem at Saint Kilda?'

I nodded. 'Yes, I've heard some talk, but I was just about...'

He frowned. 'Well, we're looking for at least one or perhaps two men in connection with it. We can't say too much as this is a matter of national security. Do you understand?' he said, looking at me intently. He knows, I thought. I nodded and looked down at my prescription pad.

'You'll know that we've already found one body. We've also recovered an inflatable dingy. It was washed up further down the coast. It was bloodstained. We've run tests and the blood on the dingy is from a different blood group from that of the body. So we're looking for at least one other man. Probably someone who may be injured,' he said picking up his pipe. He struck another match, and this time was successful in lighting the pipe, and he began puffing smoke into the room. The other man coughed. I felt sick. He pulled the pipe from his mouth, 'We think it's unlikely that he'll seek medical advice, but if you have any suspicions about an unregistered patient presenting with a wound it's important that you contact us or the police immediately. Do you understand?'

'Of course.' I smiled. He did not. But Captain Ellery did. He had a warm smile. Mr Simpson cleared his throat. He was trying to attract my attention. Reluctantly I shifted my gaze from the captain. Mr Simpson was holding out a business card. I took it and placed it beside the phone.

'This is the number that you must call. Do you understand?' he asked in a stern tone. I was immediately transported back to my headmaster's office.

I nodded, 'Yes of course,' I replied. The captain looked embarrassed by his colleague's tone.

'Your help would be very much appreciated, Doctor,' said the captain. He smiled again as he stood up, and offered his hand. I shook it and looked at Mr Simpson who was juggling with his pipe and briefcase. He dropped the briefcase as he walked to the door and bent down to pick it up. As he did so I saw the ghost of a smile flicker across the captain's face.

They left and I sat back on my chair and let out a long sigh. My hands were shaking. There was a knock at the door. Oh no! Had they come back? Mrs Murray stuck her head round the door.

'Are you free to start the surgery now?'

I nodded.

'They looked very official. English were they?' She came in and closed the door standing with her back against it.

'Yes, just a medical matter. Introductions just in case there were any incidents involving the soldiers while they are on the island. They don't have a medic with them, so we'll be their first port of call, so to speak,' I said.

'Ah, well let's hope there won't be. Did they say anything about the body?'

'No. I don't suppose they'll know anything without a post mortem.'

'That'll take a few days by the time they get the remains to Inverness. I heard that they wouldn't let the GP in the town do this one. Something's going on,' she muttered. 'I've never seen the likes of this before. They didn't tell you anything at all?'

I shook my head. 'The next patient, Mrs Murray?' I said.

'Aye. There's only one. The power cut's still keeping them away. Every cloud has a silver lining, I suppose,' she said, and she reluctantly left the room to call the next patient. Joanna MacPhee was a plump, middle-aged lady who had her grey hair corralled tightly under a paisley patterned head square. She was married to Lachie the postman. She had five children and had nursed both her parents at home before they'd died. From her notes, it appeared that she was suffering from depression. I saw she was a long time patient of Doctor Robertson and she was on uppers and downers. Probably she'd benefit from some psychiatric input, but as the nearest psychiatrist was located in the hospital in Inverness, that wasn't an option.

'It's my nerves, Doctor,' she said twisting the handle of her black handbag.

'Is there anything I can do to help?'

'No, if you could just give me more of the tablets that Doctor Robertson gave me, I can get a night's sleep. And then the other ones perk me up in the morning.'

It seemed like a pretty good regime to me. Why make her miserable by weaning her off them? Easier just to write another prescription.

'Are you sure you'd not like to come back in another day and have a chat? Or if you'd prefer I could refer you over to Inverness.'

'Good heavens no, Doctor! All I need is some more tablets. There's nothing wrong with me. Lachie's mother was in that mental hospital on the mainland. Dreadful place. We went to visit her. Lachie brought her straight back home, and Doctor Robertson gave her some pills. She was as right as rain after that.

A bit quiet, but then she never was much of a talker.'

She smiled as I handed her the prescription. 'Thank you, Doctor. Lachie will be pleased. He hates it when I'm sad.'

Right as rain. I wondered if we'd any more of these in the drugs cabinet. Perhaps I'd have a look later on...

Chapter 20

Thankfully there weren't many patients that day and the surgery progressed with a less than usual round of repeat prescriptions and coughs and sniffles. Colds are the bane of a doctor's life. Patients are keen to come and tell you that they're infected with the cold. They share this information, and their germs, with you and as many of the waiting room occupants as possible. Why they can't sit at home till their cold has passed, I have no idea. That's another thing they don't teach you at medical school.

Mrs MacLeod was one such example—a walking germ dispersal unit. I could hear her explosive sneezes through my closed surgery door and my immune system shuddered in anticipation. She entered clutching a soggy, cloth hankie, shook it, sneezed and loudly blew her nose. I flinched. The sodden rag in her hand was no shield against the germs which had now invaded my space. A middle-aged woman with sharp birdlike features and a mole on her cheek, she was the village postmistress and probably knew more about the state of health of the inhabitants of the village than I did. There were rumours circulating of mail late arriving that looked as if it had been steamed open, then inexpertly resealed. Hence her nickname—Mrs Kettles. Nothing had ever been stolen but I suspected she must have garnered a lot of information over the years. She spent ten minutes telling me she was suffering from the cold, interspersed with complaints about the problems decimalisation had caused Her Majesty's Post Office. I tried to evade a prolonged bout of coughing by pretending to drop my pen under my desk. I resurfaced when I thought the coast was clear to catch the end of a diatribe bemoaning the demise of the ten shilling postal order. I tried to sound vaguely sympathetic, but I had no interest in either, and just wanted her out of my surgery before she coughed in my face again. I wrote her a prescription for antibiotics and quickly shooed her and her germs out of the door. Thankfully I just managed to shut my surgery door before she launched into another sneezing fit.

The last patient of the day was Caroline MacDonald. I'd met Caroline, one of the primary school's two teachers, during my first week on the island. It was at a fund raising evening held in the school in aid of the lifeboat.

This was one event that I hadn't been able to avoid. We were a fishing community, and if an emergency arose it was the lifeboat that went out to help. The boat was stationed in the town. The crew were volunteers, and flares were sent up from the station which summoned them in an emergency. I remembered Mairi telling me about a plumber who was on the lifeboat crew. He was in a house in town midway through changing a dripping tap. There was a problem and he couldn't find the stopcock to shut off the water. Suddenly there was the bang of a flare overhead. He pushed a rag into the poor housewife's hand and told her to keep it pressed against the water spurting out from the top of the tap and told her not to move till he got back. It was two hours before her husband arrived home and rescued his damp and distressed wife.

But a social evening in the school had for me the lure of home-baking, and I'd popped in on my way home in the hope that I could find something to eat that would save me having to cook my supper. I'd been in luck. Someone had made a quiche. This exotic item had been viewed with suspicion and ignored by most in attendance who preferred the more familiar sandwiches or even the vol-au-vents which somehow had managed to leap the cultural divide, unlike the unfamiliar quiche.

The quiche hadn't been my first choice, but as I'd leaned forwards to pick-up the last sausage roll, it had been snatched from the plate in front of my out-stretched hand by Mr Macleod. He'd the look of a man who'd eaten many sausage rolls, most of which now seemed to have taken refuge in the folds of skin under his chin. So I sought compensation in the lonely quiche.

Sitting in the school dining room on a tiny seat with my knees almost touching my nose, I gained an insight into the world of Gulliver. Caroline and I had laughed at the adults crouched on the little chairs. Like me she was an incomer, an Australian. She lived in a small white cottage close to the harbour and was married to Duncan, the owner of one of the biggest of the local fishing boats. He was a large man who each year won the strength competition at the local games. I could understand why Brian Bain had said that he wasn't keen to take him on without some form of assistance.

Unlike the archetypical Australian: Caroline was tiny. Her blonde hair made her easy to spot in a crowd where the indigenous hair colour palette ranged from black to brown with the odd red-haired person thrown in for variety. I'd enjoyed my evening sitting next to her and discussing the difficulties of settling into island life and we had agreed to meet for coffee but hadn't yet got round to it.

The woman who'd entered my surgery bore little resemblance to the bouncy woman that I'd met before. Caroline gingerly eased herself into the chair opposite me. Her blonde hair hung limply onto her shoulders and there were dark circles under her eyes.

'Hello Caroline, how are you?' I asked. She looked up at me. Her lips quivered, she tried to speak and burst into loud sobbing tears. I got up and walked round the desk and handed her a paper hanky from the box and sat on the edge of the desk patting her shoulder until the sobbing subsided. I could see this was going to take some time. 'Cup of coffee?' I suggested. She nodded, noisily blowing her nose. I handed her the box of paper hankies and went through to the kitchen. The surgery was empty. Mrs Murray had gone home for the night.

I took my time making two mugs of coffee.

'I'm sorry,' said Caroline, blowing her nose as I backed through the door, mugs in hand.

I put a mug of coffee on the desk in front of her. She picked it up and took a gulp.

'I just had to speak to someone, I don't know what to do.' She put the coffee back on the desk then pulled up her jumper, exposing some angry bruising on her ribs. I examined her carefully. Thankfully none of her ribs appeared to be broken.

'Do you want to tell me what happened?' I asked.

'It's Duncan. There's problems with the boat and with money. He's got a lot of debt and the boat needs a new engine. Now he's started drinking again. He used to drink heavily before we were married, but he swore he'd change. For six months before our engagement, he didn't touch a drop. And he stayed dry for nearly three years. But he started again at new year. The stress...the stress it's making him upset. Angry. And if he's very angry he'll sometimes slap me. But last weekend he went nuts. He kicked and punched me. I locked myself in the car and hid. I spent the whole night on the back seat. He couldn't find me but I heard him shouting that he was going to kill me.'

I remembered Brain Bain's comments about his worry of tackling Duncan if he was drunk, and Brian was a good foot taller than Caroline. 'Have you spoken to anyone about his behaviour?'

She nodded balling the paper hankies rolled in her hands. 'On Monday I went to see Reverend Macleod to see if he could help... perhaps talk to Duncan and try to persuade him to cut back on the drink. But he told me it was my duty as Duncan's wife to stand by him. That we're all prone to human frailties.' She looked up at me shaking her head. Large tears were rolling down her cheeks.

I nodded. 'What are you going to do?'

'I have to leave him. I can't stay another weekend. I don't know what to do or where to go. I've no family in Scotland and all my friends are here on the island. I'm frightened if I stay he'll get drunk again and kill me.' She started to cry again.

'You're certain you want to leave him?' I asked.

She nodded. She picked up her mug of coffee. It was shaking in her hands and coffee was spilling onto her lap. I took it from her, frightened that she was going to drop it. I knew there was nowhere on the island for her to go. There had been an unsuccessful attempt by a women's group to get funds to establish a women's refuge. This had been refused by the all-male council. The applicant, herself a victim of domestic abuse, had received an official letter advising her that there was no need for such a facility on the island.

I patted her shoulder 'I know of a place in Glasgow which helps wives who've been beaten by their husbands. Do you think you could get down to Glasgow?'

'Yes, I can tell Duncan that I have a school trip to Inverness. By the time he finds out it's not true I'll be away,' she said.

'Do you want me to contact the home?'

She nodded and I quickly wrote a letter to Elizabeth, the manager explaining Caroline's circumstances and asking her to shoehorn another woman into the already crowded home. I handed the letter to Caroline and she stood up and hugged me.

'I don't know how to thank you. You've saved my life,' she said.

'Good luck,' I said as I let her out of the locked surgery door.

Outside, the light was starting to fade.

I watched as she drove off down the hill. I suspected that she wasn't the only woman I had on my list who suffered from domestic violence. Caroline was smart; hopefully she could start a new life. One problem solved, but I still had a larger problem waiting for me at home. I sat for a while sipping the tepid dregs of my coffee. I looked at my watch. It was later than I thought. I yawned then lifted the phone, it was dead again. Mrs Murray had been right. I let myself out and locked the door.

Chapter 21

My stomach rumbled. I was starving. Food, I needed to buy more food. As Andrey's health had improved, so had his appetite. I'd thought that Russians lived on a diet of cabbage and pickles. Just my luck to have landed a gourmet one who wasn't going to be happy to live on my tinned food diet. I'd have to expand my recipe range. That meant I'd have to explore the more exotic, as yet, uncharted aisles of Macleod's shop. More importantly than provisions, I needed information about what was happening, and Macleod's Stores was the best place for this, but I'd have to be careful not to arouse Mr Macleod's suspicions with a sudden increase in the amount of food that I was buying and a change in my eating habits.

As I walked in, the smell of paraffin hung heavily in the air. Mr Macleod had dotted paraffin lamps about the shop so that it was just possible to make out the stock on the shelves. Peering through the gloom, I saw Mr Macleod's bulk leaning on the counter with the fragile flicker of an almost deceased fag end dangling from his lips. Three other orange glows, hung in the air around him, like indolent fireflies, indicating he had company. A burst of laughter from the group of men was cut short as I entered. Then the conversation resumed in Gaelic, and there was another burst of laughter.

I wandered round the shop peering at unfamiliar labels and products. I remembered seeing a cookery book of Mairi's somewhere in the kitchen. Perhaps I'd take a look at that when I got home. I grabbed some tired-looking carrots and onions. A bag of rice caught my eye, and I also threw in some tinned tomatoes and a tin of corned beef into the wire shopping-basket.

Sandy Ears, who was standing polishing his glasses as I approached the counter, said, 'I hear they're sending up soldiers from the mainland to start a search. Supposed to arrive tomorrow evening. They're telling everyone it's an exercise, but I reckon it's probably got something to do with that body.'

'The one they dredged up?' said Mr Macleod.

'Aye, my cousin Iain B phoned over from the town. He's in the army reserves. He says they're sending up bloodhounds too.'

'Bloodhounds?' said Mr Macleod, 'Never seen one of them in action.'

'Can't beat a good collie,' said Calum Mhor, the tallest shadow.

'They're not coming here to round up sheep, you idiot. Fat lot of good a collie would be at following a scent. I read somewhere, think it was in the Reader's Digest at the dentist, that them bloodhounds can follow a scent that's days old. Collie's only interested in sheep.' He dropped his cigarette and ground it out under his heel.

My stomach tightened. Soldiers, bloodhounds—I'd need to get back to warn Andrey.

'They're all being billeted in the old army camp at the point. He says there could be fifty, maybe even a hundred of them. Good for business, eh, Angus?' he said, looking at Mr Macleod. They all turned in my direction as I approached the counter.

'Aye,' replied Macleod taking a final draw and extinguishing the life of his cigarette. 'Every cloud has a silver lining. Have to stock up if we're getting military guests.' He smiled at me.

'Army camp?' I said putting my basket on the counter.

'Aye,' said Sandy Ears, sticking his glasses back on. 'During the war troops were billeted here. In fact some of the b—sorry, Doctor, some of the soldiers married some of our local lassies and took them off the island.'

'Aye, and some of them soldiers never left. Knew which side

their bread was buttered on,' said Pimple, the third shadow. I'd met him at the shop before and thankfully his childhood nickname was now dermatologically incorrect. 'Though most of them moved into town,' he continued. 'Didn't get on so well with some of us local boys.' He stuck out his chest and cleared his throat. I thought he was about to spit on the floor, but he then thought the better of it.

'Is that all, Doctor?' said Macleod. He'd produced a torch and was shining it in my wire basket, looking at the contents. 'Looks like you're going to be making yourself a nice wee dinner,' he said.

'It's my aunty,' I stuttered. 'She's very particular about what she eats and she's coming up soon on a visit, so I'm going to practice some cooking. I've found Mairi's recipe book and there's one or two nice recipes in there.'

'Aye,' he nodded, 'don't suppose you've got much time to cook for yourself. Dr Robertson was always being invited out to tea by Mrs Murray's sister.' He weighed the vegetables. He rang through the contents of the basket, but I noticed that as he packed the shopping he slipped two brown paper bags from under the counter into the cardboard box where he'd put my shopping. He winked at me as I paid him. When I got back to the car I opened the bags and looked inside. Nestled amongst the tins and food inside the two bags were two bottles of gin and some packets of cigarettes. I smiled. It looked as if we'd established a system.

My mind was in a turmoil as I drove along. Soldiers, bloodhounds—Andrey would have to leave now. Approaching the cottage, I could see some flickering lights in the kitchen. When I opened the back door, I paused and sniffed—cooking smells, overlaid with peat, and topped with cigarette smoke. In the kitchen the fire was exuding a rosy glow. Andrey was sitting beside the stove, reading a book.

'You've been busy,' I said, the smell of food momentarily dissipating the fear from my stomach.

'The medicine has started to work and I feel a lot better,' he said smiling. 'You're a good doctor.'

'We have to sort something out...make a plan. I've just been in the shop. They say they're sending up troops to start a search for you. With bloodh—dogs,' I said. He paled and sat up.

'When?' he said.

'Tomorrow. What will we do?'

'Eat! The first thing we must do is eat. Good food must never go to waste,' he smiled. 'I found your freezer and took out some meat this morning. It will melt with this power cut. I have made a...what do you call it? A casserole?'

'Stew. In Scotland we call it stew.' Sometimes I wonder about my sanity. All hell is about to rain down on my head and I'm discussing the semantics of boiled meat with a Russian.

'You Scots with your different ways,' he laughed.

But where was George? The house was quiet. There hadn't been barking followed by his usual over rapturous welcome

'Have you seen George?' I said.

'George, your husband?' he said looking puzzled.

'The wee dog.'

'Wee?'

'No, George the dog. Wee is Scottish for small.'

'Your 'wee' dog was barking at the door, so I opened it,' he said.

No further explanation was needed. George must have taken off on another amorous adventure. I'd not yet removed his gene sharing equipment and once in a while he would disappear and come back with a smile on his face. In Glasgow he'd once disappeared for three days.

But just before we sat down to eat there was a scratching at the back door and my errant canine Casanova walked slowly in and flopped down onto the rug in front of the fire. The only obstacle preventing him from having a post-coital cigarette was his lack of opposable thumb.

Dinner was strange. Sharing a candle-lit dinner with a Russian fugitive was not something I had ever imagined. Andrey had more of Alasdair's whisky, and I reverted to gin and tonic as we ate. It was a long time since I'd sat face to face across a table from someone of the opposite sex who didn't want to discuss their medical problems with me. I smiled. Then my smile quickly faded as I thought back to the last meal that Tom and I'd shared. I saw Andrey look at me as I frowned but said nothing. I felt he would understand if I told him, but this was neither the time nor the place. It was strange, but somehow it felt that time was suspended, encapsulated. If I was going to be thrown in the Tower, to be pecked to death by the ravens, I wanted the whole of Andrey's story. Mine could wait.

'Tell me what happened after you left Saint Kilda?'

'I'm not sure. Things are mixed up in my head,' he said, putting down his glass. 'We were on the boat. I tried to get as far away from the island as possible. I knew I had to try to reach land before the storm broke. The compass on Dimitri's wrist was smashed, I didn't know what direction to go. So I just let the tide take us and I just rowed and rowed. I think fear gave me strength. At first Dimitri kept crying out. He was in a lot of pain, but gradually he got quieter and I thought he had gone to sleep. The sea was so rough I kept being sick and I had to keep bailing to stop us sinking. When the sun came up, I could see the high cliffs of St. Kilda in the distance and knew that we were too far away for them to see us.

'Then I saw Dimitri in the daylight. His face was so pale. He felt cold. I felt for his pulse, there was none. I knew that he was dead,' he sighed, lowering his head. 'He was so big, so heavy, he was weighing the boat down. More and more water was coming in as the waves got bigger. I said a prayer for him and his family and pushed him into the sea.'

'But what about the device?' I asked.

'It was only after his body disappeared that I realised my mistake. The device was still attached to his waist.'

'I think we need another drink,' I said standing up and pouring another large glass of Alasdair's whisky for Andrey. He continued.

'My leg was starting to give me more pain and I realised that things were not good. The wind was growing stronger and the waves were coming more and more into the boat. I thought I was going to drown. I was feeling so sick. I didn't realise my leg was infected and that I was so ill. It was dark when the boat landed on your beach. I holed the boat with the knife that I had taken from Dimitri's body, then hid it under some rocks and crawled up the shore. I just kept crawling until I came to your henhouse. You saved my life, Doctor.' Taking my hand he kissed the palm. He stood up and held out his hand. I took it and he pulled me close to his chest. My mouth found his. I forgot the ravens, the soldiers and even Mrs Murray, as I followed him upstairs.

Chapter 22

My mind was empty but my body felt warm. I stretched my arms and yawned. Smiling, I lay for a few moments with my eyes closed listening to the noise of gentle rhythmic breathing beside me. It had been a long time since I had shared a bed with anyone. I'd forgotten how good that could be. I reached my arm across the bed and felt...fur. George was lying on the pillow—legs in the air, not a care in the world. There was no sign of Andrey.

Perhaps he'd left. I'd been through this post-coital scenario many times in the past. Disappearing amnesiac lovers who never phoned. Damn—now I could add unprotected sex with a Russian spy onto my worry list. Idiot, idiot, idiot! How many times had I counselled patients not to be careless? Sex was not something I had planned for. There were times I didn't need my mother to tell me how stupid I was. Fingers crossed I should be okay and get away with it. Where was Andrey?

Footsteps were coming slowly up the stairs. The bedroom door swung open and Andrey appeared holding two mugs of coffee. I pushed George off the bed. There was a thud and a yelp. I mentally added cruelty to animals to my list of unattractive attributes. George slunk out the door, throwing me a quick *I can see that I've been replaced* look. His tail was firmly between his legs. Andrey followed him downstairs and returned with a plate of oatcakes spread with marmalade. I sat up in bed, pulling the covers around me.

'I found it in a jar. It looks like jam but it's orange,' he said, looking at it suspiciously as he passed me the plate.

'Marmalade. We eat it on toast for breakfast. What's the time?' I said, raising my head from the pillow and realising that things felt less fuzzy again this morning as I'd not taken any sleeping tablets. But I'd slept soundly and for a few moments I had been happy. This feeling quickly evaporated as things were now coming thudding back into focus. I felt my blood pressure starting to elevate—work, spies, pregnancy, soldiers.

'Eight o'clock,' he said. He sat down on the edge of the bed.

I started to eat the oatcakes.

'I'm sorry.' He took my hand and held it and touched Tom's ring. 'I'm so lonely. I haven't...talked...with a woman since my wife died. We were so close and now there is no one. I didn't think...to meet...to meet someone.'

'I know. I understand,' I said. What else could I say: *send the Russians a note that you've decided to stay in the Outer Hebrides and you won't be back. p.s. You've lost a piece of equipment of strategic importance*?

Reluctantly I pulled my hand from his. 'I've got to get moving—morning surgery. Tonight we must talk. We must try to work out how to get you home.'

He nodded and left the room. I drained the coffee hoping that the caffeine would kick in. I didn't want to get out of bed. I didn't want to leave the house. I wanted to stay here wrapped in Andrey, but that wasn't an option. I threw the bedclothes to one side and shivered as the cold air hit my skin.

Driving to the surgery, I'd to pull in sharply when I met two speeding army trucks on a bend. The lead one sounded its horn at me as they roared past. 'Bloody road hogs,' I muttered. Things were moving a lot faster than I'd anticipated. Andrey had to get off the island as soon as possible.

Mrs Murray was smiling as I entered the surgery. This was unsettling but I hid my surprise.

'Would you like the good news or the bad news first, Doctor?'

'Let's make it the good please,' I said.

'The phones are working again.'

'That's good, but I've just nearly been flattened by an army truck.'

She looked startled, Yes, I've heard they arrived last night. They're all up at the camp and the search is starting today. Wild goose chase if you ask me. Russian spies my giddy aunt.'

'And the bad?' I said.

'Bad what?' she looked at me quizzically.

'News.'

She nodded towards the waiting-room, which was full of people. 'The patients are back,' she said in a low voice. She saw my face fall. I didn't need a full surgery, I needed time to think, but that wasn't going to be an option today.

'I'll show the first one in and bring you a coffee and a biscuit.' She took another look at my face. 'Two biscuits.'

The day sped past. I had no chance to think. I had patients. Updating records and dictating and signing letters. I realised how busy I was when Mrs Murray walked into the surgery and placed a ham sandwich and cup of tea in front of me.

'I'll hold the next patient for ten minutes till you eat this,' she instructed. I ate while I wrote.

Five o'clock came and the last patient of the day left, and my thoughts returned to Andrey. The reception lights were still on when I closed my door but thankfully there was no sign of Mrs Murray. I had almost reached the outside door when there was a cough and Mrs Murray's head appeared from the tea room.

'I trust that you're remembering, Doctor MacAllister?' she said, her tone expectant.

I nodded. 'Yes, of course. Remembering?' I said, desperately trying to remember what I was supposed to remember.

'You're drawing the raffle at the ceilidh on Saturday evening in the community hall,' she said, impatiently.

'Oh yes. Of course. What time?' I asked.

'Eight o'clock. Doctor Robertson usually gave us a tune on his accordion. He was very good and we always looked forward to it,' she said.

'Well I'll be there, but I'm afraid that I'm tone deaf and can't play a note,' I said ruefully. This probably didn't come as a surprise to Mrs Murray and would be added to my ever-growing list of shortcomings.

'Eight o'clock,' she said. 'Don't forget.'

I nodded, my stomach sinking. An evening in a draughty hall surrounded by my patients was not my idea of a good time when instead I could be stretched out on the couch beside Andrey and George. But I couldn't arouse suspicion, so I'd better be there.

'Saturday evening, I'll see you there.' I was anxious to get home to Andrey. Soon my life would revert back to work and George. I wasn't sure how much more of that I could cope with. My short time with Andrey had unsettled me. I had to do something, but what?

Perhaps Andrey and I had a week together, perhaps a fortnight. Perhaps he would stay. I shook my head and forced myself to concentrate on the road.

My stomach dropped as I drove up the hill towards the cottage. The car of Ewan MacDonald, the fiscal, was parked outside the house. Worse still the car was empty. As I walked in I could hear muffled voices in the living room. I hesitated, then opened the door. The conversation stopped. The game's up. How could I explain away a spare Russian in my kitchen? Tower of London, here I come. Had he already phoned the police?

'Hello, Helen,' Ewan said smiling and standing up with his arm outstretched. He was holding a mug of coffee. We shook hands and he sat back down. 'I had to come over to meet with the military.' I quickly checked the room. There were no police.

Andrey was sitting in the other armchair, legs crossed, clasping a mug of coffee.

'I saw smoke as I drove past and thought you were in,' he said. 'Thought it would give us an opportunity to have a quick chat about the current situation, but it gave me a chance to talk to Andy.' He smiled in Andrey's direction. 'We've both got an interest in Arctic birds.'

'Yes, Andy...birds,' I stammered, reddening.

'He tells me that you were at university together.'

I looked over at Andrey who nodded, 'Only for a year while I did my Engineering Ph.D,' he said, uncrossing his legs.

'You'll need to introduce him to Magnus in town. He's Norwegian, and I'm sure would enjoy a yarn with another Norwegian.'

'Em, good idea,' I nodded. I noticed the little colour that had been in Andrey's face was fading rapidly. He'd pushed up his sleeves and was scratching the scar on his arm.

'Eczema? Suffer from a touch of it myself.'

Andrey shook his head.

'Andy was telling me,' continued Ewan, 'that he arrived last week but has been laid low with flu.'

'Ah yes, flu. Nasty stuff, really high temperature. Still you're on the mend now, aren't you Andr...Andy?' I said to Andrey, smiling stiffly.

'Yes, in another couple of days I will be returning to Norway.'

'Call in if you're over in town and I can introduce you to Magnus. I can show you my picture of the Steller's Eider that I took last year. It's on my office wall in the sheriff court.'

At the mention of the word court, any remaining colour in Andrey's cheeks now vanished.

'Never known one of them land here before. Might have been blown off course.' He stood up. 'Better get moving, stuff to do in the office. The regional fiscal's over tomorrow. This Russian thing is causing quite a stir. The last time I saw this much brass it was playing a tune.' He laughed at his own joke. I squeezed out a smile. Suddenly Ewan moved towards Andrey, his hand outstretched. Andrey's body stiffened, I froze. Then exhaling rapidly, he shook Ewan's hand.

'Nice meeting you, Andy. Let's hope they find this bloody Russian soon, so that we can all get back to normal. At least we've got electricity in town,' he said, looking at the candles. 'I'll pop into the surgery when I'm next passing, and then we can have that chat,' he said picking up his briefcase and heading for the back door. George was close on his heels, sensing an open door opportunity and another romantic interlude. He whined when I grabbed his collar until I heard the back door slam.

'Andy? Norwegian? University? That was too close for comfort. We have to try and get you off the island as quickly as possible.'

'I am attending to that.'

'How?'

'The phone rang today,' he said. I looked at him sharply.

'I didn't answer it. But now it is working, I made a phone call to a friend in London.'

'A friend?'

'Yes. A friend who will be able to help me travel back home. Back to Natalia. I am worried about her, for her safety. I pray that she has not been harmed.' He wrapped me in his arms. 'I wish that things could be different, but I don't see what else I can do?'

I nodded. 'I know you must go home. The longer you stay here, the longer you are in danger and if you do not return—your daughter.' I leaned my cheek against his chest. 'Oh God!' I gasped and broke away from him. 'Look!'

I pointed out of the window. 'They've started the search.'

Through the gloom outside, on the hills, I could just see figures waving torches, sticks in hand advancing up the slope in a line. In the distance, carried by the wind, I could hear the barking of the bloodhounds. I shuddered. 'You must not go outside while they're here.' I said, 'They'll finish and then move on. I don't think they'll pick up a scent as there's been so much rain, but we can't risk it.'

We stood for a moment watching the beams of the torches dancing on the hill. Then I drew the curtains and locked the back door.

Chapter 23

'What will happen when you go back to Russia?' I asked picking at a loose piece of thread on Andrey's shirt. We were lying entwined on the settee, basking in the glow of the peat fire and crammed full of yesterday's warmed-up stew. The remnants of this lay in a pan on top of the stove, being carefully guarded by George. Two large coffees and a slice of apple pie from MacLeod's Stores had finished our meal. The evidence of the apple pie was on Andrey and I wiped the sugar moustache from his upper lip with my moistened finger tip. The noise of barking dogs and the light had both faded. The candles were burning lower and flickering in the draft.

To go with the coffee, we were drinking more of Alasdair's best malt whisky. Its overpowering odour of peat filled the kitchen, bringing back memories of the antiseptic I'd faithfully but futilely dabbed on my adolescent pimples.

In the last few days my short leet of character faults had grown to a long leet and was still expanding rapidly. Theft of whisky was small beer in comparison to lying to policemen, aiding foreign spies and treason, to name but a few.

'But are you sure it's safe for you to go back to Russia?' I asked, licking the remnants of sugar from my finger.

Andrey shook his head. 'I'm not sure. Dimitri's bosses will not be happy. The mission was not successful, but I hope they will understand that the device was lost when his body went into the sea.'

'There's been no word of anything stolen from St Kilda, only how they found a body washed up, but if it's top secret I doubt if they'd mention it. They're hardly likely to broadcast on the BBC news that a piece of equipment affecting national security's been stolen, are they?'

He shrugged, 'It will be at the bottom of the sea. I don't suppose it will take your government long to develop another one. But it will probably take our engineers about five to ten years. But that's probably not a bad thing.' He stood up and started to pace up and down.

'What's wrong?' I asked.

'I just need to get out,' he said. 'We were on the submarine for a long time. Now that I feel a bit better, I just need some air.'

'It's dark. The dogs have gone. Why don't you take George for a walk along the beach? Stay below the seaweed, along the tideline. The sea will come in later and cover your scent. George knows the way. I'll clear up.'

At the mention of the magic word 'walk' George leapt to his feet, his tail wagging like a metronome on speed. Andrey pulled on Alasdair's jacket and woolly knitted hat, and they exited in a flurry of excited barking. Suddenly there was silence.

Silence. I'd better get used to it, I thought taking another sip of whisky. No one else in the house; back into singleton mode. I wasn't looking forward to it. Although I loved George dearly, there was a limit to having a small dog as my plus one. But, just as importantly, could I get used to living in a community where people said 'Bless you,' before I'd even sneezed? How much longer could I stay here? Mairi and Alasdair would be back home in the summer, and I would need to move out. Maybe I could get a job down south; a big town perhaps. Somewhere where I knew no one and where I could live life on the edge and buy a newspaper and a pint of milk on a Sunday, and where I didn't have to worry if the toilet roll ran out on a Saturday night, as had happened to me on my second weekend. Rationing toilet roll had not been something I'd ever envisaged.

I could go somewhere where they ran evening classes. Join one on motor car maintenance. Meet a gorgeous hunky man, with a lovely shiny car. Preferably an open top sports car...

There was a loud bang at the back door. Then another. No, it couldn't be Andrey; he knew the door was unlocked. Brian Bain? Another emergency? No, there was no need for him to visit, now the phones were working. The third bang sounded as if someone was kicking the door.

'It's alright. Hold your horses! I'm just coming,' I shouted. I put the whisky glass down and picked up a candle, and went to the door. As I turned the handle, the door was kicked open with such force, that it felled me backwards, bouncing my head off the wall. The candle rolled along the floor and went out.

'Bitch! You bloody bitch, I'm going to kill you,' slurred a hoarse male voice as the dark figure pushed his way into the hall and stood looming over me. The wind now whistling in through the open back door snuffed out most of the candles. Edging into a sitting position, my nose was almost level with the top of his yellow wellies. He raised his foot, and I braced for the blow, but at the last moment he swung round and kicked the door shut. I started backing away from him, pushing myself along the floor, hoping somehow that he wouldn't see me. Leaning forward he caught a handful of my hair and dragged me into the kitchen, knocking against the table. Andrey's empty whisky glass toppled onto the floor, smashing. My head was pounding and I felt sick. He let go, and I managed to crawl onto the settee, and lay there shaking. He walked over and stood swaying in front of me. He was a large man well over six foot tall. He reeked of body odour. But who was he? I didn't recognise the voice, but he had a local accent.

'She's gone, you bitch,' he said, jabbing his finger at my face, just missing my eye. I smelt stale whisky on his breath.

'Who's gone?' I barely managed to whisper. He bent over, and suddenly his fingers were round my throat, compressing it. I was struggling to breathe. I clawed at his fingers trying to force him to slacken his grip.

'Caroline, you bitch. You told her to leave me. She's gone,' he slurred, shaking me by the throat. I gasped for air, pawing desperately at his hand. My ears were ringing; I was becoming oxygen deprived. He let me go and stood swaying in front of me. 'I'm going to kill you, you bitch.' He swayed over to the table crunching through the broken glass and picked up the whisky bottle almost knocking over the remaining candle. Slugging from it, he choked and whisky erupted from his mouth.

I couldn't remember his name. What had Caroline said her husband's name was? I suspected I was concussed from the bang on my head, but I knew he was vicious and this was probably not going to end well. I played for time.

'Why don't you sit down and we can talk?' I said. I doubted if any of my calming skills would help here, he was so drunk. I was right.

He walked over, bared his teeth and slapped me. I screamed, desperately looking around for something to defend myself with. There was nothing. He was muttering to himself. Staggering backwards across the room he punched the mirror above the fireplace. It cracked but didn't shatter. I flinched and cowered deeper into the settee. Duncan. His name was Duncan. Unsteadily he moved round the room, still mumbling and bouncing off the furniture. I watched him, praying that he would go. He bent over and picked up the knife Andrey had been using to chop the vegetables. He waved it as he staggered across the floor shouting unintelligible words in Gaelic. I couldn't move. I grabbed a cushion and clutched it in front of my chest and closed my eyes.

Suddenly the noise of snarling filled the room. I opened my eyes to see George launching himself across the floor and sinking his teeth into Duncan's trouser leg. Duncan was swatting at him but George clung on. Duncan stumbled round the kitchen, trying to kick George off his leg.

'Bloody dog,' he said, raising the arm holding the knife.

'Leave him! No!' I screamed. Suddenly everything seemed to happen in slow motion. The hand bringing down the knife froze in mid air, held by another hand which twisted it up and behind his back. Duncan lashed his heel back against Andrey's shin. There was a shout in Russian, and Andrey pulled Duncan's arm and twisted it further up behind his back. There was a scream and more swearing in Gaelic as I heard a crack and recognised the sound of a shoulder dislocating. Andrey removed the knife from Duncan's hand and pressed it to my assailant's throat. Andrey was panting hard and Duncan had started snivelling. George had backed off and was now hiding under my legs but I could feel his body shaking.

'Please, please stop...it hurts. Stop!'

'Andrey, let him go.' I was barely able to get the words out. Andrey looked at me for a moment. I wasn't sure that he could even see me. I thought he wasn't going to let him go. Then, lowering the blade, he pushed Duncan towards the door.

'You bitch, you'll pay for this,' said Duncan giving me one last look before he staggered out of the door, holding his injured arm to his chest.

My teeth had started to chatter and I was shaking. I slumped back onto the sofa.

'Who was that? An old boyfriend?' said Andrey, his eyebrows raised quizzically, as he placed the knife on the kitchen table.

'No, just the dissatisfied husband of one of my patients.' I managed a small smile. I sat stroking George who had now planted himself in my lap, still vibrating with fear.

Andrey, sat down beside us. 'You have George to thank,' he said stroking George's muzzle. 'He suddenly turned round and ran back here. I followed him and saw a van parked at the bottom of the hill. I thought you had a visitor and was going to wait outside till they left. But George ran up the hill and when I got here, the door was open and I heard all the noise from outside and realised something was wrong. Not a very friendly man. But I don't think he will come back.'

'Where did you learn to fight like that?' I said.

'I was in the judo club at university for a year. Glad I remembered some, but I've never felt a shoulder crack before.'

'Thank goodness you both came back,' I said.

'Perhaps George has, what do you call it in English, six senses? Do you Scottish have another word for it?'

'No,' I said, 'but we do have more than one way of saying thank you.' I smiled as I took his hand, and blew out the last of the candles.

Chapter 24

I hadn't been late recently, but I was today. It was a long time before we'd slept last night, and I'd fallen into a deep dreamless sleep in Andrey's arms. George barking at a feral cat in the garden had woken us both up with a start. I swore when I saw the time.

Now I was speeding along the road trying to make up lost time. Hopefully Andrey would feed George and the chickens. His domestic skills seemed more honed than mine. It was already past nine, and I knew that Mrs Murray wasn't going to be a happy bunny. I'd nearly reached the surgery and was turning the blind corner at the bottom of Calum Mhor's croft when I saw, just yards in front of me, a wooden barrier stretched across the road. I stood on the brakes, and my car slewed towards it. The two soldiers standing in front of it abandoned their rifles and leapt for their lives into the ditch. I shut my eyes. The car came skidding to a halt inches in front of the barrier. I heaved a huge sigh of relief. Then I saw the faces of the soldiers as they emerged from the ditch, wiping mud from their trousers. Glowering, they walked slowly towards my car stopping to pick up their rifles. The soldier with pockmarked skin rapped on my window. I rolled it down. My stomach was knotting.

'In a bit of a hurry, love? Got a train to catch?' he asked in a broad Yorkshire accent, peering inside the car.

This was not the time to point out we were on an island and the nearest railway station was in Inverness. I smiled and took a closer look at them. They looked like young squaddies not long out of school. Not bright enough to pass an exam, but old enough to be entrusted with the large rifles that they were now both leaning on. Hopefully someone had shown them where the safety catch was. If not, they looked in danger of shooting off a toe.

'Sorry, I didn't expect this to be here,' I said, pointing at the barrier, 'and I'm late for work.'

'And where would that be, love?' the taller one asked in a Liverpool accent.

'The surgery,' I pointed, 'just up there.'

'Ah, another nurse. This has cheered us up, ain't it, Steve?' he said, winking at the other soldier.

'Change from 'em bloody sheep,' Steve nodded in reply, looking faintly embarrassed.

'We might call in later for a cup of tea, eh, Steve? Seen any dangerous Russians on your travels, love?'

I thought of Andrey and shook my head vigorously.

'What's your name, love?' asked the tall one.

'Helen,' I stuttered.

'Okay, Helen, love. My name's Terry. On you go, but you mind and let us know if you find any nasty Russians hiding under your bed—we'll come and sort 'em out for you,' he laughed, and I forced a smile.

They slowly lifted up the barrier and waved me through. I drove carefully up the surgery road, my blouse pasted to my back with sweat.

'Good morning, Doctor MacAllister,' said Mrs Murray as I opened the surgery door.

'Sorry, Mrs Murray. Bit of a delay with the road block.' I waited for a complaint about my tardiness.

'How are you today, Dr MacAllister? You've met the soldiers. Thank goodness they're here. I'd thought it was stuff and nonsense—all this talk of a Russian spy. But my husband says the Russian's escaped and he's on the island, I feel a lot safer now the soldiers are here. The thought of Russians running around trying to murder us in our beds is frightening. I've even started to lock the house door and told Iain to leave one of the dogs in the house with me when he goes out.'

I didn't like to say that in a standoff between Mrs Murray and a Russian soldier, my money would be on Mrs Murray every day of the week.

'Yes. Worrying,' I nodded.

'You're looking a bit pale,' she said. 'Was there an emergency last night?'

'No, none,' I said. 'Quiet night.'

She glanced across at the waiting patients and dropped her voice to a whisper. 'I heard that Duncan Macdonald had a fall last night. Sandy Ears found him lying plastered on the road just along from your house. His car was parked nearby. Not sure why he didn't take him up for you to have look at. Sandy Ears said he wasn't making much sense when he found him, he was so drunk. But he insisted that he wanted to go to the hospital. Just as well. When they x-rayed him they found that the stupid blighter got a dislocated shoulder. He's been drinking like a fish for the last few days. I heard yesterday that Caroline, his wife, packed her bags and got on the ferry. No one knows where she's gone. Rumour is that she left a note, but he hasn't shown it to anyone.' She stopped talking and looked at me. 'She was in to see you a couple of days ago, wasn't she?' she said peering at me over the top of her glasses.

'Yes, but nothing related to all of this. Better be getting on,' I said looking towards the patients.

She ignored me and continued. 'What? Well, yes, I've got my suspicions. Duncan's always been a bit too handy with his fists. Got a nasty temper on him, especially with a drink in him. Goes way back. He broke Shoe Lace's arm in second year at school. Bad to his dogs too. No wonder he's got problems keeping a crew on his boat. Last fellow working for him took off to Barra after Duncan whacked him. Didn't settle his wages either,' she said, handing me the bundle of patient files. I withdrew to the consulting room, closing the door behind me to gather my breath, but not for long as there was a knock on the door and the first patient of the day came hobbling in.

The surgery was busy, and I tried my best to concentrate on the patients, but my mind kept wandering back to last night's incident in the cottage. Duncan was a big man and I wondered what would have happened if Andrey hadn't intervened. I could hardly report him to the police in case they wanted to interview Andrey and ran some sort of check on him. I didn't think that Duncan would be anxious to report the incident to the police either as he'd have some explaining to do as to why he was in my house uninvited. I'd need to make sure that my doors were locked from now on. My hand started to shake again. I suspected that he was the sort that would bear a grudge though I didn't think he would be back soon. He was a bully and like most bullies picked on people weaker than him. Andrey's presence would deter him meanwhile.

Finally, the surgery finished and I started to write up the notes and dictate some letters. My concentration was shot and my mind kept revolving back round to Andrey. He would leave soon. My choice of boyfriends had sometimes been interesting, but even by my standards this was spectacularly stupid.

Boyfriend—I'm not sure that I could even call him that. Perhaps, I could run off to Russia with him. No, it was difficult enough living in the Hebrides where half the time I couldn't understand what was being said. It would be even worse in Russia. And colder. Was I ready to be mum to a six-year old Russian? No, probably not. Better to write it off as a sort of Russian fling and concentrate on getting Andrey home.

There was a knock at the door and Mrs Murray appeared with some letters and put them down for signing.

'Another cup of tea, Doctor?'

I nodded.

'Lachie the Post has just been in and says that the army are about to start a house to house search for the Russian.' I dropped my pen. It rolled across the desk and fell onto Mrs Murray's foot. She picked it up and put it on the desk.

'Hopefully that'll flush him out. Though Angela says there's a rumour going round town that he was seen on the ferry with Caroline. But you know what this place is like for rumours,' she said, as she closed the door.

House to house. I had to warn Andrey. I grabbed the phone and dialled, winding the cord between my fingers. No answer. He could be in the barn or on the beach. What if the bloodhounds caught his scent? I grabbed my bag and coat.

'Emergency call, Mrs Murray, please apologise to the patients,' I said, running past reception.

'But, Dr MacAllister you can't...'

The door slammed behind me.

Chapter 25

I set off down the hill, my tyres screeching on the gravel as I pulled out of the surgery carpark. I imagined Mrs Murray clenching her ill-fitting dentures at the noise.

As I approached the roadblock, I could see the two squaddies whom I'd nicknamed Laurel and Hardy marching up and down, stamping their feet and slapping their arms round their shoulders in an effort to keep warm. The autumnal Hebridean wind was clearly not to their liking. They were experiencing the effect of wind-chill; the wind's ability to plummet the temperature several degrees below what the thermometer read. It sometimes bordered on the vicious. Combine this with a rainy day, and a walk on the beach felt as if someone was slapping you around the face with a wet fish. From the grim expression on their faces, Laurel and Hardy looked as if they were experiencing this piscatorial phenomenon. Their rifles were propped against the large truck, and when they saw my car approaching they quickly grabbed them. I slowed the car down to a standstill and wound down my window. They approached but smiled when they recognised me.

'Hello, nurse Florence—nice to see you again. Didn't take you long to sort 'em out. Them patients all better now are they?' The tall one with the big ears was now leaning one hand on my car roof, his head poking in my window. I instinctively moved away. He poked his head closer. 'What you doing on Saturday night, love? How about we get together for a drink and...?' He quickly withdrew his head, looking embarrassed. Then I realised that he'd seen Tom's ring.

I looked down at the ring, smiled ruefully and said, 'Sorry I'm in a bit of a hurry. Got a sick patient that needs urgent attention.'

'Okay, Miss, on you go.' They put their rifles down and raised the barrier and waved me through. As I was pulling away, I saw Mary, our other district nurse, driving towards them. She waved as she passed me. In my rear view mirror Hardy stepped into the middle of the road, his hand raised and the brake lights of Mary's green Cortina lit up. Meeting Mary would cheer them up. At twenty-three, Mary was our youngest nurse. From Uist, soft spoken, with long dark hair and dark eyes, she was innocent looking but with a wicked sense of humour. She was also a lover of disco music as I'd discovered one day when she'd given me a lift to a meeting in Stornoway. My ears were still ringing two days later from my enforced session.

My attention was on the road, but as I was driving along I could see more soldiers in lines spreading out over the hills and along the beaches. Their search seemed to be widening. What was I going to do with Andrey? How would I get him back to Russia?

I accelerated as fast as my elderly car would allow, but then had to swerve to avoid a sheep lying in the middle of the road on a bend, and nearly ended up in a ditch. I stopped the car and turned off the engine. My hands were shaking. Pull yourself together, woman! I had to get home, but in one piece. I waited a few moments, concentrating on slowing down my breathing, then I turned the key, restarted the engine and slowly drove down the hill.

I'd nearly reached home, but when I saw the road leading up to cottage, my heart sank. There were two large covered army trucks parked at the bottom of the road, blocking it. I'd need to pull over and make the rest of the journey on foot. I parked and as I hurried past them, I could see that they were empty. There was no one in sight, but in the distance I could hear the sound of whistles and barking. They must be searching further over the hill in the next village. I started running up the hill but had to stop. I'd need to give up the fags—I was starting to wheeze worse than some of my patients. My heart, which had already sunk, almost stopped when I reached the top of the hill.

Four armed soldiers stood facing the barn, their rifles aimed at the door. A fifth soldier was struggling to hold onto the lead of a large Alsatian dog.

Oh God...Andrey!

The soldier had both hands on the lead, but the dog was so strong it was almost pulling him off his feet.

'Jesus, Brutus, will you just lie down,' he shouted, yanking at the lead. Brutus clearly had other ideas and began to bark as he slowly dragged the soldier towards the barn. If Andrey didn't get shot, he'd be torn to pieces by this slobbering brute. I panicked and ran towards them waving my arms and shouting. 'No! Don't hurt him! Please don't shoot him!' The soldiers swung round and pointed their rifles at me. I stopped and instinctively put my hands up. Years of watching western movies as a child had instilled this reflex. The soldiers perceiving no threat, turned their guns and attention back to the barn. Two more soldiers had appeared from round the side of the house. They blocked my way and grabbing me by the arms dragged me away from the barn.

'For God's sake, please don't hurt him,' I shouted towards the soldiers holding the rifles.

They ignored me and the one with stripes on his arm raised his hand. 'Ready?'

They nodded, grim faced.

'Safety-catches off,' he instructed. There were four answering clicks.

I screamed then my knees buckled, but I was prevented from falling by the two soldiers gripping my arms.

'For the last time. We have you surrounded. Come out with your hands held above your head,' shouted the sergeant. There was a scuffling noise from inside the henhouse. The Alsatian's barking morphed into snarling, and his handler was pulled forward again, almost losing his balance.

'Here he comes,' shouted the blonde soldier nearest to the barn. 'Get ready.' They raised their rifles to shoulder height aiming at the door.

'No,' I screamed. I felt sick and my head fell forwards. There was an ominous silence, and then the Alsatian's barks intensified and it was difficult to hear anything else. I closed my eyes and every muscle in my body tensed waiting for the gunshot. Suddenly there was a burst of laughter.

'What the hell?' said the sergeant. I looked up and saw that creeping out of the door on his belly was a very frightened-looking George. This was a streamlined version of his usual self, ears tightly flapped back to his head and his tail clamped firmly between his legs. He furrowed his way across the yard towards me.

'George,' I shouted. The soldiers released their grip. I knew that tomorrow I'd have ten purple fingertip bruises on my arms where they had held me. George gave an excited yelp and ran towards me and leapt into my arms. His tongue rasped my face. The soldiers lowered their rifles. 'Is this your spy, Jonesy?' said the fat one, whose avoirdupois ensured that he'd never be in danger of blowing away in a gale.

'Shut up, you bastard,' replied the soldier holding the Alsatian's lead. 'Oh sorry, ma'am. Who are you?'

'I'm Dr MacAllister. I live here.'

But where was Andrey? Was he safe? Where the hell was Andrey?

'You'd better speak to the captain, ma'am. He's been looking for you.'

Game's a bogey, I told myself. Get the Tower ready. Ravens here I come.

The door of the cottage opened and the captain emerged and strode quickly in my direction. He did not look happy.

'Doctor MacAllister, I need a word with you,' he said.

Suddenly the Alsatian lunged forward. The soldier who'd been holding it lost his balance and fell forwards letting go of its lead, and the Alsatian ran snarling into the barn.

Oh God! Was Andrey in there after all? I froze, clutching George tighter in my arms.

The captain moved in front of me. 'Search the barn.' The dog handler and another soldier still holding his rifle strode forwards into the barn.

A voice called out, 'Captain, I think you should come and see this.' The captain signalled to another soldier, who raised his rifle and followed him inside.

'What exactly is this Doctor MacAllister?' came the captain's voice from the gloom inside.

Oh no! Andrey must have been hiding in the barn with George. I clasped George tighter and walked inside. The four men were gathered round a bucket at the back of the barn. The Alsatian was barking and snapping at it. The captain moved forward and lifting the lid exclaimed, 'What the hell is this?' he backed away with his hand held over his mouth

'Guga,' I said. It's a delicacy and is being stored here.'

'Delicacy, it looks and smells like old shoes. What is it?'

'I think it's a sort of bird. My cousin gets them from a man who lives in Ness. I think he catches them on another island or something. There's a crowd of them go out and stay there and bring them back.'

The captain shook his head. 'They actually eat this?'

I nodded.

'Well, it's sure as hell spooking Brutus,' said the handler dragging the dog out of the barn.

I put the lid on the bucket and followed everyone outside. Where was Andrey? Perhaps he was hiding up on the hills. I quickly scanned them but could see no movement.

'Doctor MacAllister,' said the Captain turning round. 'I think you still have some questions to answer, don't you?' He shouted an order and Andrey, followed by a soldier, came out of the cottage.

The captain stood with his arms folded. 'Well, how exactly do you explain this, Dr MacAllister?'

Chapter 26

I froze. The Alsatian stopped barking. It dropped to the ground, panting heavily, its large pink tongue lolling through a fence of teeth. The captain's frown was deepening as Andrey and the soldier approached. He was standing so close to me I could smell the odour of wet wool from his coat and see the droplets of rain sliding off his cap brim.

Game's up. Here we go, I thought. My voice was unsteady, 'Em I can explain, it was...'

'I thought you were asked to contact us if there was anything suspicious?' he said, raising his voice and turning towards Andrey.

I nodded, 'Yes, but I ...'

He interrupted. 'Your friend Mr Iversen here,' he said, nodding at Andrey, 'has just been explaining to me that there may have been an intruder in the barn.'

'An intruder?' I said.

'Yes, an intruder. He told us about the blood in the barn and said tha—'

'The blood? Mr Iverson? The barn?'

'Yes, but if you would just let me finish a sentence, Doctor,' the captain said, folding his arms.

'Sorry, sergeant,' I said still looking at Andrey who was standing casually watching our conversation or lack of it. He winked at me.

'Captain Wells, not sergeant,' said the soldier.

'Well, Captain, I...'

'Wells,' he said.

'Well, Captain, er, Wells, we have problems with...with mink.'

'Mink,' he echoed.

'Yes, mink. There was a mink farm on the island a few years ago, but they escaped and have been attacking the chickens ever since.' He still looked suspicious. 'If you check with any of the crofters they'll tell you what a pain it is. My friend Andy...Mr Iverson is Norwegian but lives in Glasgow, and he refused to believe that one mink could have caused such a mess in the barn, and was convinced we had an intruder.'

Andy, formerly Andrey, was nodding intently.

'Being from the city I'm just not used to all these...things...rodents,' he shrugged.

I laughed, 'Yes that's what happens when these city slickers visit us country folks.'

'Yes,' said the Captain, 'I can see why finding the dried blood in the henhouse might have made you jump to the wrong conclusion.' He smiled at Andrey who raised his eyebrows and shoulders simultaneously.

'Would you like a cup of tea, captain?' I said, hoping that he would refuse.

He looked at his watch. 'Sorry, no time. We have more premises to check before nightfall. Someone mentioned seeing a suspicious figure near their peat stack. We have to investigate that too before it gets dark. Still better to be vigilant like Mr Iversen.'

Andy, alias Mr Iversen, nodded and shook the hand proffered by Captain Wells.

'Better be off.' He turned to the soldiers. 'Right, sergeant, get the men back in the truck and let's investigate the next sighting. Where the hell's croft number forty-four? Bloody map's useless here. The house numbers are haywire. Croft thirty-six B next door to forty-one. Number twelve squeezed in behind twenty-one C! Can't find a bloody thing! Don't know how they ever get a letter delivered.'

If I'd been kinder I could have given him a look at the tattered photocopy of a hand-drawn map that I carried in my bag. Mrs Murray had given it to me on my arrival. It was a location map of all the croft houses in our local villages, drawn by one of the reserve firemen. The ambulance station in town had a copy too. The locals didn't need it, they knew where everyone lived, but on more than one occasion the map had saved me valuable minutes when I was making an emergency house call.

The sergeant barked an order. Andrey and I stood together watching them as they headed off down the hill, rifles leaning on their shoulders, wind trying to whip off their caps. We had to stifle a laugh when the Alsatian in its anxiety to chase a sheep tripped up its handler who tumbled into the ditch. He stood up dripping. Even from this distance I knew that his language was both graphic and colourful. He kicked at the poor dog, and the Alsatian suitably chastened slunk at his heel till they reached the van. They all mounted and drove off at speed, tyres churning the loose gravel on the road.

'I think we both need a drink, but coffee will need to do.' I put George down and he led the way into the cottage 'What the hell happened? What's that smell? The whole house stinks of it. You smell just like my dad,' I said sniffing Andrey's neck.

'Shaving lotion,' he said. 'I was in the bathroom and heard the trucks and barking. I thought it was the bloodhound, so I tipped a bottle of shaving lotion over me to try to hide my scent.

I took another breath of him and coughed, backing away.

'They just appeared,' he said. 'George was outside and must have hidden in the barn. They burst into the house. They said that a man had told them there was someone strange here, so I smiled at them and explained we had gone to university together.'

'A man. What man?' Then a slow dawning realisation. 'Bloody Duncan. I bet it was him.'

Andrey's face hardened.

'It is getting more and more dangerous.' We need to get you away from here and back home as soon as possible. Any word?'

'It is difficult,' he said. 'Tomorrow they will phone and tell me what to do. A few days—a week at the most.'

'Good,' I lied, and turned away. I didn't want him to go, but he couldn't stay. Once more I had the crazy fantasy of asking him to take me with him back to Russia. Could it really be any worse than staying here? Could it be any more foreign? Gaelic. Russian. What was the difference? Would I notice? Would I care? I suddenly realised Andrey had stopped talking and was looking at me questioningly.

'Sorry, I was lost in my head. There's so much going on, sometimes I just can't keep up. Sometimes I don't want to keep up.' The last word came out as a sort of hiccup and I burst into tears.

'I'm so sorry,' I sniffed, rubbing my nose with my sleeve. 'I don't usually cry. Well, only occasionally, but then only at really sad films and only in the dark.'

He smiled and pulled me towards him, and I buried my head in his shoulder.

'It's just that...well, I just don't want you to go,' I said, and pulled my head away from his shoulder and looked into his eyes.

His eyes looked down into mine, and he stroked my hair, 'I don't want to go back either. You must know that.'

I nodded.

'But I have to or they will kill Natalia,' he said.

'I know,' I said. 'I'm just being selfish. I need a drink, but at this time in the morning it'll need to be coffee. Would you like some?'

'Yes, but perhaps the coffee can wait for a while?' he said, smiling and pulling me closer.

'Yes, perhaps it can,' I said.

Suddenly I leapt up. 'Oh God, she'll kill me!'

'What is it?'

'Mrs Murray will kill me! I've left a surgery full of patients. I'll need to get back. Sorry!'

'Go,' he said, kissing me on the forehead and smiling. He gently pushed me towards the door. 'Your patients need you.'

Chapter 27

'Here,' I said, pushing the box of hankies across the desk. 'Blow your nose. Take your time and try again.'

I looked at the surgery clock. It was late and I was anxious to get home to Andrey. My last patient of the day was sitting with tears running down her face. A teenager in her school uniform, she had been shown into the surgery by Mrs Murray. They had been chatting together cheerfully in Gaelic, but the minute the door had closed and I'd asked her how she was she'd burst into tears and become unintelligible.

'How about a cup of coffee?' I suggested. There was a vigorous nodding of the head, and I escaped from the surgery and headed to the kitchen.

I hate tears. I hate death. Why I became a doctor I sometimes wonder. Perhaps I should have opted for hairdressing. I'd once read an article that said that hairdressers were happy at work whereas doctors and vets were often depressed and prone to committing suicide. Probably something to do with all the sad, sick people and pets that hang around surgeries, I thought. Bit of an occupational hazard. But to look on the bright side, at least I only had one physiology to deal with. Vets had loads. One minute a horse, the next a rabbit. Could lead to embarrassing mistakes. I smiled. And at least I didn't have to put my patients down.

'You're looking happy, Doctor. The kettle's still warm, just boiled it. Thank goodness for bottled gas,' said Angela. She was standing cigarette in one hand, mug in the other, leaning against the fridge where we kept the refrigerated drugs and the milk. She exhaled. I sniffed appreciatively and immediately felt the need for a cigarette.

'How are things?' she said.

'Busy day, last patient but I was desperate for a coffee,' I omitted to mention the sobbing.

'You've got young Hetty, my niece, in. Nice kid. Off to Edinburgh after the summer. My sister's so proud,' she beamed. 'First one in the family to get to university.' She stubbed out the cigarette.

'Got to go,' I said, picking up the mugs. 'Trying to finish surgery before the shop shuts'.

'Right, here we are,' I said, backing into the surgery, a mug in each hand. I sat down. Thankfully the crying had subsided. 'Shall, we try again?' I said, handing her a mug.

'Thanks. I...I think I'm pregnant,' she said, looking down. Somehow I'd already guessed that might be the problem.

'I've missed my period.' She looked at me. 'What shall I do?' The sobbing started again. I took the mug from her hand before the coffee slopped onto her lap. I explained I'd need to send a urine sample to the hospital for testing and it would take about a week.

'Did you use any protection?' I asked.

She blushed and shook her head. 'The chemist in town sells condoms, but my boyfriend's aunty works there. Dr Robertson was against contraception. There's a Family Planning Clinic in the hospital, but that's over an hour away on the bus and my mum knows some of the nurses in the hospital.'

She sighed, 'I didn't mean for this to happen. Rondo and I—we're almost engaged. He works on a fishing boat and we were waiting till I came back from university to get married. He really doesn't want me to go away to uni. Says his uncle could get me an office job in town.'

'What are you going to study?' I said.

'Medicine.'

She blushed. 'You must think that I'm really stupid,' she said.

'Em, no,' I said, her potential pregnancy predicament lying closer to home than I would like. 'Come back in a week.'

Before she left, I labelled her urine and I handed her some condoms which I kept in the cupboard, well away from the prying eyes of Mrs Murray who didn't approve of such things. I suspected that hanging above Mrs Murray's bed there was a cross stitch panel proclaiming:

SEX = PROCREATION NOT RECREATION.

'These will help till you can get advice when you go to university. Go to the Family Planning Clinic.' Inwardly, I laughed. Even the name was a bit of a misnomer. Family Planning Clinic—more like Children Avoidance Clinic.

I thought back to the Family Planning Clinic which I had attended at university. This had been on my 'to do' list along with buying books, filling out library applications and learning to drink alcohol.

The clinic was held in a large draughty hall on a Monday evening. I'd gone along with some other first-years from our halls of residence. We were working on the safety in numbers theory. I recognised other female students, who were definitely not there to plan their families, scattered amongst the tired-looking women, many of whom had brought some of their unplanned family with them.

I didn't want Angela or Mrs Murray finding out about the pregnancy test, so I'd post it off under the name of Caroline Macdonald marking it personal and asking for a sealed reply. I was sure Caroline wouldn't mind, and anyway she wasn't here to complain. I locked Caroline's and Hetty's notes in the bottom drawer of my desk. Hopefully Mrs Murray wouldn't notice their absence.

By the time I'd finished my paperwork the lights were out in reception and Mrs Murray had gone home. As I was walking past reception the phone started ringing and I picked it up.

'Dr MacAllister speaking,' I said.

'Doctor, thank goodness you're still there. It's Ben. He's in a lot of pain. I don't know what to do,' said an anxious male voice. 'I think it's his mouth, but he won't let me near him and I'm worried.'

Damn, I thought, so much for getting home quickly. 'What age is Ben?' I said.

He hesitated. 'He's seven, I think.'

I was used to fathers not knowing the ages, or more often the dates of birth, of their children. I'd yet to meet a mother who couldn't remember them. Was it something to do with the experience of labour?

'Right, I'm just leaving the surgery and I'll pop in on my way home,' I said. I scribbled his name and address down. I never liked to leave a child in pain. I'd heard rumours about the work of our local dentist, none of them complimentary, so rather than send him there, I'd take a quick look first, and if necessary organise some pain relief.

On my way to the patient it seemed there were more army trucks on the road than yesterday. Laurel and Hardie were still on their checkpoint at the bottom of the hill. If anything they looked even more miserable, their shoulders drooped dejectedly as the water dripped off their raincoats. They brightened when I stopped the car.

'Hello, Miss. If it's not our favourite nurse. Is that you finished for the day? asked Laurel leaning against my car.

'Sorry, off on another emergency call,' I said. He jumped back and lifted the barrier and waving me through.

I'd had a quick look for Ben Macdonald's file before I'd left the surgery, but couldn't find it. Another point I'd need to raise with

Mrs Murray, but perhaps I'd leave that meanwhile. I had other things to concentrate on like Andrey and the small matter of breeched national security.

Like many doctors I wasn't fond of child patients. In a child, unlike most adults, there was no attempt at reserve. You tell an adult that *you may experience some discomfort*, but this is medical speak for *this is going to hurt like hell*—most adults just grit their teeth and we, the doctors, plough on regardless. But if a child is in pain, he'll let you know he's in pain, usually very vocally. In A and E on more than one occasion, I'd found myself and the young patient's mother chasing an injured child round the clinic in order to capture it before I could treat it.

Still, on the bright side, at least Ben was seven and could tell me where it hurts, always a huge plus when it came to diagnosis. Hopefully it wouldn't take too long and I'd soon be back with Andrey. Our time together was precious and I didn't want to waste a minute of it.

Chapter 28

Approaching the croft, I could see two rusting cars lying abandoned. Apparently there was nowhere to scrap cars on the island. I'd heard a rumour that in one of the villages the wreck of a crashed plane was being used as a hen house—surely that couldn't be true? As I pulled up, I was sure I saw a chicken's head bobbing up and down—like a fairground target—in the rear window of one of the wrecks. In the front garden an irritated looking ram stood tethered by a chain, its gritted teeth hoovering the grass close to the house. Bringing forth my knowledge of geometry, I did a quick mathematical calculation that Pythagoras would have been proud of, to check that its chain wouldn't stretch as far as my car, before gently easing open the door and stepping out onto the grass. I needn't have worried; the ram gave me a disinterested look then returned to its task.

I went round to the back door of the house. There was no point in going to the front door; I knew it would be locked. I knocked and waited. There was no reply. Opening the door, I stepped tentatively inside shouting, 'Hello, it's Doctor MacAllister come to see Ben. Is there anybody home?'

Still no reply, and I was unsure if I'd got the right house. There was a battered-looking pot bubbling fiercely on the stove, its lid jigging away. The smell of scotch broth permeated the kitchen.

'Hello,' I shouted again, this time louder.

A door opened, and an older man wearing an Icelandic jumper and well-worn jeans stuck his head round the door. He put a finger to his lips with one hand and beckoned me through into the living-room with the other. I followed him in. The flag of his shirt tail was peeking out from between his braces.

I recognised him as Seonaidh Beag. He was the clerk of the local grazings committee—a big noise in a tiny community. He was in charge of organising the grazings and fanks. Fanks I'd learned from Alasdair were the gathering of sheep together in the wooden pens when they needed to be attended to or sheared. They were also an opportunity for crofters to get together and swap news. The sort of Hebridean equivalent of a men's club, but until today, I hadn't realised that Seonaidh was married or had a son.

He was frowning and shaking his head, 'He's asleep. He didn't sleep at all last night. He was in so much pain. Poor boy.'

I nodded my head sympathetically. 'It's always a worry when they're ill. Where is he? Sitting with his mum?' I said.

'No,' he said looking at me quizzically. 'I'm not married. He's lying in front of the fire. I gave him some whisky and that seemed to make him a bit better, Doctor.' I frowned, my concern for the child was growing. Giving whisky to a seven-year-old, even if he was in a lot of pain, was not acceptable—in fact it was dangerous. 'There,' he said pointing his finger. I looked, following his pointed finger. There was my patient fast asleep in front of the fire. Yes, he appeared to be about seven years old. But he also had four legs and a tail. A sheepdog. I stifled a giggle. 'Ben's a dog?' I said. The old crofter looked at me as if I was stupid.

'Yes, he's a great dog but he's got the most terrible toothache, Doctor. He's been howling with pain. I can't afford the vet, and I don't know what to do.' He looked at me.

'But I'm not licensed to treat dogs,' I said.

'It's okay, Doctor, I won't tell him that. If you could just pull the tooth. He won't let me near his mouth, it's so sore.'

As if to emphasise this fact, the dog started shuddering. One eye opened. He whimpered then, catching sight of me he folded his lips back from his teeth and snarled. The animal was clearly in pain, and I couldn't leave man and dog in distress. On the bright side, I remembered attending a lecture at university from a visiting professor who'd spent a year as a doctor as part of the Antarctic Survey Team. He'd been called in one evening to extract a tooth—from an extremely unhappy polar bear. I suspected that I wasn't carrying enough anaesthetic to knock out a polar bear, but reckoned I could manage a collie.

'I don't think he's going to let me near him, but I think we're going to have to get that tooth out. I'll get my bag from the car. Have you got a pair of pliers?'

He nodded.

'You'll need to make sure they're clean and disinfected. We don't want him picking up an infection. Give them a scrub and dip them in some whisky'

I followed him outside, and he headed in the direction of the barn. I fetched my other bag from the car, and followed Seonaidh back into the kitchen. The dog was now sitting up and fixed me with a suspicious glance as I prepared something to relax him, guessing at the approximate dose for a border collie.

'You'll have to hold the sharp end while I stick this into his bottom—sorry! Hind quarters. I hung well back until Seonaidh had the dog's head firmly tucked under his arm and was holding his muzzle clamped shut. The animal's legs started frantically scrabbling and a low growl was emanating from the dog. I moved quickly forward, knelt down and inserted the needle. The dog gradually went limp and we both relaxed back onto our heels. Seonaidh handed me the pliers which reeked of whisky. I opened the dog's mouth. I gagged at the smell. The rotten tooth was near the back of his mouth. Why anyone would want to become a dentist is beyond me. Years of training followed by mining for rotten molars, not to mention, the bad back that seems to be an occupational hazard. Still, on the bright side, dentists' patients, unlike doctors' patients, don't want to spend hours telling you how depressed they are.

I tugged at the tooth, and luckily it came away in one piece. I threw it on the fire. The skin round the tooth space looked inflamed so I gave him an injection of antibiotics in case there was an infection.

'That should do it, but I'll just wait till he comes round to check that he's okay.'

'You'll have a wee dram and a cup of tea, Doctor,' said Seonaidh.

'Thanks. Just a wee one while we wait for the lad to waken up,' I said.

An hour later the patient was fully recovered although he was still regarding me with suspicion as I left the house carrying a joint of lamb, which Seonaidh had pressed into my arms.

He waved to me as I drove off. Another satisfied customer and another depletion of the drugs cupboard that I'd have to explain to Mrs Murray. I wasn't sure what her view was on doctors treating unregistered canine patients, though I suspected that I already knew the answer.

I was shattered when I reached home. The surgery had been busy and the stress of hiding a stray Russian was beginning to tell. I was used to spending quiet evenings at home with George and some gin. Now I was sharing my space again, even if it was in a rather unconventional manner. I'd got used to my own company and the raw gaping wound which had opened with Tom's departure had started to heal over since Andrey had arrived. I supposed he was like a temporary plaster. It would be interesting to see what would happen when he left. I suspected I already knew the answer to that too.

I was still smiling when I walked into the kitchen. 'I've just had my most interesting patient yet,' I announced to Andrey, and told him the story of Ben and his tooth. He laughed and looked relaxed, as did George who was lying across his thighs. Then, the moment disappeared and I remembered that there were far more important matters to be discussed. 'Do you have any news?' I said.

He shook his head, 'No, perhaps tomorrow. We should eat. I've put some of the things from the freezer in a saucepan and have heated it up. I have no idea what it is.' He shrugged his shoulders.

'I don't care. I'm starving and could eat a scabby horse,' I said.

Andrey looked puzzled, 'You Scots, you are like the French. You eat horsemeat?' he said.

'No,' I laughed, shaking my head. 'It's a Glasgow expression meaning that you're very hungry.' I lifted the lid of the pan. 'Lamb. Smells nice.'

'Stew!' he said, smiling.

I laughed. 'Yes, you're really starting to master the Scots language.

He smiled and patted the sofa beside him. 'Sit and tell me more Scots words.'

'Okay,' I smiled, bending down taking his face in my hands and kissing him. 'But some of these words should never be repeated in public.'

Chapter 29

Next morning driving to the surgery, I was on auto-pilot. My mind and body were still back in the cottage with a sleeping Andrey.

Another night without drugs: no morning brain fog to wade through. It was a lot easier to wake up in the morning, but a lot more difficult to leave the warmth of a rumpled bed when there was someone in it. But the patients wouldn't heal themselves, and I had to try to act normally so as not to arouse the military's suspicion. I drove to work, my windscreen wipers conducting the drumming rain. Near the bottom of the road leading to the surgery, there was no sign of Laurel and Hardy. The barrier across the road was up and I drove through it and up the hill. Perhaps some kindly local had taken pity on them and they had found somewhere warmer and drier.

The car park looked quiet. Hopefully I could get the surgery over with quickly and get back to the cottage. I was humming to myself as I pushed open the door.

There weren't many patients this morning, but my heart sank at the sight of one small man in his dark suit. This might take a bit longer than I'd hoped. Calum Twig was sitting flicking through the pages of one of the women's magazines which I'd started bringing into the surgery. I knew that Mrs Murray wasn't very happy. Nothing had been said, but I'd come in some mornings and the magazines had disappeared overnight. When I'd first arrived the only reading material on the waiting room table was The Christian Herald or the bible. Calum usually arrived with a newspaper or magazine cutting about an illness which he'd convinced himself he'd contracted. Last week it had taken me twenty minutes to persuade him that malaria had not reached the islands and could not be contracted from a midgie bite. Fingers crossed it wasn't a prostate problem.

'Morning, Mrs Murray,' I said lifting the patient files and moving towards my room. She beckoned me back. Then leaning forward conspiratorially across the reception desk whispered, 'Have you heard?'

'Em, no, I haven't. Heard what?'

'The army's going to start rounding them up and questioning them. Taking them into town,' she said, and leant back folding her arms, the information having been dispatched.

'Rounding up who?' I asked.

'Any man who's not local. There's not been anything like this since the last war. I remember they rounded up Luigi the Italian who owned the cafe in Stornoway and took him off to a camp somewhere in England. Said he was a foreign threat. Only weapon that poor man was capable of working was his cappuccino machine.' She laughed at her joke. I did too. A Mrs Murray joke was a protected species. It might be a long time till I heard another one.

'PC Bain's just been in. He says that the army's setting up a cordon. They're rounding up all men over eighteen not on the voter's roll and taking them into Stornoway for questioning.'

God, I had to get back to the cottage to warn Andrey. I dumped the patient files back on the reception desk and started backing towards the door.

'Dr MacAllister, where are you going?' said Mrs Murray. 'The surgery's about to start.'

'Emergency, Mrs Murray, can't stop. Be back later.' I pushed open the surgery door and ran to the car. I had to get back to the house before the army reached there. I drove at speed, aware of every bend in the road and the time the drive was taking. I didn't see any army vehicles or soldiers on my way back, but as I drove through the valley I could see the unmistakeable shape of two army trucks in the distance parked across the road. I slowed down as I approached, and when I stopped the car two soldiers approached from behind the barrier. I recognised Laurel and Hardy. They were about to wave me through when there was a shout and Captain Wells appeared from round the back of a truck.

'When I said search every car, I meant every bloody car.' He glared at the two soldiers.

'Bastard,' muttered Laurel under his breath. He smiled at me and shrugged his shoulders. 'Sorry, Miss, but orders is orders and his captain-ship is being a pain in the Arsenal.' He walked round to the back of my car, opened the boot, closed it, then waved me past. I smiled back, trying not to speed as I drove home. I could see there was movement further along the valley where the crofters were working on their sheep at the fank. As I drove past, Seonaidh Beag raised his arm in greeting.

Andrey was standing in the kitchen, still dripping from his bath, a towel wrapped round his waist, looking out the window at the soldiers in the valley below. He smiled as I ran into the room but when he saw the look on my face his smile quickly vanished.

'What's wrong?' he said.

'They're doing a house to house and rounding up any man who's not local. They're not far away and they'll reach here soon.'

Andrey sat down heavily on the sofa, his face chalk white. I had to do something.

'They'll kill her, I'll never see her again,' he said, then started muttering in Russian.

'Shut up! I need to think. Save that for later,' I said, and started to pace up and down the room. There had to be something. Yes, but what was it? I looked round the kitchen.

Alasdair's blue overalls were hanging on the hook at the back door. I grabbed them and thrust them at Andrey. 'Quick—get dressed.'

He opened his mouth. 'No time to explain. Stick these on.' I grabbed Alasdair's grey Harris Tweed cap and handed it to him. With Alasdair's wellies on his feet, he looked the part of a Hebridean crofter as long as he didn't open his mouth. 'Right, into the car, we're heading for the fank.'

'What's a fank?' he said, jamming the cap on.

'I'll explain on the way. Move!' I implored.

I drove down the hill to where three battered vans were parked. I was about to get out of the car when out of nowhere a collie appeared and jumped up at my car door snarling. I recognised Ben my dental patient. He leapt up again, his lips curled back exposing his teeth. I shrank from the window and Andrey muttered something in Russian at the dog.

'Shut up, idiot. You're supposed to be Norwegian remember.'

Seonaidh Beag turned round and shouted something at the dog in Gaelic and it dropped from the car door and crept sullenly to his side where it lay down. But all the time its eyes were following me. Seonaidh walked over smiling and puffing on his pipe.

'Sorry, Doctor, Ben's still a bit sore and not back to his usual self. You can get out now if you want.'

I smiled and slowly got out of the car, pulling up my hood against the pelting rain.. Ben was tracking my movements with his eyes, but didn't move. I followed Seonaidh over to where the other man was leaning on one the fence poles.

'I've got a problem,' I said, 'The soldiers are rounding up people, who aren't local, and I don't want my friend Andy, who's here on holiday, to be carted all the way to the town. I've got a surgery this morning and I haven't got time to waste going all the way over to fetch him back. He's Norwegian. Not much of a way to treat a visitor is it? Can you help?'

Seonaidh took a draw on on his pipe and looked over at Andrey who was sitting in the car.

'Doesn't look like a foreigner to me,' said Seonaidh. 'Bring him over.'

I turned and waved at the car. Andrey opened the door and Ben immediately sprang forward running towards him. Seonaidh shouted something in Gaelic and the dog dropped onto its belly as if it had been shot. Andrey walked over, his gaze not leaving the dog.

'See these rocks?' said Seonaidh waived his crook at a rocky outcrop, half way up the hill.

Andrey nodded.

'Get up there, on the rocks, close to these two sheep,' he said to Andrey, pointing with his pipe to where two sheep were grazing.

Andrey started to run up the hill. Immediately there was a snarl and Ben took off after him. Seonaidh angrily shouted the same phrase and the dog stopped dead. Its tail dropped between his legs and he slunk back to his master's side. I watched Andrey run up the hill towards the sheep, who started to move away as he got closer to them. Andrey's fitness was in no doubt. Most people after the illness he'd had would still be sitting by the fireside recovering but he was scrambling quickly over the rocks and was soon blurred by the distance.

He had just reached close to where the sheep had been when there was the sound of an engine and an army Land Rover rounded the corner approaching the fank. I recognised the driver—it was Captain Wells. The vehicle stopped a few feet from us and Captain Wells opened the car door. There was a bark and Ben threw himself towards the vehicle. Captain Wells quickly withdrew his legs to the safety of the car. I waited for the call back shout from Seonaidh. None came. The dog circled the car snarling. Then it quietened, lifted its leg and relieved itself on one of the tyres before rearing up onto its hind legs and scrabbling at the driver's door, its muddy paws mosaicking a pattern onto the paintwork. Seonaidh slowly walked over and stood about ten feet from the car still smoking his pipe. The captain began to roll down the car window. The dog's barking and scrabbling intensified and he quickly rolled it back up again.

'Will you call that bloody dog off,' shouted the captain but it was difficult to hear him from inside the car. He rolled the car window down an inch.

'Sorry, Major—the dog's got toothache and won't take any notice of me. Doesn't trust strangers. Careful or he'll have your hand off,' said Seonaidh apologetically. The barking intensified and Ben had recommenced circling the car and snapping at the wheels.

Seonaidh walked a couple of feet closer to the Land Rover and shouted at the dog. It ran over and dropped at his feet, still growling in Captain Wells' direction.

'Not good with strangers you said,' declared Captain Wells, rolling down the window of the car but keeping a wary eye on the dog. We're verifying people's identities,' he lifting a clipboard and pen from the passenger seat. 'And you're?' he said to Seonaidh.

'James Macleod, croft 29. That's Iain Macleod, croft 24,' he said nodding at the other crofter, who grunted in the direction of the car.

'And that's Alasdair Macdonald,' he said, pointing at Andrey with his pipe. Lives at croft 38. He's a cousin of Doctor MacAllister and...'

'That's all I need,' said the Captain, and he rolled up the

window and attempted a three point turn, which wasn't, and drove off wheels spinning, being chased down the track by Ben.

'Well, Doctor, you can tell your friend Andy that if he ever wants a job there's a place for him here,' he said, looking at Ben. 'It would save me having to get another sheep dog.' The dog had returned and was lying at his side, its long pink tongue lolling from the side of his mouth, panting heavily. If I didn't know better, I could've sworn that it was smiling.

I looked up, Andrey was on his way back down the hill.

'He's not good with strangers,' said Seonaidh, patting Ben on the head, 'but, then, sometimes that's not a bad thing.' He hit the bowl of his pipe off a fence post, pulled out a pouch of tobacco and started to refill it.

'But once he gets used to you he's fine,' he said and winked.

Chapter 30

Andrey was white faced and shivering by the time we got back to the house.

'Change out of your crofter's uniform into something dry, and I'll make you a coffee to heat you up,' I said. I filled the kettle. 'Well, now we know you we can get you a job as a collie if you ever give up engineering,' I laughed, grabbing a towel and throwing it at him. He caught it, looking puzzled. 'Get you a job as a sheep dog—a collie dog.'

He nodded, still breathing heavily and started to peel off the sodden overalls.

'It is getting more difficult...with the soldiers...I will phone them again today,' he said, towelling his hair.

'I'm worried. I don't know what they'll do next. I feel that they're starting to close in. It's getting more and more dangerous,' I said, as I ran the water into the kettle.

I smacked my forehead with my hand. Damn. Not again. 'Mrs Murray and the patients,' I said looking at my watch—half past ten. 'She will be hopping mad.' I dialled the surgery number. Waited for the phone to be picked up then said hello, and held the phone well away from my ear. I couldn't hear the words, but I understood the message. Mrs Murray was not pleased.

'Yes, I know. I'm sorry, Mrs Murray. It was an emergency. Please tell the patients I'm on my way,' I said, and hung up the phone. I turned round and bumped into Andrey who was standing behind me. He pulled me towards him and hugged me. Once again I was aware of the strength returning to his muscles.

'You have saved me twice, Doctor MacAllister,' he kissed me hard. Then stepping back, he held me at arms' length, looking at me. He smiled in a lop-sided way and started to pull me back into his chest, then shook his head. 'You must go back to your patients,' he instructed, as he lifted a strand of my hair which had escaped, and tucked it back behind my ear. He pushed me gently away, then his arms dropped to his sides. I stood feeling simultaneously dazed and bewildered.

'I must go,' I whispered backing towards the door. I pulled it closed behind me, and sought the safety of the car where I sat feeling breathless. I shook myself again, rather as George does when waking from a dream. Where was George? I hadn't seen him this morning. I hoped he hadn't found another dead fish on the beach to roll in. A similar incident last week had cost me a whole bottle of shampoo and several squirts of Mairi's expensive perfume. This was much to George's obvious distaste as he spent the rest of the afternoon wandering round the house sneezing.

My head was crowded with thoughts on my drive back to the surgery. It was probably too fast and too distracted and I'd no recollection of the journey when I stepped out of the car. Luckily, when I pushed open the surgery door Mrs Murray was on the phone, deep in conversation. I quickly grabbed the bundle of patient records from her desk and had taken the first patient into my surgery before she could say anything. But I knew I'd have to wait a while for a cup of coffee to be delivered to my desk.

My first patient Effie Macdonald, an elderly woman sat before me, dressed in black, her handbag clutched to her chest, eyes downcast. She reminded me of pictures of mourning women, I think they were Greek or Italian, that I had seen in my geography book as a child. They had the same sad look, whatever their nationality—the light in their life had dimmed. I looked at her notes, it was over ten years since she'd been to the surgery. I'd apologised for the delay, but she said she'd been happy chatting to one of her cousins.

'I'm sorry to bother you, Doctor,' she said. I smiled. It was usually the apologetic patients who were not a bother. She explained that she hadn't been to see Dr Robertson as she was too embarrassed to arrange an appointment.

'I didn't want him fiddling down there, Doctor,' she said, dropping her eyes. 'Him being a bachelor.'

I locked the surgery door, and drew the curtains round the examination couch. I asked her to get undressed and asked her to popup onto the examination couch. She looked troubled. I handed her the blue wool baby blanket which the practice nurses used to protect the patient's modesty. She seemed to relax. I was unsure about the hygiene element of this but I knew that the nurses used it and that it was laundered weekly. So, why not? Anything to keep the patients happy. It's hard enough sometimes to do an internal and anything which helps a patient relax can only be a good thing.

I'd attended gynaecology clinics as a young medical student and marvelled at the skill which some nurses had developed to protect the modesty of their female patients; or in some cases to counteract the lack of sensitivity of some male doctors. Similar to the dance of the seven veils, the patient's modesty was shrouded from view by sheets or blankets.

Today's examination over, I explained to Effie Macdonald that I would have to refer her to the gynaecologist in the hospital. Unfortunately, he too was male but at least she didn't have to face him every Sunday morning in church, as she had Doctor Robertson who sat in the pew behind her. Lack of female doctors was a problem, but more so in single-handed practices. I'd noticed from the patient records that a number of women were visiting the surgery, many of whom hadn't been for an appointment with the doctor for a number of years, and they usually wanted to discuss gynae problems.

There was a polite cough and I looked up. Effie was dressed. Still flushed from her ordeal she reached into her handbag and brought out a small square packet wrapped in greaseproof paper.

'Some of my homemade shortbread,' she said placing it on my desk. I had a quick peek before the next patient. It was golden and crumbly and might be able to keep me going to lunchtime, even if home-baking rations were being withheld by Mrs Murray. I crept out to the kitchen and quickly made myself a cup of tea and was wiping shortbread crumbs from my mouth as the next patient came in.

No cup of tea arrived that day and I knew things weren't good, and I had to face the music. After the last patient I approached the reception desk. Mrs Murray looked up and I waited, tensing for the onslaught.

Chapter 31

My ears were still ringing from Mrs Murray's tirade about my disappearance from the surgery. I explained that it had been a family emergency and she seemed to calm down after that.

Driving home listening to Simon and Garfunkel's *Bridge over Troubled Water* and trying to unwind, I was still mulling over the events of the last week when I narrowly avoided smashing into a speeding van on a bend. I almost ended up in the ditch as I swung the wheel over to avoid a collision. In the process, I managed to stall my car. Many of the island roads were single track with passing places, so sometimes near misses were unavoidable, but this van was being driven almost as if they wanted to cause a collision. Then I recognised the driver as the van zoomed past. It was Duncan. Scowling at me, he raised his fingers and gave me a V sign. Pig! Since the night of his nocturnal visit he hadn't been back to the cottage, and so far I'd managed to avoid him when I was out. But I'd heard that he was still drinking heavily since Caroline had left the island.

There were no lights on. I'd got used to seeing the beacon of light as I drove up the hill. Well, I'd better get used to the idea that this welcome wasn't going to last much longer.

But, surprisingly, there was no welcoming bark or cooking smells when I opened the door. I turned and looked along the beach and at the far end through the gloom, I could just make out the figure of Andrey jogging back along the shore line, his feet kicking up a spray. George was probably worrying another piece of seaweed somewhere in the machair. I went into the kitchen and put the kettle on. Then, remembering that I hadn't fed the hens that morning, went out to the barn, while the kettle heated up. I knew that I'd get a rapturous welcome as they must be hungry. But unusually there wasn't a sound.

They were all huddled outside the barn and didn't move as I approached. 'Don't tell me that George has taught you how to sulk.' I laughed and went inside. By the fading light, I could just see their feed bin. I opened it then dropped the lid with a scream. There was something lying behind it. I stepped back warily. Was it a mink or rat? My breath quickened. Despite my scream it didn't move. Hesitantly I bent down to take a closer look. I laughed. It was George. I'd caught him having a nap in the barn.

'Come on, George, let's get a biscuit.' I said. He didn't move. I knelt down, and touched him. No response—something was wrong. His body was warm. I felt for a pulse. It was thready. His chest was barely moving. Then I noticed there was vomit round his mouth. Oh God! I couldn't lose George. He was only two years old but we had been through a lot together. Of the two of us George had always been the more sensible. He'd been my only friend through the last two difficult years. His body twitched and he vomited again. His eyes fluttered open and he whimpered. I wiped away the vomit with a rag and gently picked him up and carried him towards the door. His body went rigid as I stumbled out of the barn. He seemed to be fitting. Andrey ran over when he saw me.

'What's happened? Is he ill?' he said.

'I...I don't know—I thought he was dead,' I said, collapsing onto my knees, and holding his now floppy body close to my chest. All of the grief and feelings flowed out as I sobbed uncontrollably. Andrey looked shocked, as he knelt down and wrapped his arms round me.

'Let's get him into the house,' he said softly. I nodded stroking George's fur before reluctantly holding up the almost lifeless form to Andrey who took him into his arms. I followed them into the house, wiping the tears away. I had to pull myself together, focus, try to help George.

'I don't know what's happened,' I said. 'I suspect he might have ingested poison. Let's try giving him some milk. He's vomited already. He might stand a chance if he's brought most of it up.'

I filled a small jug with milk dribbled it into George's slack mouth while Andrey held his muzzle. I sat holding him. Andrey disappeared out of the room. George vomited again. This time there was bits of bone and fur.

Andrey came back into the kitchen, shaking his head. 'I looked, there was a dead rabbit in the barn which I think he was eating.'

'Strange. Rabbits never go in there.'

'It smelt funny. Poison for rats? Do you have that in the barn?'

'No, I'd never put that stuff down,' I replied. Then I remembered Duncan's near miss with my car. 'I think it might have been Duncan. I met him, driving away from here. He was at the bottom of the hill. The idiot nearly drove into my car. But I've no proof it was him.'

Andrey nodded grimly.

There was a whimper and George opened both his eyes. I gave him more milk, and this time he managed to keep it down.

I stood up. 'Keep an eye on George but hopefully as he's been sick he might have got most of it out of his system before ingesting it. I think we might have caught him in time, but we won't know until the morning. I need to get some more milk,' I said, standing up and looking at the empty jug.

Andrey nodded and knelt down beside George and gently stroked his head.

The shop was closing as I arrived but Mr Macleod, smiled and waved me in. 'Just in for a few things,' I said.

He nodded, and reached towards the gin.

'No thanks, not today, though I'll take some cigarettes and milk.' I paused. 'I'm having problems in the barn. Something's stealing the hen food and the eggs,' I said.

'Aye you'll want a pack of this,' he said, reaching under the counter. 'It'll be a rat from the shore. This'll kill the wee buggers stone dead. Must be an epidemic, you're the second person in today looking for the stuff.'

I stiffened.

'Someone else having problems?' I asked.

'Duncan,' he said. 'He was in this morning. Surprised he could even keep the car on the road. He was too drunk to walk. Just as well he was driving. Bought more whisky and the poison. Did you say you were wanting a pack?' he said, holding up a cardboard box with a skull and crossbones on it.

'Er no,' I said, 'I've changed my mind, I'll leave it. Just the milk and cigarettes.' I paid him, grabbed the bag and ran out of the shop.

Andrey was standing at the sink, busy chopping vegetables as I burst into the kitchen. There was no sign of George. I dropped the bag and burst into tears. Andrey looked startled.

'Oh God, no. Don't tell me he's dead.' I clutched the chair for support.

'No, no,' said Andrey putting down the knife. He pointed at the floor. George was lying at his feet. I let out a huge sigh and stroked his fur and his tail started gently sweeping the floor.

He attempted to raise his head but that seemed to require too much effort and he laid it back on the floor. I stood up. 'He might have got it out of his system quick enough. The bastard! I shouted, standing up Andrey looked startled. 'It was him. Duncan tried to kill George,' I said.

'How do you know?' he asked leading me over to the sofa and gently pulling me down.

'I went to the shop. Mr Macleod said Duncan had been in buying rat poison this morning.'

Andrey muttered something vehemently under his breath. It was in Russian. I didn't understand the words, but there was no mistaking the sentiment as he slowly walked over picked the knife up again and began to chop more vegetables. I was thankful it was a large wooden block as I think his knife might have cracked a thinner one.

'Why George?' I started to cry again.

'The man is a b...' He said something unintelligible in Russian and his chopping becoming even harder.

Placing the knife down on the board, he knelt down and patted George, who made another unsuccessful attempt to raise his head.

'I will sleep down here beside the wee dog tonight. If anything happens, I will come and get you. There is no point in us both being tired tomorrow.'

I nodded, exhausted. I just prayed George would still be alive in the morning.

Chapter 32

I was exhausted. Although I didn't think I would, I'd slept. I woke up with a start and put out my hand to feel the pillow—nothing. There was light outside. The clock said half seven and the room was silent. No Andrey. No George.

My stomach tightened. There was no excited greeting from George when I opened the door. This wasn't a good sign.

I walked into the kitchen. Andrey was prone, fully dressed, on the sofa, in almost the same position that I'd left him last night. A half-folded map of the island was lying discarded on the floor. George lay across his knees. I couldn't tell if he was breathing or not. Both their heads lifted when I walked in. I burst into tears. George slid off Andrey onto the floor, and made his way to the back door. He was doing a good impersonation of a Glasgow rubber man—someone who's had too much to drink—but his tail was wagging as he tottered outside and I followed him at a discrete distance. He seemed to be getting steadier on his paws, and even took an interest in the hens when I fed them. Things were looking up, but I kept an eye on my canine invalid just in case.

Returning to the back door out of the wind, I pulled out a packet of cigarettes from my dressing gown pocket and lit one. I turned to offer one to Andrey who had come to stand beside me.

I noticed that his face was ashen. I wondered if the infection had returned.

'You look pale. I'm just going to take your temperature,' I said, turning to go inside.

He caught my arm and shook his head. 'She phoned when you were out with George.'

184

'Who?'

'Natalia.' His voice softened. 'I spoke to her. She's well. Frightened, but well. They have taken her from my parents' house. If I do not meet the submarine as arranged, they say they will kill her.' We went back inside the house, and he sat down heavily on the sofa.

'God, she must be terrified.' I crouched down on my knees in front of him, and took his hands in mine. I could feel the sweat on his palms.

'My parents are with her. They have all been taken to a government house. I don't know where it is. I have to go back. You understand?' His eyes held mine.

I nodded.

'I spoke to Asimov, the section head,' he continued. 'He is very unhappy that I do not have the part. They know it is lost, that the mission has failed, but he said I must return.'

Andrey looked down at me, his voice trembling. 'I spoke to my father after I spoke to Natalia. He told me that he is sure Asimov will kill her if I do not come back. He said that he has seen him with a knife. Helen, she is all I have. They cannot kill her.'

I squeezed his hands together. 'You have no choice. I understand.'

He looked haggard. 'He is a...' he punched the sofa arm and I jumped.

'She was so frightened. They dragged her away from the phone. I could hear her screaming. I have to get back, or Asimov will kill her.'

Any last hope, that I could somehow persuade him to stay, evaporated at that moment, and I knew that all I could do was concentrate on getting him successfully to the rendezvous point.

'Look we'll do it. Things will be okay,' I said, using my best GP reassuring voice—the one that I used while mentally crossing my fingers. It usually worked well on patients and seemed to work with Andrey.

'Thank you,' he smiled.

'What happens now?' I asked.

'They are sending a submarine for me. I have the coordinates and I have worked out where it is.' He stood up and picked up the map and pointed his finger to a spot on the map just round the headland, not too far out, but hidden from sight of the road. I leant against him, feeling the warmth of his body, aware of the fact that he would soon be gone and that I would never see him again.

'They have checked the weather. It is good. They will only surface and wait for ten minutes. They know that it is dangerous and that there are more patrols. It is my only chance. It is Natalia's only chance. If he kills her...'

I shivered, he was speaking in a low voice barely no louder than a whisper, but the tone of his voice frightened me. I knew that I would not want to be in Asimov's shoes if something happened to Andrey's daughter.

'When will the submarine be here?' I asked, praying that it would take days to arrive.

'It has already set off. It will be here tonight at midnight,' he said.

'Tonight?' My heart sank. I was going to lose him. But he had to go.

'I must leave. You know that I must leave,' he said, looking at me.

I slumped further down and hid my head in his lap. I couldn't cope with this. He stroked my hair and gently lifted up my chin with his hand and wiped away my tears with the sleeve of his jumper. 'You knew I must go back,' he said.

I nodded numbly.

'Yes, but did it have to be tonight? Why so soon?'

I started to cry again.

'I phoned. They said the tides are right and they will come for me. I must go. I have no choice,' he said looking at me intently. 'You know this.'

I nodded.

'Bugger! bugger!' I said.

He looked startled. 'What?'

'God! The ceilidh—I forgot about it. It is on tonight. I have to attend or people will be suspicious.'

'What is this ceilidh?' he asked, looking puzzled.

'Singing, dancing, drinking,' I said.

'Ah we do that at home too. Is someone getting married?'

'No, in Scotland we don't need an excuse! I have to draw the raffle.'

'You are drawing too?' He looked more bemused.

'No—pick a prize,' I said.

'You get a prize?'

No, I can't explain. I can't think straight. We have less than twenty-four hours and then you'll be gone.'

He nodded.

'I have to go to the ceilidh, but I'll leave early, and be back in plenty of time to drive you to the rendezvous. If anyone asks I'll just say that I have to check on a patient. The soldiers won't be bothered; they've seen me driving to home visits. We'll get you to the meeting point safely. Don't worry everything will be okay.'

I'd said it again. This time I instinctively crossed my fingers. 'You will see Natalia. You'll get her back.' I stood up, 'I need a drink. We both need a drink.'

He nodded, 'Perhaps it would be better if we had breakfast instead. It is only eight o'clock and it is going to be a long day. If things had been different...'

'I know,' I said, and pressed my finger to his lips. 'But they're not. Another time, another place, things could have...would have been different. But they're not and you have to go back. At least they understand that the device was lost.'

He looked at me intently. 'They are not happy. It sets them back ten years behind the English. But the world is safer while we do not have it,' he said, shrugging his shoulders.

'We must eat,' I said.

'Yes, but perhaps it would be better if I cooked?' he said, lifting his head and smiling.

'Good idea.'

'Perhaps we have time before we eat,' he said, standing up and pulling me gently towards him. 'I will miss you Doctor MacAllister,' he said, kissing me on the forehead. 'In Russia it is important that we say goodbye properly. We do not rush these things,' and he kissed me hard on the lips.

Chapter 33

Damn, damn, damn! My last evening with Andrey, and I'm spending it in a draughty hall with twenty people and an out-of-tune accordion. Just my luck. If it wasn't for communism, western civilisation and nuclear missiles, my life could be so much simpler.

Well, I'd just better get on with it. The sooner I started, the sooner I'd finish. I'd stick my nose in the door, do one circuit of the hall, smile sweetly, draw the raffle. I checked my watch, it was half-past seven. Half an hour, and then I'd head home. Only five hours to the submarine rendezvous. That'd be plenty of time to get Andrey to the pier, so he could 'borrow' a boat to meet the submarine. I just wanted the next bit over as soon as possible. I hated goodbyes. I just wanted to fast-forward the next few hours. I stubbed out my cigarette in the car ashtray and walked across the school car park.

I could hear what in Glasgow would be called heedrum hodrum music overlaid with laughter, but I couldn't see inside as all the windows were greased with condensation. The heat and cigarette smoke cloud enveloped me as I pulled open the heavy wooden door. It was difficult to see as far as the band at the other end of the hall, the cigarette haze was so thick. The olfactive cocktail of Brut shaving lotion and perspiration hung in the air. There was also something else—a sort of peaty smell, but I couldn't work out where that was coming from.

'Dr MacAllister, glad you came. How are you?' said an overstuffed, red-faced man in a shiny suit, shirt buttons straining for freedom. He pounced on me, grabbing my hand and shaking it vigorously. He returned my hand which now hung rather limply at my side.

'Em, fine thanks,' I muttered recognising Calum Thin, the digger driver and chairman of the hall committee. In a small tank, little fish can be very important. I attempted a smile.

'Glad you made it. You'll have a wee drink, Doctor,' he said. I nodded, and followed him through the heaving crowd to the side of the hall where I could see a large trestle table serving as a bar. It was scattered with bottles of beer and cans of soft drinks. Calum stretched over, I hoped his buttons would take the strain. He took a glass from the cardboard box on the back of the table. Then, reaching underneath the white starched tablecloth, he drew out a bottle wrapped in a brown paper bag, and poured a generous measure, and handed me the glass. Ah, now I knew why I was smelling peat—it was malt whisky.

'We haven't a licence to sell spirits,' he winked. 'It didn't matter when they did all this licensing control stuff from the mainland, no one ever bothered their shirt tail about us. Out of sight, out of mind eh? But this new licensing lot in the Stornoway council are just a wee bit more enthusiastic. PC Bain's told us that he's got orders to do a surprise inspection of the hall to check that we're obeying their rules and not selling any spirits,' he said, looking at his watch. 'Ten to nine. Brian'll be here in about ten minutes to do his surprise inspection then, after he's gone, we can all relax.' He drained his glass and smiled.

Without warning, someone barrelled into my back, knocking the glass from my hand and sending me flying into the arms of Calum Thin. Luck and his avoirdupois prevented us both toppling over. I looked round.

'Bitch,' muttered Duncan as he staggered past me, weaving towards the bar, leaving a waft of whisky and rank body odour in his wake.

'Are you all right?' asked Calum as he peeled me from his jacket.

'Yes, fine thanks. Just didn't see that coming,' I said, accepting a replacement glass.

'I'm sorry, Doctor. He gets out of control when he gets a drink in him,' said Calum, shaking his head. 'We should really put him out, but we don't want a fight. No one'll take him on when he's like this. He has a nasty streak in him.' We watched Duncan pin-balling into the other dancers as he staggered across the floor.

We stood chatting for a few minutes. I was trying to take an interest in local sheep prices and failing miserably. I was aware of my time with Andrey egg-timing away. I could see Duncan coming back across the dance floor bouncing off dancing couples. As he passed me, he leaned into my shoulder and slurred into my ear, 'How's that wee dog of yours, Doctor? Not barking now eh?' He laughed, then lost his balance and swept over the top of the table beside him, smashing glasses in his wake, and narrowly missed skiting into Mrs Kettle's lap before thudding onto the floor where he miraculously landed in a sitting position still clutching his half empty glass. Muttering, he rocked forward and tried unsuccessfully to get to his feet. He swore loudly. All eyes were now upon him and the dancing stopped. He was the centre of a moat of space which had cleared around him, and no one was willing to cross this to assist him. He made another attempt to stand up, then fell back, his glass spinning from his hand. The nearest dancers shrunk further away from him. Then out of the corner of my eye, I saw two figures approaching from the other end of the hall. It was my military friends—Laurel and Hardy. I hadn't recognised them out of their uniforms.

'Evening, nurse. This fellow giving you grief?' said Laurel, as they both bent down beside Duncan. 'We'll just give him a bit of a hand outside.'

'Come on, mate. Let's go get some air,' said Hardy as they each grabbed one of Duncan's arms. It wasn't an easy task as he started to swear and tried to kick out, but they pulled him up and quickly pinned his arms behind his back. Still swearing loudly, he was marched to the door, where he was batter-rammed through it. The dancers had parted to let them through and the door slammed behind them. The hall seemed to let out a collective sigh of relief and the music restarted. I stood half-heartedly chatting to Calum, hoping that they would draw the raffle soon.

Archie the accordionist stood up, wiping his forehead and announced a Strip the Willow. A cheer went up from the crowd. The women removed their high heels, the men their jackets. The sexes lined up like two opposing tribes preparing for battle. The accordionist struck the first note and they were off. The men spinning their partners and everyone clapping and tapping their feet in time to the music. The dance was fast and furious. I hoped that there wouldn't be any casualties. Eventually it was no longer possible to hear any conversation as the music was getting louder and louder and the dancers were whooping as they spun in their sets. It looked like a combination of human ping-pong and skittles as the dancers ranged up and down the set. Occasionally a dancer let go of their partner while birling in the centre of the set and they'd both lost their balance— spiralling outwith the set walls, before quickly regaining their momentum and their partner.

I'd recognised the name of the dance when it was called by Archie. It was one I'd learnt at secondary school in P.T. class. But at school we had gone through the motions of the dance in a lukewarm fashion under the watchful eye of Mrs O'Donnell our P.T. teacher. The teenage boys, their acne intensified by their blushes, had been reluctant to ask the girls to dance, holding them at arm's length. They were annoyed that their football practice had been cancelled.

But here, dancing was being practised with an almost religious fervour though I remembered hearing that some of the churches opposed dancing in case the dancers became too aroused. It had been likened to sex with clothes on, but to me it bore more resemblance to a sporting event. I looked on. Sweat was now glistening on the foreheads of some of the dancers, and there were damp patches spreading on the backs of the men's shirts.

The hall door swung open, and Laurel and Hardy reappeared looking slightly bemused at the whirling dancers.

'Thank you,' I mouthed to them as they passed me on their way to the bar.

'Your friend's just having a wee nap,' said Laurel, rubbing his knuckles. 'We've tucked him up, for a little nap, in his Land Rover.'

'Yea, we even read him a bedside story,' said Hardy. They laughed and walked back over to a table clutching their drinks and sat down beside Angela and Mary. Angela waved and I waved back. Hardy turned round and I saw Mary pointing at me and shaking her head and laughing. Hardy shook his head then laughed. Smiling, he raised his glass of beer to me and I raised my glass back. I suspected my cover as a nurse had been blown. The music stopped and the dancers returned to their seats and thirstily grabbed their drinks, and the band put down their instruments and announced that they were having a break.

'We'll just have a few tunes from some of the children. Then we'll draw the raffle at the interval,' said Calum. 'Dr Robertson used to give us a tune...I don't suppose you...' He looked at me hopefully.

'Em, no. I'm afraid not. Never got past the recorder at school. I'm afraid I can't stay too long. I've to pop in to check on a patient on my way home.'

'Evening, Calum,' said Brian Bain, I hadn't noticed him coming into the hall. He was in uniform, his cap tucked under his arm. 'Everything going well?'

Calum nodded and smiled

'Evening, Doctor,' said Brian looking round the hall. 'Sorry. Didn't see you there when I came in. Warmer in here than outside. Just seen Duncan being helped into his Land Rover.' He gave a wry grin. 'These army boys have their uses. I've to fill in a report for the boss confirming no spirits on sale.' He winked, glancing round the room. 'All looks in order to me. Off home for a cup of tea. Are you staying for the dance, Doctor? Looks like a good ceilidh. Doctor Robertson used to play the accordion you know,' he said.

I smiled. 'Tone deaf,' I muttered. 'Blame my parents.'

He put on his cap, turned and headed towards the door.

Once Brian had left, Calum tapped his glass for attention and announced, 'The children will now play some tunes.' This was met with enthusiastic clapping from the crowd. I stood and listened, not expecting much and was pleasantly surprised. Some sang unaccompanied, some played the accordion and one wee boy sang and played the guitar. Their age, like the level of accomplishment varied. Some of the singing was in Gaelic. I couldn't understand a word but it was achingly beautiful and I could feel my eyes filling with tears. All the songs seemed to be about the loss of young men at sea. I supposed this was an occupational hazard of living on an island where hardly anyone could swim. There wasn't a swimming pool and most of the year you wouldn't want to dip a toe in the water, it was so cold.

I was trying to find a hankie without success when there was a polite cough at my side, and I turned round to see Ewan proffering a neatly ironed white cotton hankie. I was reluctant to take it but the alternative was the back of my sleeve. So I took it and blew my nose. He looked a bit startled by the noise and took a step back.

'Sorry—George nearly died,' I said.

'I'm so sorry to hear that.' He stood looking embarrassed. 'Was he a close friend?'

'He is my dog.' More tears started. He took another step back. 'I've just remembered I've got to do an urgent house call. Would you explain to Calum, I've had to go.' I held out his crumpled hankie.

'It's probably best if you just hang onto it,' he said.

I could feel the tears welling up again. 'Goodnight,' I sniffled as I turned and fled from the hall to the safety of the darkness.

Chapter 34

My ears were buzzing and I felt sick. I shook my head. Not a good idea. The bees buzzing inside my head got angrier and I felt sicker. Bright lights were now exploding inside my skull.

I vaguely remembered leaving the dance. I was anxious to get home to Andrey. I needed to get him to the rendezvous point on time.

I'd been distracted as I'd driven along the cliff-top road, so busy thinking about Andrey and whether the submarine would arrive on time and if he'd get away safely that, initially, I hadn't noticed the car headlights following me until they filled my back windscreen, bouncing off my rear-view mirror and blinding me. I put my hand over the mirror to shield my eyes and drove with one hand. The car behind me was going at speed and before I could pull over to let it pass, it nudged my rear bumper and my car jerked forward. I swore, grabbing the wheel with two hands. I thought it was some drunk trying to get home. He'll pull back and I can let him pass at the next passing place, I thought. But no. The car sped up again and this time rammed my bumper hard. I heard a crack. I lost control of the steering and one of my back tyres rolled over the cliff edge. Screaming, I instinctively leant away from the drop and gripped the steering wheel desperately trying to regain control. I pulled the tyre back onto the road. Thank God. I let out a huge sigh of relief. Suddenly I bounced off a rock and the car veered back towards the cliff edge. Slamming on the brakes, the back end of the car began to veer round. Then the car went over the edge. After the first turn I must have lost consciousness.

I must have hit my head as the car rolled. God, I was lucky to be alive. The car was on its side and my head was resting on the driver's window. I was strapped into the seat.

By choice, unlike most drivers, I always wore my seat belt and so hadn't been thrown out of the car. I'd once spent an interesting morning in theatre watching an eye surgeon picking glass out of a casualty's eyes. The patient had gone through a windscreen. It wasn't a pretty sight.

First thing, I had to get out of the seat belt. I felt for the release button, pressed it and fell against the car door. I lay there, not moving.

Above the buzzing in my head, there was another noise. The car engine! It was still running. I opened my eyes, peering into the gloom. I couldn't see outside the car—the headlights must have smashed on the way down. But by the dim blue light of the dashboard I could just make out the car interior.

I felt something wet on my head. Blood? Was I bleeding? I wiped it with my hand. God, did I have a head wound? I peered at my hand. It was too dark to see if it was blood. Then I smelt something else. Petrol!

I swore. My hands began frantically flailing for the ignition key, but I couldn't find it. I was hyperventilating. I concentrated on slowing my breathing down and trying not to panic. In...out...in...out. I had to get out of the car in case the petrol ignited and I was fried. I didn't want to end up as a roast joint on a slab being poked at by a disinterested pathologist. I'd heard from an off-duty fireman that I'd met in a pub that humans smell of roast pork when they burn. I gagged.

The pounding was strengthening in my ears. I imagined the front page of The Islander, our weekly newspaper: *Doctor identified by dental records*. Finally, my fingers found the ignition key and I turned off the car engine. Silence, apart from the rasping sound of my breathing. Without the dashboard light, the interior of the car was coal black.

I was still trying to pull together my thoughts. Now that the immediate risk of being flambéed was averted, was I injured? I flexed my arms and legs. No broken bones. I could wiggle my toes—spine seemed okay. I took a deep breath, nothing caught. Good, no broken ribs. I ached all over but nothing serious.

I knew that I was in shock, but hopefully adrenalin would kick in. I shifted position and groaned at the pain across my chest, but put that down to my body hitting the seat belt. My neck hurt too. Still, at least I was alive. If I couldn't get out, I'd just have to wait till the morning. Someone going to work would see the car and pull me out. Andrey would be gone by the time I got home. He would wonder why I hadn't come back to pick him up. He'd probably already set off to walk to the rendezvous point. I'd never see him again. I started to cry. I should never have gone to the ceilidh; I should have waited with him.

It was so dark, I couldn't even check the time on my watch. Then I remembered the torch that Mr Macleod had given me and reached across the passenger seat and pulled it out of the glove compartment. Would it work? I pressed the switch and squinted against the light which flashed on, bouncing off the car windows. Now I could see the passenger door handle. With difficulty, I manoeuvred myself across the car, I put my hand up and pulled at the handle, then with two hands tried to push the door open. The door didn't move an inch. The smell of petrol seemed to be getting stronger. I tried pushing the door harder, this time with my shoulder—using all my weight—nothing. Something was holding it closed. My heartbeat quickened and I was starting to hyperventilate again. With shaking hands, I shone the torch through the glass. I could see sand and sea weed. Luckily it hadn't landed on the rocks. It must have rolled down onto the beach, the sand breaking its fall. I tried the handle again, still no movement. I shone the torch up—the door was buckled and jammed. The window—I'd use that. I'd roll it down and crawl out. I grabbed the handle and tried to turn it—no movement. I gritted my teeth and tried again, summoning all the strength I had, I wrenched at the handle with no result. I shone my torch outside the car again. The waves seemed to be coming closer across the beach. There was already water surrounding the car.

The tide was coming in.

I screamed.

'Get a grip woman,' I urged. A plan. I needed a plan. I could turn the lights back on, but I was frightened that a spark from the ignition would ignite the petrol. Shining the torch around the car, I looked for something to smash the windscreen. The jack—I could use that, but it was locked in the boot. The noise of the waves seemed to be getting louder. The tide—it was getting closer. If I wasn't going to be burned to death, I was going to be drowned.

'Help me! Please help me,' I screamed, banging my fists and feet against the glass, but there was no one to hear me. I was lying entombed in a metal and glass casket waiting for my fate.

Chapter 35

Suddenly, the sea lit up with the soft glow from an approaching car's headlights fanning out through the darkness. Now I could see more clearly the waves inching their way up the sand. The car was passing above me on the cliff road. My heart leapt. I let out a long sigh of relief. They'd see my car and come down to rescue me. I'd soon be home. Would Andrey still be there? Perhaps I'd be able to say goodbye. I shone the torch on my watch but the glass was smashed and the hands crushed. I edged up into a sitting position poised to welcome my rescuers. I wondered who it was. They had probably been at the ceilidh.

My heart plummeted as the light receded and the beach slipped into darkness, and they drove on ignoring me. I tried the car horn. It was dead. I battered on the windows in frustration till my knuckles ached. Why hadn't they come to help? Why had they driven past? Then the slow, cold, dawning realisation that if I couldn't see them, then they couldn't see me. My car was tucked in at the bottom of the cliff completely hidden from anyone driving past. Even in the daylight nobody would see me from the road. No one was coming to help me. In the distance I could see the lights of the cottage, but Andrey would be preparing to leave and not looking out the window. Even if he did there were no headlights and he wouldn't be able to see me. I had to get myself out of this mess.

Bracing myself I started kicking the windscreen as hard as I could with my feet. It always looked so easy in films. The glass stubbornly resisted.

I peered through the window—the waves were closer and starting to nibble round the car. I reached down with my hand and realised my woollen coat was getting wet. Gasping with horror, I saw that rear back window on the driver's side was smashed; water was slowly starting to trickle into the car, and a puddle was beginning to form inside the car. Panicking I tried the horn again. I leant on it with both hands. Nothing. Then suddenly it burst into life, before dying away just as suddenly, and leaving only the sound of the wind and the waves. I frantically started kicking the windscreen again. My feet and ankles were hurting and I finally gave up in exasperation. I pounded the car horn again with my fists.

I buried my head in my aching hands and sobbed. I didn't want to die. I didn't want to drown in a bubble of salt water like an inverted goldfish. How long did I have left? Ten minutes? Twenty minutes? I started to shiver as the freezing water slowly began to inch up the windows. More water was channelling inside and wicking up my coat. I took it off and stuffed it into the broken window to try to stem the flow of the water. Memories came back to me of the Dutch story where the little boy used his finger to block the flow of water from a breeched dike. Well, he clearly had more success than me.

Death. I wasn't a stranger to it—no doctor is—but I hadn't planned for my own just yet. Hadn't even made a will. The way my life was at present, George was likely to be my executor and sole beneficiary. I wasn't sure if that was allowed in Scot's law. Shame we weren't in America: there was bound to be a state where it was perfectly acceptable to leave your worldly wealth to your dog and make him responsible for all the administration too. I wondered just how many dog biscuits I was worth.

Oh God! Was it too late to take up religion? I should have accepted Mrs Murray's offer of accompanying her to church. Would I even qualify for a church funeral? The only one I'd been to since I'd arrived hadn't seemed like much fun, so perhaps missing out wouldn't be such a bad thing.

Outside the car, something flashed. Was I imagining it? No! A light was slowly weaving down the cliff path. Someone was coming. I could put my funeral plans on hold. I wiped my nose with the back of my hand. My spirits lifted. I quickly flashed my torch on and off a few times to let them know that I was alright. The torch light flashed in reply. Thank God! I'd soon be home and in warm clothes. My teeth were chattering; I didn't know if it was the cold or shock or a combination of the two.

The figure reached the bottom of the cliffs and was now wading through the seawater towards the car. I rubbed off the condensation and strained to see out of the window, but I couldn't see their face. It seemed to be a tall man in a dark jacket. My spirits plummeted. Was this the person who'd run me off the road coming back to finish the job? I turned my torch on trying to search out their face, but the light bounced off the glass back into the car making it difficult to see. He reached the car and pulled at the door, but it was still jammed. Shouting, he kicked at it angrily. The light from his torch was shining into my eyes and blinding me. His face was completely hidden by a scarf and hood.

'Help me,' I screamed. He ignored me and turned and walked towards a pile of rocks. Bending down he pick up a large boulder. Staggering under its weight, he came towards the car. He struggled as he slowly heaved it above his head and brought it down towards the windscreen. Oh God! It was him—he was going to kill me. I looked round the car—there was nothing to protect myself with. I pulled the sodden travel rug over my head and held my breath, trying to make myself as small as possible. I screamed. There was a crash. The windscreen shattered and sea water flooded in.

Chapter 36

I felt the shattered glass hitting the rug. The noise of the sea and the wind ripped in through the broken windscreen. Like a hunted animal I desperately tried to burrow deeper under the rug. A hand reached in and was clawing at me, pulling the cloth from between my fingers and shining a torch into my eyes. I couldn't see his face, but I knew he was going to kill me.

'Leave me alone. Please don't hurt me.' I tried to roll myself into a ball and tensed waiting for a rock to smash my head.

'Helen, Helen,' shouted a voice. I looked up, squinting against the light. It was Andrey, standing shining a torch into the car. I shielded my eyes from the glare.

I let go of the rug. He pulled it out of the car and wrapping it around his hand he punched out the remaining pieces of glass surrounding the edge of the windscreen.

'Quick, there is not much time,' he shouted. 'Hold my arm.' I struggled to clutch it with my numbed fingers as he pulled me out through the gap. I gasped as I fell onto my knees into the freezing cold water. He hauled me up.

'Can you stand? Are you hurt?'

'I'm okay. Thank God it was you. I thought they'd come back. Somebody tried to kill me. They drove me off the road.' I clung to him. He shone his torch towards the back of my car, there were deep gashes along the Beetle's yellow paintwork.

'I know. I saw it happen from the window,' he said. Tugging my arm, he pulled me. 'Hurry, we must climb. The tide's coming in. We can't stay here.' Pulling and half carrying me, we waded towards the bottom of the cliff path. The light of Andrey's torch lit the way and we struggled to the bottom of the cliffs. I kept stumbling, and more than once my legs gave way and I pitched forward, but was prevented from falling by Andrey's firm grasp. The waves were now past my knees as we splashed through them. We reached the bottom of the cliff and started to climb the rough path back up towards the road. Andrey led the way, shining his torch and I followed close behind, one hand clinging tightly onto his jacket. All the adrenalin was leaving my body and I was starting to feel weak. Halfway up the cliff face, my breathing became ragged and I felt my grip slackening. There was a pounding in my ears and things were starting to swim around my eyes. I knew that delayed shock was setting in. My hands fell to my side and I stood, nausea gripping me. Andrey turned round and his torch beam lit me up as I was swaying on the edge of the path. He shouted at me in Russian. Lunging forward, grabbing my arm and pulling me back to safety, he knocked me to the inside of the path where he fell on top of me.

'We must keep going,' he urged, pulling me to my feet. He pushed me in front of him, and I staggered the rest of the way to the top of the path where I flung myself face down onto the grass whimpering.

'Get up,' said Andrey tugging on my arm and lifting me to my feet. 'We have to get to the house.'

I could see the lights of the cottage windows cutting through the darkness at the top of the hill as I stumbled along the road half leaning, half carried by Andrey. His grip on my forearm was hurting as he dragged me along the road. My teeth were chattering and my legs kept buckling. When I tripped and fell for the third time, skinning my hands on the gravel, he stopped. Stuffing the torch into his jacket pocket, he muttered something in Russian, swung me over his shoulder and carried me for the last hundred yards. There was no romance in his action. I felt more like a sack of coal being delivered.

Finally, we reached the cottage. The kitchen light blinded me as Andrey kicked open the back door, and we both collapsed inside onto the floor. The warmth of the house surrounded me, but I was freezing cold and shaking. Andrey hauled himself up, and I pushed myself up onto my knees and onto the sofa, where I sat arms wrapped round my knees. He came back with a towel, and helped me peel off my sodden clothes which clung tightly to my goose bumped skin. I resembled more an uncooked chicken than a human being. It reminded me of days on the beach when as a young child you returned to your mother and stood chittering, covered in sand, waiting to be rubbed down by a rough towel that felt like a piece of sandpaper. Andrey massaged my skin hard with the towel to restore the circulation as I sat shaking.

'Oww, that hurts,' I protested. He ignored me and continued rubbing my skin. The colour was starting to return as my circulation was restored. Then he helped me into dry jeans and jumper which he'd pulled off the dryer beside the stove. Feeling was returning to my fingers and feet. They were still white cold, but now they were starting to tingle, and I'd stopped shaking. Andrey knelt in front of me and held a glass of whisky to my lips. I took a huge mouthful choking on the liquid heat.

'Slowly, slowly,' he urged, holding the glass back to my lips.

'How did you know where I was?' I asked.

'I was standing at the window watching for you. I saw it happen, then I saw a light on the beach.' He looked at his watch then groaned. 'It is too late,' he said.

'What time is it?'

'Half past eleven,' he said, his head lowering.

'What time will they be there?'

'Half past twelve. The submarine will surface for ten minutes, then they will leave. We are too late.'

'Right, we need to get to the pier and borrow a boat,' I said.

'But how? How will we get there?'

'Well, we can hardly phone a taxi,' I retorted. I was still feeling weak and sick. 'Quick throw me over my bag,' I instructed.

He brought it over, and I searched out a pack of uppers and shook some into my hand. Needs must, I thought to myself; after all, this was a medical emergency, a matter of life and death. I offered him some tablets but he shook his head.

'Right,' I said. 'The barn.' He looked puzzled but followed me as I stood up and staggered out ahead of him grabbing one of Mairi's waterproofs from the pegs by the door. I was starting to feel better as the booze and the tablets kicked in. There were gentle clucking noises from the sleeping chickens as we approached the barn. These turned into disgruntled squawks as I flung open the barn door, but I ignored them and headed for the back of the barn. I began tugging hard at the heavy tarpaulin with both hands dragging it off. Andrey shone his torch. There, gleaming in the torchlight was Alasdair's pride and joy—his motorbike.

Chapter 37

'What! Is it yours?' asked Andrey, his torch light bouncing back off the chrome.

'No, it's Alasdair's, but he was frightened it'd be stolen if he took it down to Glasgow.'

'Does it work? Can you drive it?' he asked, dubiously.

I nodded. 'Hopefully...it's been a while,' I said, grabbing the handlebars and pushing the bike off the stand and out of the barn, Andrey's torch lighting the way.

Yes—I could ride a motorbike. I'd never passed my bike test, but this probably wasn't the time to worry about such technicalities.

The key was in my hand. I stuck it in the ignition, turned on the fuel and, saying a prayer, pressed the starter. Three times it failed to start, but on the fourth attempt the engine caught and it roared into life.

'Come on,' I mouthed above the noise, waving to Andrey to get on. He hesitated but there was no choice. He climbed on and his arms encircled my waist. We set off slowly down the hill. I braked sharply a couple of times to test the brakes and his grip round my waist became vice-like.

'Trust me,' I shouted over my shoulder to him. His grip didn't relax. Gathering more confidence, I accelerated. Andrey's grip tightened so much that my breathing was in danger of becoming constricted. I knew the road and it would be easy to spot the lights of any oncoming cars in the darkness. I increased my speed. We had less than an hour to get to the submarine and make the rendezvous. We needed a boat. All the village boats were moored at the pier. Only one problem remained—I could drive a bike, but not a boat. Hopefully Andrey could. We didn't meet a single car coming in the opposite direction, and reached the pier in a time that I reckoned even Brian Bain would have been proud of.

I slowed the bike as we drove down the pier road and Andrey's grip around my waist began to relax. I stopped, and we both dismounted. I remembered to leave the bike in gear to stop it rolling down the hill, and propped it against the wall. Duncan's van was there. We walked over to it. The driver's door was lying wide open. Andrey put his hand on the bonnet.

'Still warm,' he said. Then he shone his torch on the crushed front bumper, there was a slash of yellow paint on it.

'Bastard! He could have killed me.'

Andrey muttered something in Russian and looked at his watch. 'We have forty-five minutes,' he shouted. Turning he ran to the pier and jumped onto the deck of the first boat. I followed the light of his torch as he scrambled from boat to boat. Five minutes later he hauled himself back onto the pier.

'No keys,' he said angrily.

'Who lives there?' he asked pointing at the lights of the house at the head of the pier.'

'Duncan.'

'Him?'

I nodded.

'He has a boat?'

I nodded and pointed at The Girl Morag, a dilapidated wooden fishing-boat tied to the furthest mooring on the pier.

'Stay here,' he instructed. He set off towards Duncan's house jogging up the path. A rectangle of light appeared as he opened the door and went in. I paced up and down. Duncan's temper was well known. Andrey was still recovering from illness. Would he be any match if Duncan assaulted him? Fearing the worst, I picked up an iron rod propped against a wall, and started to walk up the hill. Then the door of the house opened and a figure appeared—it was Duncan. Oh God! What had happened to Andrey? But as he got closer I realised there were two figures. Andrey was immediately behind Duncan, bending Duncan's arm up his back. Duncan was shouting at him in Gaelic. When they got to the pier Andrey threw him onto the deck of The Girl Morag. He lay there stunned and not moving, holding his arm. The swearing had stopped.

'Duncan's going to take me out to meet the submarine then bring the boat back,' he said. He took a step towards me. 'I have no time,' he said. 'I'm sorry. I must go.' He pulled me towards him into his arms, the strength of his kiss bruising my lips. He let me go, and I backed away stunned. Before I could say anything he jumped onto the boat. In the light I saw him pick up Duncan by the scruff of the neck, and drag him unprotestingly into the wheelhouse.

Shortly afterwards the boat engine started and it headed out of the harbour. The boat had no lights on but I stood and watched it till I couldn't see its shadowy form any more. In the distance I could still hear the faint humming noise of the engine above the sound of the waves. Tears were running down my cheeks unchecked. I stood for about an hour, but the boat didn't come back in. Part of me wished that the submarine hadn't made the rendezvous, but deep down I hoped that Andrey had made the transfer.

But where was the boat? What had happened to Duncan? Probably passed out in the wheelhouse and sleeping his hangover off.

Finally, before I lost all the feeling in my fingers and toes, I turned and walked over to the bike. I took one last look at the sea, then I rode slowly home alone. I carefully put the bike back under the tarpaulin before heading into the house. George raised his head as I entered, then put it back down on his paws.

I felt empty. I sat down, put my head in my hands and sobbed. I felt that I was going to break. At one point I was aware of George's nose nuzzling the top of my head. Eventually, exhausted, I stopped. I went into the bathroom, and pulled off a long strip of toilet paper, and noisily blew my nose. I looked away from the red-eyed woman who looked out accusingly from the mirror. I went back through to the kitchen, and got out the gin bottle, and poured a large glass of gin and tonic. Then I opened the kitchen drawer, where I'd thrown in the sleeping tablets. I took out the bottle, unscrewed it and shook two into my hand. I hesitated. Did I really want to start using these again? But I knew I couldn't face a sleepless night on my own. It had been bad enough when I'd lost Tom but this time it felt far worse. I placed them in my mouth, then washed them down with a large gulp of gin. I left George downstairs. He was lying facing the door, waiting for Andrey's return. Slowly I climbed the stairs. I crawled into bed fully clothed. I pulled the blankets around me. I could still smell Andrey on them. I bunched them up and hugged them tightly to my chest and waited for the blackness to engulf me.

Chapter 38

The boat wobbled again on the waves, and I lost my balance and grasped the side for support.

'It's a pain that the fiscal's in court,' said Brian, 'but we want to get the body up and certified, before dark.'

I nodded and turned my face out to sea. We were standing on the deck of Duncan's boat, The Girl Morag. She was anchored round the headland just out of sight of the pier. Scooby and Dan, two local fishermen had motored us out in their wooden fishing boat, and then brought us alongside, and we'd scrambled on board Duncan's boat. I'd been frightened that I'd fall between the two boats, but the men held them together and helped me across. Then Scooby had moved his boat away and was now watching us, his boat gently rocking from side to side on the waves. I could just see the puffs of smoke coming from the roll-up hanging at an angle from the crease of his mouth.

Brian and Terry, an overstuffed, pasty-faced policeman from town who looked as if he was no stranger to a doughnut, were struggling with the anchor winch. Dan tutted impatiently and said something to them in Gaelic, waving them away with his hand. He took over the winch which began creaking as it slowly wound the anchor chain.

Brian came over and leaned against the wheelhouse. 'Aye, Scooby went out fishing this morning. Duncan's boat was moored here, but he thought nothing of it. Duncan's got some lobster pots laid nearby,' he said, wiping perspiration off his brow with the back of his sleeve. 'But when he came back at one, he saw that Duncan's boat was still anchored in the same spot. He shouted but couldn't see anyone, so he came on board her to check everything was okay. That's when he saw something in the water. Looks like a body. The anchor chain's wrapped round it. It's quite far down and it's going to be a bugger to get it up,' he said, moving over to the front of the boat and looking down.

I was shaking as I watched the chain gradually coming out of the water and winding round the winch. Was it Andrey? Please no. Let it be Duncan. Had they both gone overboard? Bile was in my throat. I needed a drink. I needed to sit down.

'Stupid bugger. He should never have taken her out when he was plastered,' Dan said, shaking his head as he worked the winch. The blue veins in his neck were standing out.

'Aye, probably still drunk from the night before,' said the town cop.

'Don't know what got into him. Usually when he's drunk he goes home and sleeps it off. Never known him take his boat out,' grunted Dan, scratching his head, 'but he's been on the booze since Caroline left.'

'Surprised his liver hasn't packed in,' said Brian, turning to me as if seeking medical verification of this. 'You alright, Doctor?' he asked. 'You're looking a bit pale. Soon be finished then we can get you back on shore.'

'I'm not good on boats,' I said, my voice almost a whisper, as they continued to haul the anchor chain up.

'Got him,' shouted Brian as a pair of wellingtons appeared. Oh God, Andrey. I swayed, then realised that they were yellow not black. The light was fading but I recognised the figure of Duncan as it gradually emerged, dressed in seaweed. The anchor chain was wrapped round his legs and his arms hung down on either side of his head. Almost as if he was trying to dive back into the water. The boat lurched as the three men moved to the side to haul the body onboard. I grasped the edge of the boat with both hands. I was starting to go cold and clammy. I wasn't sure if it was shock or sea sickness. I tried closing my eyes but that wasn't helping. I leant over the the side and threw up then sat down heavily on an upturned bucket and concentrated on not throwing up again. The sooner I got back onto land the better.

Brian had brought a large black body bag with him and they unfolded it and placed Duncan's body on top of it. Terry took a large camera from a scuffed black bag. There was a flash and the sound of the spool being wound on as he took some pictures before they unwrapped the chain from his legs.

'The fiscal likes to be at the scene of a body recovery before we move it when there's a sudden death. But these'll have to do him instead. At least this time I remembered to check there was film in the camera,' he laughed.

I looked at Duncan's body. The water was ebbing from his clothing and flowing onto the deck. It didn't need a doctor to see that he was dead, but procedure was procedure, and I looked at my watch and said, 'Three thirty-five pm.'

Brian confirmed the identity of Duncan and wrote it in his notebook. The formalities completed, the bag was zipped up and the two policemen, helped by Dan, struggled to lift the body onto the other boat which Scooby had brought back alongside.

I went into the wheelhouse. I was frozen. I sat down on the torn leather seat at the wheel. Something caught my eye. Just sticking out on the shelf holding the charts was the screw top of a half bottle of whisky. I looked round. Everyone was still busy with the body. Need must, I thought and quickly took a gulp. I sat holding the bottle thinking of Andrey. Where was he now? There was a cough behind me.

'You never get used to death,' said Brian holding out a form. 'Could you sign this for me please, Doctor?' He looked at the bottle in my hand then glanced away, and I hurriedly screwed the top back on, and jammed it back in beside the charts. Was

Duncan's death an accident or was Andrey responsible? No, Andrey would never kill anyone. But then I remembered the look on his face when he'd seen the crumpled bumper of Duncan's van. No, Duncan must have attacked Andrey. Everyone said how vicious he was when he was drunk. There must have been a struggle and his legs got tangled in the chain as Andrey fought him off. God! Was Andrey okay? He could have gone overboard too. He might be dead. I started to cry. Brian looked surprised. 'It's okay, Doctor, he wouldn't have known what happened it was so quick.' He pulled out a folded white cloth hankie and handed it to me. 'Always have one just in case,' he smiled.

'Thank you,' I snuffled, as I blew my nose. I proffered it back to him. He shook his head and I stuffed it into my pocket.

'What happened to you last night?' he asked, looking at me intently.

God! What did he know, I wondered.

'Saw your car being winched up from the beach by Seonaidh's pick-up,' he said.

I slowly let out a breath. 'I was lucky. Swerved to avoid a sheep on the way home from the dance. Car went off the road and rolled, but I managed to get out through the windscreen. Think it's a write off. I'll need to hire a car till I can get a new one.'

Brian turned and shouted out onto the deck, 'Hey, Dan, you still got your auntie's old car or did you sell it?'

'No, it's still in the barn, taking it to the mainland next month to sell it. Why?' he said sticking his head into the wheelhouse.

'Doctor here hasn't a car. Written off last night in an RTA. Can you help?'

'Sure, we can drop in to my croft on the way home and you can pick her up, Doctor. It's a red Mini. The gears are a bit ropey, but it will get you around till you get another one.'

I muttered something about payment.

'No need, Doctor. Just stick some petrol in the tank. You can borrow it till you find yourself another one. Can't have the medical profession walking to their patients, can we now?' he said, smiling.

I was about to say something about insurance, then I took another look at Brian's face, and realised that it was unlikely to be an issue.

'Okay if I take her back to shore?' Dan said heading back on deck.

Brian nodded. 'Right let's get you back onto dry land, Doctor,' he said.

'Helen, Brian. Helen will do,' I said.

'Okay, Doc—sorry, Helen?' he smiled, and went back on deck. I slumped back onto the seat as Dan started the engine, and we headed back towards the pier.

Chapter 39

In the medical profession there are times when you literally hold a patient's life in your hands. Perhaps as part of a surgical team in a brightly lit operating theatre trying to stop a patient haemorrhaging, or continuing with CPR on a weakened body in a RTA, long after it should be stopped, in the desperate hope that the patient will revive.

Thankfully this heavy responsibility doesn't often happen to a lowly GP, but today I was sitting at my desk holding a patient's life in my hands. Or to be more exact in one hand. The other held my mug of coffee.

I was looking at the brown envelope bearing the hospital stamp on it and the words PRIVATE and CONFIDENTIAL typed in capitals along the top. Usually the post didn't reach us till about three o'clock. Yesterday afternoon, Mrs Murray had marched Boadicea-like into my surgery clutching two brown envelopes in one outstretched hand and a cup of coffee in the other. I'd thanked her and taken them from her. She then stood expectantly in front of my desk with her arms stapled across her chest, but her face had fallen when I'd pulled open the top drawer of my desk and dropped the unopened envelopes inside. I took a sip from the mug of coffee and smiled. Pursing her lips, she'd turned and exited muttering about overdue filing.

Twenty-four hours later I'd almost forgotten about the envelopes. I was trying to force myself to concentrate and block all the other thoughts apart from those relating to work out of my brain, but thoughts of Andrey kept breaking through. My concentration was shot to pieces.

Thankfully, my worst faux pas today had been asking an

octogenarian when her last period was. There had been a long pause before she'd replied. 'I think it was 1949, Doctor.'

I was interrupted by a knock at the door and in came Hetty Matheson, her shoulders drooping, large dark circles under her eyes.

'Sit down. How are you?'

Perched on the edge of the chair, she looked at me and shrugged. 'Not great, Doctor. I was sick again just before leaving the house,' she said, her fingers picking at a thread on her black anorak.

I opened the drawer and fished out the envelope, tore it open and extracted her pregnancy test results.

'Well, you'll be pleased to know that your experience with babies is going to have to wait till you do your maternity placement,' I said, smiling.

'But I was sick.'

'Nerves. You've been through a lot of stress. Our bodies all act in different ways, but you might want to take some more of these.' I nodded towards my bowl of contraceptives discreetly nestled behind some files, well hidden from the eagle eyes of Mrs Murray. 'It'll save you visiting the Family Planning Clinic until you go to university.'

'Now off you go.' I stood up and patted her on the shoulder. 'Good luck with university, but file this experience—it'll make you a better doctor in the future.' I didn't hold with the god-like demeanour with which some of my male colleagues held themselves, and on more than one occasion had been embarrassed, if not angry, witnessing the treatment of patients by these insensitive oafs. Doctors may be in the top one percent intellectually, but many were in the bottom one percent emotionally.

I remembered watching a young woman lying trembling on a

bed in an obs and gynae clinic her dignity barely covered by the thin, green, cotton robe supplied by the hospital. Twelve students stood and watched the consultant as he performed an internal examination. The young woman's face was chalk white and her eyes were brimming with tears as the surgeon barked at her to relax and spread her knees. I and the other three female students blushed and looked away in sympathy. I studied a plaster crack in the ceiling. Just as I thought that it couldn't get any worse the surgeon finished then turned to our class, peeled off his rubber gloves and dropping them into the metal bin asked 'Now does anyone else want to perform an internal?' We all froze and waited. Thankfully, there were no volunteers. 'Right then, let's see what the next one's got to offer,' he said, handing the patient's file to a nurse and launching himself at the swing doors.

I swore I would never treat a patient with such insensitivity. Talking of insensitivity brought me back to Captain MacDonald. There was a knock at the door and he marched in and dropped into the chair.

It was midway through the morning, and for once my clinic was running on time, so tardiness on my part wasn't the reason for Captain MacDonald's glowering face. He'd pulled the chair forward and was drumming his fingers on my desk.

'Well?' he demanded.

'Good morning,' I replied, 'I'll just find your results, one moment please.'

'Just get on with it, Doctor—I'm in a hurry,' he barked.

Very occasionally you can just be pushed a bit too hard by a patient's rudeness. We doctors are only human after all. I opened his file.

'I'm sorry Captain MacDonald, I just don't seem to be able to lay my hand on your results,' I said, shuffling the papers on top of my desk and moving his file on top of the other envelope Mrs

Murray had given me from the hospital also stamped PRIVATE and CONFIDENTIAL.

'Now I have a full surgery, and I'm afraid I don't have time to look for it just now. If you're in a hurry, I can ask Mrs Murray to do it. It'll probably be a bit quicker,' I said, rising to my feet and picking up his file.

I could see from his expression that he wanted to shout at me. This was clearly a man who wasn't used to being kept waiting.

'No. I'll wait till you have time,' he said through clenched teeth.

'Thank you,' I smiled. 'I'm sure Mrs Murray will make you a cup of coffee.' He left my surgery, closing the door forcibly behind him. I moved the file and picked up the envelope, tore it open and extracted the results. Nothing. No infection. Lucky man, I thought.

Still, it wouldn't do him any harm to cool his heels for another half hour. He could wait till I'd seen another couple of patients. He could keep Mrs Murray amused. I smiled and picked up the next patient's file.

Chapter 40

It was half six when I drove up the hill to the cottage. I was still driving Dan's auntie's red Mini, which I'd bought with the insurance money from my old car. I liked the car, my only problem was remembering that, unlike the Beetle, the boot was at the back of the car. Last Monday morning, I'd been late arriving for work and had skidded into the car park, leapt out and tried to open the bonnet to get my bag. The waiting room had been treated to the sight of me kicking the car tyres and swearing at the car. Strangely no one mentioned it as I passed through reception into my room, but I noticed Mrs Murray brought through my coffee earlier than usual that morning.

I still missed Andrey. The days weren't so bad, it was the evenings when I returned home to an empty house which were the worst, but gradually I was adjusting to living on my own again. George had spent a week after Andrey had left sniffing round the house. I still slept with the Aran jumper he had worn, but any scent of him had long faded.

Christmas came and went. It was easy to ignore it on the island. The surgery was decoration free. Mrs Murray, being a Free Presbyterian, didn't allow them. I'd waited for Christmas trees to start beaconing in house windows. None did. Coming from Glasgow where for many households Christmas seems to start shortly after the summer holidays, I found the lack of decorations strange. But this year it fitted my mood.

There were no Christmas tree lights in the town either. Not even a municipal tree in the square. A couple of incomer proprietors bucked the trend and their shop windows displayed tinselled trees with their rebellious lights sparkling.

A few days before Christmas, I'd had a phone call from Mairi.

'Hi Hel, we've decided to stay down in Glasgow for Christmas. The weather forecast's pretty poor. There's going to be strong Southerlies, and Alasdair reckons that the ferry might be cancelled, and we don't want to be stranded in Ullapool, or stuck on the ferry.'

I wasn't in the mood for company and had been happy to work through Christmas and New Year, and had declined invites from Angela and Brian.

But that evening as I turned up towards the cottage, I saw that I'd a visitor. The fiscal's car was parked outside my back door. A well polished blue Ford Escort. I compared it to my grimy, mud-splattered Mini. I suspected his social life was as dull as mine, but car polishing was never likely to become one of my hobbies.

I hadn't seen Alasdair's cousin, Ewan, since the Fatal Accident Enquiry into Duncan's death. It had been held in the Sheriff court in the town. The sheriff seated in his elevated position in the court wearing a Victorian-looking wig and gown had returned a verdict of death by misadventure. I'd been called as witness to confirm the time of death. But, as I'd sat in the stuffy witness room before giving evidence, I'd felt sick as all the emotions of that night had come flooding back. I tried not to think about what had happened to Andrey. Had he survived? I would probably never know.

Ewan, had been busy in court and had only nodded in passing. After the verdict was announced by the sheriff, he'd been approached by one of the other solicitors, and quickly gathering up his papers he bowed to the sheriff and left the courtroom deep in conversation with the other solicitor.

I wondered if Caroline would come home. She'd come up to the island for Duncan's funeral, but had quickly left the following day. I hadn't been able to speak to her alone. Then she'd sent me a Christmas card with a letter saying that she'd found a flat and got a teaching job in Glasgow. A school in a rough area on the edge of the city with a class which she described in her letter as 'challenging' and she had decided to stay there for a while and let out her house meanwhile. It was probably best to let things settle down a bit. From comments I'd heard it seemed that while most people sympathised with her predicament, some people blamed her for Duncan's death, saying her absence had driven him to drink. But I suspected most people who knew him were just glad that he was gone.

As I drew up, Ewan got out of his car.

I turned off the engine. 'Hello Ewan, nice to see you. How are you?'

Leaning back into his car, he pulled out his briefcase. He was frowning as he approached me, the briefcase clutched to his chest. 'Good evening Helen. There's something I'd like to discuss with you, if you have a few moments?' From the tone of his voice this was clearly an instruction rather than a request. He was as formal as ever. I suspected that he didn't only live by the book but probably slept with it as well. Not my type. He just lacked any spark. But I wondered what had brought him all the way from town to my house rather than to the surgery.

'Sure, just give me two minutes to dump my bag and feed the hens. I forgot to do them this morning. I was running a bit late.' When I came back into the kitchen, Ewan was standing in front of Alasdair's record collection. He was holding one of Alasdair's albums in his hand and reading the back cover.

'Shostakovich. Russian—too morose for me. I prefer my music Scottish,' he said, putting down the album.

I picked up my cigarettes and lit one.

'Coffee?' I suggested.

'No, thanks.' He shook his head.

'Any word of Alasdair and Mairi coming home at...

'It's not a social visit, Helen.'

'Oh...'

'I just thought you might want a look at this. It came in the post from London this morning'

He sat down and pulled a form from his briefcase.

'What's this?' I asked.

'The Official Secrets Act. You have to read it and sign it before we can talk further,' he said.

My breathing quickened. I felt sick

My hand shook as I stubbed out my cigarette. I took the silver pen from his outstretched fingers, my bitten nails contrasting with his carefully filed ones. I hesitated, looking at the document headed *Official Secrets Act*. He coughed, and tapped his foot.

His lips pursed, and he stared at me intently. 'It's up to you, Doctor.' His black leather briefcase sat at his feet, and he bent down and pulled out a thin buff coloured file and placed it on his lap.

Perhaps it held the answers to all my questions. I had no choice but to go ahead and sign it. I was aware of my heart beat accelerating. I scribbled my signature on the line and handed the form back to him. He folded it and placed it in his briefcase then handed me the file.

'Thanks,' I said.

He nodded. I took a deep breath, opened the file and began to read. My hands were shaking. Paper-clipped to the first page was a post mortem picture of a man. Oh God I thought - they've found Andrey's body. But no, this was a picture of an overweight middle aged man which had clearly been in water for some time. It was the body that had been found by the fishing-boat in their net. The sea and rocks hadn't been kind to his features, but a scar, which I presumed to be from an appendix operation, was clearly visible.

There was also a black line and bruising round his neck. I looked over at Ewan who sat grim-faced. I lifted the photograph and saw that the sheet was headed Andrey Grekov, Aeronautics Engineer.

'Poor bugger had been garrotted before being thrown into the sea. Post mortem shows he was dead before he hit the water,' he said, clicking his biro.

I turned the page. On the next page there was a fuzzy picture of Andrey. My heart rate increased. I'd almost forgotten what he looked like. But the page was headed Dimitri Nikitin. Under distinguishing features there was a reference to a childhood injury on his left forearm. My stomach dropped and I gasped involuntarily. Ewan caught my eye, and I looked back down at the file. The report detailed missions that he had been on and others that he was suspected of. He had killed many people and was wanted in a number of countries. Andrey wasn't Andrey but Dimitri, a top Soviet spy.

The colour drained from my face. Andrey had swopped identities. But why? A cold chill sped through my body. He'd killed the engineer to save himself and avoid detection.

Ewan coughed. I looked up. He was staring at me.

'Interesting reading?' he said.

'Yes,' I whispered.

'They think these are the two men who landed on St Kilda and sabotaged the security device. Shame the photograph isn't a bit sharper. Can't really make out who it is. Looks vaguely like your friend Andy, doesn't he? Got a scar on his arm too.' His eyes held mine and I blushed and looked at my lap.

'Tide must have taken him off. Sometimes these bodies are washed-up months later. Nasty character—wouldn't have wanted him here,' he said.

I nodded, closing the file. He took it and slipped it back into his brief case and snapped it shut. He stood up.

'This is confidential and cannot be discussed with anyone. Do you understand? If you hadn't been related to Alasdair and Mairi things might have been different.'

'Yes, but...' I said.

'No one on the island has clearance to see this file apart from me.'

'Yes,' I rasped. My mouth had dried and my tongue was stuck to the roof of my mouth.

'I'll let myself out, shall I?'

I nodded. I wasn't sure if I could stand up. He left, closing the door. I heard his car crunching on the stones as he drove off. I stood up to make myself a coffee. My hands were still shaking as I filled up the kettle. While I was waiting for it to boil I noticed one of Alasdair's books lying facedown on the table where Ewan had been sitting. He must have been looking at it while I was feeding the hens.

I picked it up. It had an interesting cover. I looked at it closer. It was called, *I Robot*. I wasn't interested in science fiction and had never bothered with looking at Alasdair's books. Then I looked at the author. Isaac Asimov. Andrey had told me the man that was going to kill Natalia was called Asimov. There was no Natalia. I dropped the book. It had all been lies. Nothing had been true.

I sat for a while. I was numb. Then I started to sob. Chest-tearing sobs as tears poured down my cheeks. Eventually I stood up. The light was fading. I picked up the album cover which was lying on the table and pulled out the record and placed it on the turntable. The sound of Shostakovich filled the room. He had used me. He hadn't loved me.

I went into the kitchen and under the sink found the half drunk bottle of gin. I poured a large glass, and sat down, and slowly drank it letting the music wash over me. Then I couldn't bear the sound any longer. I picked up my glass, gripping it so tightly I thought it might shatter. How could I have been so stupid? It had felt so right. I threw the glass at the record player. It smashed and the music stopped.

Chapter 41

My life dragged into February—supposedly the shortest month of the year, but it didn't feel that way. Two months of storms and dark, leaden days. On some days there was so little daylight that I needed to keep the lights on all day to examine my patients and their notes. It reminded me of my youth when all photographs and televisions were black and white. Only they weren't black and white. They were just like life—varying shades of grey. The cold was grey too. It wasn't a blue and white freezing cold, but an unrelenting damp that seeped into your bones. Like living inside a mouldy sack—but a sack that was pegged out on an exposed washing-line and constantly battered by the wind.

My patients sat in the waiting room complaining of their arthritis and aching bones. I would have liked to prescribe hibernation or emigration—for them and me—but neither was available on the NHS. Because the Gulf Stream flowed round the island and raised the sea temperature, there was little snow. Snow would have been preferable—it would have been drier and brighter—but this unrelenting dreich weather had completely sapped what was left of my depleted spirits.

Each day I dragged myself out of bed and into work. I hadn't resorted to the sleeping pills again. I was anxious to avoid those as they muddled my brain. I was probably drinking too much, but the only person who witnessed that was George. The system that Mr Macleod and I had established for my gin delivery was working well and each Friday night I came home and sitting in brown bags on the kitchen table there would be some groceries and three bottles of gin.

I struggled to keep my professional work face firmly attached like a mask. It was an effort. Even Mrs Murray—a woman not known for her caring nature had asked me on more than one occasion if I was feeling well. I'd smiled tightly, assuring her that I was well and eventually she'd stopped asking. But she kept me well supplied with coffee and scones.

The cottage was cold and damp. Some nights I could see my breath as I huddled under a blanket in the living-room. It took too much effort to light the stove. The house smelt fusty. I suspected I probably smelt fusty too. The rusty two bar electric fire which I'd found in a cupboard didn't heat the kitchen, despite its valiant attempt at a cheery glow. In the bathroom the wallpaper was starting to peel off the walls.

Most nights I came home late. I needed to keep my mind occupied, so I'd started reviewing the patients' records. I found half a dozen who hadn't attended for some years—mainly men. I'd invited them in for a check-up, and I'd turned up a couple of cases of high blood pressure which needed immediate treatment. The last of the files lay on the floor beside the sofa. Hopefully, I'd get through them tonight. Worryingly, I might then have to start on some housework.

When I stood up to fetch another cup of coffee to heat me up, I saw that there was a letter lying on the floor, half hidden by the door mat. The postman ignored the front door which had a letter box. All mail and parcels were put inside the unlocked back door. I'd missed it on the way in. I presumed it was for Mairi or Alasdair. I picked it up. It was addressed to me, in neat handwriting but in a rather strange script. I checked the post mark but it was smudged and illegible. Probably another university friend extolling the virtues of an an exotic work placement. If the coal fire had been lit, I'd have tossed it on the flames but I couldn't throw it on the electric one, so I tore open the envelope.

I pulled out a folded lined sheet of paper. It looked as if it had been torn from a child's jotter. Opening it a photograph fell face-down into my lap. I ignored it and read the letter. The writing was small and difficult to read.

Dear Helen,
My father forgave that I had lost his birthday present and was pleased to see me.

It was from Andrey. My heart leapt—he was still alive. My hand holding the letter was shaking.

Natalia says hello. One day, when things change, perhaps we can meet again.
I miss you.
Love,
Andrey.

PS I hope you and Brian enjoyed the guga.

I put the letter down and picked up the photograph from my lap. It was a crushed grainy black and white picture about four inches square. It seemed to have been taken in a park. In the foreground was a young girl and standing immediately behind her with his hands resting on her shoulders was Andrey. There was snow on the ground and they were encased in warm clothing and Andrey, I couldn't call him anything but Andrey although I realised it wasn't his real name, was wearing Alasdair's Harris Tweed cap.

From the picture, it was easy to see they were father and daughter; you only had to look at her dark eyes. They were both smiling at the camera.

Thank God, he was alive. There was a Natalia. He hadn't lied about everything. Perhaps he had no choice in what he did. He had to protect her. But why had he killed the engineer? What had happened on St Kilda? I would never know. Tears started to prick my eyelids—I could feel a dark emotional hole opening up. A tear escaped and rolled down my cheek. George crept over from his position in front of the fire and climbed onto my lap and licked the tear away. Whining he sniffed the letter, then tried to ferret his nose into the envelope as if searching for more of Andrey's scent.

Holding the letter in my hand I sat for half an hour thinking about Andrey, the Andrey I loved. But I knew he had another side too. I had glimpsed it in his eyes, the first time he'd opened them and in his actions towards Duncan. Perhaps it was just as well that we would never see each other again. I thought about a drink. No, I'd focus on the patients' notes. Perhaps I could distract my brain. I picked up the last set of notes. It was impossible. My hand was still shaking. I couldn't concentrate.

Guga? What did Andrey mean about guga and Brian? The only guga was soaking in that disgusting bucket in the barn. Standing up, I picked up the torch and went outside, George following at my heels. The hens looked a bit bemused when I unlocked the door and went inside disturbing their slumbers. I wondered if hens snored. There was some re-arranging of feathers and mild clucking of disapproval.

The guga bucket was in the back corner of the shed beside Alasdair's motorbike. Hanging nearby on a hook beside the brush and shovel, was a pair of Mairi's yellow rubber gloves. I put them on and then, holding my breath and screwing up my nose, carefully lifted the lid off the bucket. I hadn't been near it since the visit by the soldiers and the bloodhound. It just looked like a white rancid mess. I gagged and pulled a lifeless bird from the salted solution and placed it onto the straw. Then I did the same with the next two birds. Nothing. I was about to sling the birds back in and then I noticed that George was ignoring the pile of birds on the straw. His attention was fixed on the bucket. 'Okay, just to please you,' I muttered at him, plunging my hand deeper into the bucket and swearing as fetid, freezing water ran inside the glove. Then my fingers brushed something lying at the bottom of the bucket. I pulled it out and dropped it on the straw beside the birds. It was a belt with an oilskin package attached to it. I knew what it was without opening it. Why had Andrey left it? Had he spoken the truth when he told me he was being forced to work against his will?

I put the guga back in the water and replaced the lid. Then still wearing the gloves took the belt and package into the house and gently placed it in the sink. Brian Bain would be interested in this, so would the military and the government. Two men had died and our national security was still under threat.

Chapter 42

The next morning, Saturday, I got up early and went downstairs. There was a smell of fish as I entered the kitchen. I donned the plastic gloves, untied the package from the belt, and peeled back the grey waterproof covering revealing a grey plastic box, hardly bigger than a lunch box. I placed it on the kitchen table. Then I lit a cigarette and sat staring at it.

So this was what all the fuss was about.

I stubbed out my cigarette and picked up the box. It was heavy, but I could easily lift it with one hand. Yuck! It still smelt of fish. With some difficulty and the sacrifice of two, already bitten, fingernails, I prised open the lid and looked inside. The box was stuffed with cotton-wool packing which I carefully lifted off. There nestling inside was a metal unit, about the size of a cassette case, embedded with ten miniaturised circuit boards. I'd seen circuit boards before but not anything as tiny as these. I peered at them closely, but I didn't dare take them out of the container in case I damaged them. It was difficult to believe that the removal of such a small object had placed so many people in danger.

I sat back and lit another cigarette. What next? Throw the device into the sea. No risks, no problems. Yes, the easiest solution from my point of view perhaps, but there was the small matter of national security.

My head was still reeling. Andrey's letter had raised more questions than it had answered. Why had he sent it? Why hadn't he taken the device with him? Why steal it then leave it behind? Had his time on the island changed his mind? Had he connected with the people? Perhaps even loved me?

I suspected that I would never know the answer to these questions, but I needed to return the device to St Kilda as soon as possible. But how? I couldn't take it to the police. Even Brian Bain would be suspicious about how it fell into my hands. He'd ask questions that I wouldn't be able to answer.

Obviously I couldn't post it. I could hardly stand in the post office queue and get Mrs Kettles to weigh it and ask me whether I wanted it to go to the MOD first or second class. But maybe the next best thing...

I knew that in Macleod's shop beside the stack of supplies waiting to go to the island there was also a post office sack of letters and parcels. I'd seen it when I was in doing my shopping. Sometimes it lay for days if the boat was delayed. If I could just get the device safely into the sack, then it would be delivered to the island.

The first thing was to clean the plastic box and make sure that my fingerprints were wiped from it. I fetched my bag and fished out and put on a clean pair of surgical gloves. Then I opened the box and gently took out the device and wiped both boxes with surgical spirit. Finally, I placed the box holding the device back in amongst the packing and snapped the lid shut. I remembered seeing some brown paper under a pile of newspapers in the corner of the living room. I carefully wrapped the box in one of the sheets and using my left hand instead of my right wrote:

The Officer in Charge
St Kilda
Outer Hebrides

I needed to choose a time when the shop was at its busiest. The supplies were picked up today. It was also the day that The Islander, the island's local paper, was published. It was the busiest afternoon of the week as everyone wanted to know the latest local news which seemed to be in order of popularity: deaths, weather forecast, local football results and council decisions. Living an hour from town the council was almost as remote to the village as the city of London and the Houses of Parliament. There was usually a queue to get the paper and to be the first to find out what was happening.

The shop car park was busy when I pulled in. Wearing a pair of Mairi's black leather gloves, I'd put the parcel into my shopping bag. Before I went into the shop, I checked it was still at the top of my bag and covered it with a scarf.

I picked up a wire basket and started to wander slowly around the shop. There was a queue of people at the counter and the talk was in Gaelic. No one seemed to be in a hurry. The sacks going to St Kilda were sitting at the end of the counter but the queue of people, waiting to be served, snaked past them. Then through the window, I saw the army truck arrive that came to pick up the supplies for delivery to Scooby's boat. The first soldier jumped down and slammed the door and walked across the carpark towards the shop. There was no time. How was I going to get the box into the sack without being seen? I turned and went to the other side of the shop and picked up a packet of cake mix while I worked out what to do. I looked out the window again. The soldiers had stopped to talk to Scooby who was half-sitting on a car bonnet and had pulled out the local paper and was pointing at something.

Time was running out. I moved towards the sack and then I heard a voice behind me.

'Doctor MacAllister, good morning. Lovely day.'

I turned and saw Mrs MacPhee standing in the queue, holding a bottle of milk. I grabbed her arm.

'Was that a rat?' I said, pointing at the chest freezers at the rear of the shop. Her face paled. She simultaneously shrieked and dropped the bottle of milk. The glass exploded its white contents over the floor and she ran out of the shop screaming, 'Rat! There's a rat!'

The result was better than I could have hoped. The women in the shop quickly followed Mrs MacPhee out the door, and Macleod came out from behind the counter waving a brush, shouting 'What is it? Where is it?'

'Mrs MacPhee said there's a rat behind the freezers.'

The men had gathered and were now moving the freezers. MacLeod armed with the large brush was ready to strike any emerging rodent. Looking round to check there was no one beside the counter, I skirted the broken glass and quickly walked past, dropping the parcel into the open mail sack, and headed for the car park. Outside Mrs MacPhee and the women were huddled together like a pack of frightened gazelles.

'Did they kill it?' she asked as I went past.

'No, but don't worry they've got it cornered,' I said, getting into my car. I wanted away from the shop. I drove off. I stopped the car on the cliff top and with trembling hands lit a cigarette and inhaled deeply. Okay, Andrey, parcel delivered. Let's see what happens next.

Chapter 43

What happened? Well the strange thing was that nothing really happened after that.

The soldiers did withdraw from the island two days later. They were there one night and gone the next morning. They'd all disappeared off on the early morning ferry. During the night there was the sound of their large lorries heading towards the town. They had left no obvious evidence of their visit apart from a pregnancy, but everyone, including the mum to be, was unaware of that. We were told that their exercise was finished.

I could only presume that the piece of equipment arrived safely and had been reinstalled.

Mrs Murray told me the day before they'd all left, Captain Ellery and Mr Simpson had been to see Mr Macleod. I was curious to find out why, but thought that I'd better wait a couple of days before visiting the shop to be on the safe side.

'Something to do with the St Kilda mail,' he told me when I went back into the shop the following Wednesday.

'Not sure if someone had stolen something from the mail bag. They were very cagey,' he said, packing my bag. 'They wanted to see where the St Kilda mail bag was kept. My cousin, Iain D, said that they'd also been to the sorting office in town asking questions about the St Kilda mail. No idea why. It's not as if anyone here would steal a letter or a parcel. Big fuss about nothing if you ask me.'

I smiled to myself and said, 'Probably someone had stolen something from it while it was on the mainland.'

'Aye, that's more likely, Doctor,' he said, handing me my change.

Now that things had settled down, I was able to concentrate on my work. I was getting to know the patients better and was settling into the slower pace of life. I wasn't exactly enjoying it, but I was getting used to it. My final patient that afternoon, Stub, the local journalist who wrote for the island's weekly paper, had just limped out of my surgery. I'd spent half an hour with the poor man. Luckily, being last patient of the day, I wasn't in a rush. He lived alone on the edge of the village, but his sight was badly affected by cataracts and he was due an operation the following week.

'I'll be glad to get back to work, Doctor,' he said. 'Though it's not easy to make a living here. Nothing exciting happens here. I keep dreaming that, one day, I'll get a scoop and it'll end up on the front page of the nationals. Some chance, eh?'

'Oh, well you never know, stranger things have happened,' I said, smiling as I showed him out. I shook his hand and wished him good luck with the operation.

After he left I stuck my head round the door to check that there were no more patients sitting outside. I was also hoping to avoid Mrs Murray. Thankfully, the waiting-room was deserted; Mrs Murray had gone home for the night. But there was a note in angry handwriting lying on the reception counter:

WHERE ARE THE BOOKS?

Mrs Murray and I were in the middle of another secular stand-off. After months of me bringing in magazines which then mysteriously disappeared, I'd had enough. One night last week, as I'd left I'd removed all the bibles and religious papers and substituted some women's magazines and car magazines instead. I'd tried hiding them in a cupboard in the staff room, but they kept reappearing, so last night I'd taken them all home and stuck them in the barn. The patients had seemed happy with their new reading material. Especially my older male patients who were engrossed reading the problem pages of the women's magazines, to the extent that on more than one occasion I'd not been heard when I called their name, and I'd had to stand in front of them to catch their attention.

My only real difficulty was that it had given Calum Twig, my hypochondriac, access to a whole new range of potential illnesses. Last week, I'd had to reassure him that it was unlikely that his feeling hot during the day was anything to do with the menopause. I suspected he disbelieved me and would be checking this out in a medical dictionary the next time he visited the town library.

But Mrs Murray was clearly not amused with the change of reading materials. Since I'd done this our conversation had been minimal and all supplies of home-baking had been withdrawn. I'd had to resort to a pack of digestives in my bottom drawer.

As I drove home I noticed how the days were lengthening. There was still light in the sky. I passed a field of heavily pregnant sheep. I slowed down, and stopped. I could see a lamb slowly stumbling onto its feet. I got out and leaned on the gate to watch. Nature never ceases to amaze me. A new life, whether it's animal or human, though some argue there's not much difference between the two. The unsteady creature toppled over a couple of times and then it wobbled over to its mother and began to butt her for milk.

The phone was ringing as I walked into the cottage. I dumped my bag on the table and picked up the receiver. I thought it might be the locum employment agency in London. I was waiting on word about an interview. I knew that the job in the practice was about to be advertised and rumour had it that Doctor MacLeod who was working in Inverness wanted to come back and would be applying for the job. He was male and local, so I knew that he'd get the job over a mere mainland female. Maybe it was time to move on.